THE DICTATOR AND
THE HAMMOCK

Daniel Pennac

The Dictator and the Hammock

TRANSLATED
FROM THE FRENCH
BY

Patricia Clancy

Harvill Secker
LONDON

Published by Harvill Secker 2006

First published in France by Editions Gallimard in 2003

2 4 6 8 10 9 7 5 3 1

Copyright © Daniel Pennac 2003
English translation © Patricia Clancy 2006

First published in Great Britain in 2006 by
Harvill Secker
Random House, 20 Vauxhall Bridge Road
London SWIV 2SA

Random House Australia (Pty) Limited
20 Alfred Street, Milsons Point, Sydney,
New South Wales 2061, Australia

Random House New Zealand Limited
18 Poland Road, Glenfield,
Auckland 10, New Zealand

Random House South Africa (Pty) Limited
Isle of Houghton, Corner Boundary Road & Carse O'Gowrie,
Houghton, 2198, South Africa

The Random House Group Limited Reg. No. 954009
www.randomhouse.co.uk

A CIP catalogue record for this book is available from the British Library

ISBN 9781843431890 (from Jan 2007)
ISBN 1843431890

Typeset by SX Composing DTP, Rayleigh, Essex
Printed and bound in Great Britain by
William Clowes Ltd, Beccles, Suffolk

For my brother Bernard, a very close companion.

In memory of Thierry, our builder.

Contents

I
THE NTH DEGREE

1

IT WOULD BE the story of an agoraphobic dictator. The country is not important. Just imagine one of those banana republics with a substratum rich enough to make seizing power attractive, and barren enough on the surface to be fertile ground for revolution. Let's say that the capital is called Teresina, like the capital of Piauí in Brazil. Piauí is too poor a country ever to be the setting for a tale about power, but Teresina is an acceptable name for a capital.

And Manuel Pereira da Ponte Martins would make a plausible name for a dictator.

So, it would be the story of Manuel Pereira da Ponte Martins, an agoraphobic dictator. Pereira and Martins are the two commonest surnames in his country. Hence his vocation as a dictator: when you have the same name as everyone else, multiplied by two, power is yours as of right. That's what he's always thought ever since he was old enough to think.

Later he'll be called just Pereira, his father's name. He could as easily be Martins, his mother's name, but his father is *the* Pereira in Ponte (which is three days' horse ride from Teresina), the most important family of big landowners in the region. When you have the land, the name and the money, you will have the power. This was really one of the first *ideas* Pereira had – probably the very first – a deep, burning idea, a quiet child's secret passion. A little education would be needed, obviously. You have to speak English, French and German. You have to have a knowledge of arithmetic and geography. You have to become familiar with utopias in order to prepare yourself for all kinds of threats. You have to know weapons, dancing, security and protocol. To learn all that, Pereira leaves Ponte when he is eight, grows up with the Jesuits in Teresina until he is fifteen – he's a reserved but brilliant student and a merciless chess player – then goes abroad to Europe to complete his education, and comes back at twenty-two to enter the Military Academy. He still wants power, but he has acquired the taste for being elsewhere. Italy for example. Even that little rock of Monaco, where the casino welcomes you with open arms and the Princess has given you the eye – or so he supposes.

So, it would be the story of an agoraphobic dictator who wants two things at once: power and being elsewhere. He starts with the first: as the President's aide-de-camp, he will begin to take his rightful place. As it happens, the President is a general who has neglected his own education. There's a joke doing the rounds of the salons in Teresina: 'The President has been attacked; someone threw a dictionary at him.' It's a big joke, which brings a discreet burst of laughter behind the ladies' fans. The President doesn't take offence. Many of his sentences open with:

'Pereira, you can read . . .'

The President cares little for culture. As far as he's concerned, it's 'a pastime for men with no balls'.

'I've studied men,' he says. To which he's fond of adding, 'That's why I prefer horses.'

The President distinguished himself in the war with Paraguay, then in the massacre of the peasants from the North. The peasants from the North had begun to make demands. They had actually begun by making requests, which had not been granted; then they made timid complaints, which were not heard. They begged, but in vain. And so they began to demand what they wanted. The peasants from the North marched on Teresina under the leadership of their parish priests. Teresina had been threatened with a peasant invasion. The President sent the cadets in the Military Academy to deal with it. The cavalry, sabres, a hail of bullets, then the artillery were unleashed on the villages of the North, where the peasants had retreated. With the Bishop's blessing, the President had the priests shot.

Pereira's father, old da Ponte, had condemned this massacre. Da Ponte Senior practised Christian charity. He distributed food for free from his kitchens to the starving peasants on his large properties, innocently unaware that he was the cause of their misery. As a doctor, he treated in his hospital dehydration from his plains and boils from his mountains. He listened to those who suffered from hunger and thirst, those who were sick and the relatives of the sick. Old da Ponte used to say, 'People ask nothing of a man who listens.'

By the time Pereira came home from abroad girded with his diplomas, the General had been President for four years.

Pereira killed him at the dawn of the fifth. He was almost impelled to do it. He felt that the moment had come. He appeared before the Council and said: 'I've killed that idiot.' He added, 'I offer myself to you as either the culprit or your President.'

He was holding his big automatic pistol, which was still smoking; he was a Pereira da Ponte; they made him President.

To the Bishop, who had been godfather at his baptism, he asked: 'Bless me, Godfather.'

To the oligarchy, he declared: 'Absolutely nothing will change. All I'm going to do is apply a little more intelligence.'

To the peasants, he announced: 'I've killed the butcher of the North.'

And to the population at large: 'I will be your ears.'

It was a sibylline sentence – ears spy on people even as they listen to them – but no one thought of that, so desperate were they to be heard.

So, it would be the story of Manuel Pereira da Ponte Martins, an agoraphobic dictator, who one morning would follow his intuition and seize power, just like that, because it was his secret childhood dream.

Right. But why was he agoraphobic?

2

BEFORE SEIZING POWER, Pereira was not at all agoraphobic. Quiet, yes; secretive, yes; agoraphobic, no. He had no fear of open spaces, empty streets or avenues that stretched for miles, and even less of the crowds that were always there. Not that he was particularly fond of crowds, but he was used to them. The poverty-stricken crowds of his childhood in Ponte waiting outside his father's kitchens or in the hospital corridors; the crowds of worshippers for the birth at Christmas and the crucifixion on Good Friday; the crowds of peasants at all the votive feast days, which the da Ponte family dutifully attended; the crowds at weddings and funerals, markets and fairs; the drunken crowds at the wild celebrations, when Bengal lights lit up the revellers' masks to the sound of crackers going off all around. No, he had never been afraid of crowds. When you come to think of it, apart from family meals, games of chess and time alone reading, Pereira had always, in a manner of speaking, lived among a crowd: in Teresina, with the Jesuits, the crowds of children in the schoolyard, in Europe, the silk-clad crowds at formal balls, the shivering crowds leaving the theatre, the clandestine crowds in the red-light districts, the tense crowds at the races, and even, in Paris, crowds of workers on strike . . . Actually, there were so many people . . . Periera could have counted the hours he spent alone. No, really, he had never been afraid of crowds. Nor of empty spaces.

Well then, why was he agoraphobic?

Because of something another Manuel had said: Manuel Callado Crespo, the Chief Interpreter, an extremely well-read, straight-talking man. Referring to the late President, Manuel Callado Crespo had commented: 'The stupid bastard died by the appointed hand.'

'Meaning?' asked Periera, who happened to be passing and was not supposed to have heard those words.

'Meaning that the stupid bastard was warned, Mr President.'

'And by whom, since two seconds before pulling the trigger I didn't know myself that I would kill him?'

'By Mãe Branca,' Callado replied. 'But the bastard couldn't read and never listened.'

'What will you say about me when I'm dead, Callado?' Periera enquired as an afterthought.

'Whatever impression your life has made on me, Mr President. 'And you'll do the same when you come to my funeral. There's no slander in that. The General was . . . You've seen his uniform. No, really, the term "stupid bastard" sums up his life to a T. And I say it almost affectionately.'

Mãe Branca (Old Mother White) was a Brazilian witch who came from Ceará – a white witch as opposed to a black one. It's a matter of sorcery, not of skin colour. A black witch (who may have white skin) casts evil spells. A white witch (who may be black) only makes predictions and removes spells. Everyone consults Mãe Branca: for love, family, health, money, career . . . A famous professor was even to be seen consulting a white witch to find out if he would get the Chair of Religious Anthropology at the University of Teresina, and whether he would travel all over the world giving papers at conferences. The same professor then went to a black witch to eliminate his rivals. And it's a fact that his colleagues mysteriously ceded the chair to him, and although he's very old, he is still today the only recognised specialist in his field. (But that's another story.)

Would-be dictators obviously consult Mãe Branca before a *coup d'état*. And even in democracies, presidential candidates do the same before elections. Periera realised that he had not done it. When he was in Europe he had read Auguste Comte and no longer believed in such things. Like all other non-believers, Pereira nevertheless went, out of curiosity, to see the witch. She was a small, thin (white) woman with a limp, who held her consultations in the suburbs of Teresina. Pereira went alone, incognito and at night, telling no one, but armed with the pistol that never left his side. He threw some pebbles at the witch's shutters. He paid her first, then asked two questions: firstly, what she had said to the former President.

'I told him that if he didn't read *Lorenzaccio*, he would die like Duke Alexander.'*

*Alfred de Musset's play *Lorenzaccio* (1834), set in sixteenth-century Florence, is a complex study of political power, moral virtue and corruption. Lorenzaccio kills Duke Alexander, the debauched tyrant, but later suffers a similar fate himself.

(This was real fortune-telling, since she could not read herself and knew nothing of the play.)

'And how will I die?'

That was Pereira's second question. Mãe Branca practised fortune-telling by sprinkling perfume. She plunged her hand into a big bottle of vetiver and sprinkled it all around the room. As the perfume went to her head, she began muttering to herself, turning faster and faster until she seemed to spin like a top. Then she suddenly stopped and her eyes rolled back in her head. It was only then that she called on the saints of *candomblé*.* It took a while, as there are a great many of these Brazilian deities, and their ancestors from Guinea and offspring in the Caribbean are more numerous still. Mãe Branca stood with the empty perfume bottle in her hand, trembling in every limb.

Pereira found it all as tedious as Mass on Sunday. The smell of vetiver reminded him of his childhood, when his mother had it sprayed in the bedrooms to keep the mosquitoes away. At last, when she had reached the climax of her trance, Mãe Branca vouchsafed the information he wanted:

'You will be hacked to pieces by the crowd.'

'What kind of crowd?'

'The peasant kind.'

Pereira killed her with one blow from the butt of his gun and went back to the palace.

It was thought she had had a fall. He had paid her enough for her to be given a respectable funeral. A huge crowd followed the coffin: townspeople, but also a lot of peasants who had come from all over the countryside. Pereira mingled

Candomblé is a mixture of African religions and Roman Catholicism with devotees from the coastal region of Brazil, especially the cities and the North-East, and also in the Caribbean and East Africa.

with them in dress uniform to prove to all that he shared the people's beliefs, and to himself that magic did not exist. He came back from the burial alive, as you would expect. Alive and rather admired.

So why would he be agoraphobic?

3

BECAUSE AFTER THE burial, night fell. And that night, Pereira wondered why he had killed the witch. It wasn't an attack of remorse; it was an attack of logic. Why had he killed her if he didn't believe in her predictions? And if he wasn't prepared to believe them, why did he go and see her? He had killed her as unthinkingly as he had killed the General. You could call it an instant of pure panic. He had felt sure when the time for power had come; in that moment he knew just as surely that this woman foretold its end. He had killed her instinctively, in self-protection, to ward off a spell he didn't believe in – until he committed that murder. He had brought about his own introduction to superstition.

These thoughts, which had been quietly forming in his head as he stood at the witch's graveside, now surfaced as Pereira lay in bed. He would rather have killed her for pleasure or duty, like the General, who liked murder and justice. But Pereira wasn't a killer. The total number of people he killed with his own hand in the whole of his life was three. That was very little for someone of his time and class. What is more, he'd killed them like a wild animal: hunger for power in the General's case, and the two others (the witch being one of them) because he felt cornered. It was instinct each time, innocent, animal instinct . . .

'Therefore, I believe this nonsense.'

Whereupon he fell asleep. Then came the nightmare. Pereira was being murdered by a mob of peasants. 'Obviously.' It was not surprising that he should have a dream like that, and he considered it quite coolly. He was not afraid of death. He had often imagined it coming from a single well-aimed bullet, or even a dozen aimed at his heart by a rival's firing squad. But, after all, why not a lynching? He had been born and bred in a land of revolutions. All things considered, it was a less abhorrent death than an old man's fingers clutching the counterpane. In his dream he was coming out of a hotel that stood like a cube in the middle of an empty plaza. He heard someone call his name: 'Pereira!' And he saw the peasants coming all at once from the houses that encircled the plaza – tiny single-storey adobe houses forming a huge ring around the hotel. A vast crowd was already bearing down on him. All right, he thought, as he emptied his magazine clip into the crowd, the starving populace spewing out of the houses, I'm dying from an attack of allegory. He kept firing, but the circle 'inexorably' – he loved that word when he came across it in books – closed up again around him. He was firing more on principle than in hope – one doesn't let oneself be killed without putting up a fight. The last thing he saw before the first hand grabbed him was two men standing on the edge of the plaza beneath the only street light. They were leaning on a bicycle with their backs to the scene, laughing silently as they looked at something that gave out a pale light at their feet – rather like a fire burning with a white flame. The two men's shoulders shook with laughter. 'That's real life,' Pereira thought, and suddenly he wanted to live. But the hands, feet, eyes, toothless mouths, shouts, growls, sticks, guns, machetes, the first blows, the first cuts did not explain the terror he felt. No, it was something else, something worse. The hatred . . . These men and women who were tearing at him (they pulled him by his hands, his feet and his head; the sticks broke his bones and the machetes expertly amputated his limbs) were all Pereiras and Martinses.

He woke up screaming.

Then his heart settled again into its proper rhythm.

'Right. It was only a nightmare.'

But when morning came, he had to make a real effort to confront the circular area in front of the gate to the presidential palace. The thought of all that empty space which could fill with people made his throat constrict, and he could hardly breathe.

'Shit, I'm becoming agoraphobic.'

The following night the same nightmare confirmed his phobia.

That's it. The story could end there, as Pereira died in exactly the same way as he did in his dream. But, like any man who is interesting enough to be written about, he wanted to escape his fate. And the whole story of Pereira is about that attempt.

That would be the story worth telling.

4

So, it would be the story of Manuel Pereira da Ponte Martins, an agoraphobic dictator who wanted two things (power in Teresina and travel in Europe) and, as he was destined to be lynched, would vainly try to escape his fate.

The only idea he had of finding a way out – a dictator's idea if ever there was one! – was to employ a double. The double looked like him in every way, as much as one man can look like another, of course, almost to the nth degree. No one noticed that nth degree. To make sure of that, after acquainting his double on every aspect of his life and his affairs, and training him with the utmost rigour in the art of mimicry, Pereira sent him to ask a question of all those who were closest to him. It was the same question for all of them:

'Who am I?'

The question did not please old da Ponte. He looked scornfully at the young man asking it.

'Power shouldn't make you forget who you are, Manuel. You are Manuel Pereira da Ponte Martins, the pride of my flesh and blood. Never forget it.'

The double kissed the father's hand and went off to put the same question to Colonel Eduardo Rist, the director of the Military Academy, Commander-in-Chief of the army, a friend of Pereira's since childhood. (They had studied together at the Jesuits' and spent long, silent nights playing chess.)

'You are Manuel Pereira da Ponte Martins, our liberator and President, and by knocking off the General, you made the winning move.'

'That's right, but the time for chess is over, Eduardo,'

replied the double, who knew nothing about the game. 'And by the way, you can still, when we are alone, address me as "tu" rather than "vous".'

When the double asked the same question of the Bishop (who had been godfather at Pereira's baptism, prepared him for communion and given him the symbolic two-fingered slap on the cheek on the day of his confirmation), the prelate looked deep into his eyes.

'What do you mean, who are you? What's wrong, Manuel? Do you think you are Lorenzaccio? You're surely not tormenting yourself over the death of that fool?' (He was referring to the General and former President.) 'I've already given you my blessing, but if it would set your mind at rest, I can absolve you. There you are, I absolve you. You are the one God sent to rid us of that bloodthirsty beast. Amen. Go in peace.'

Dressed as a peasant, the double approached people at random in the street. He always received the same reply:

'You are our Pereira.'

With a few variants:

'. . . and I am another.'

Or:

'You are *the* Pereira da Ponte, and your mama is a Martins, like mine.'

Or:

'You are our ears.'

Or, from the woman who sold snakes in the Teresina market:

'Pereira, I'd recognise you even if you dressed up as a mongoose. You are the heart beating in my breast.'

The double was ready. Pereira had him give the New Year message he had prepared for the foreign embassies. It was a speech of moderate tone and political erudition that made a great contrast with the happy belchings of the late President. The diplomats were all the more appreciative of its European flavour (an expression used by Sir Anthony Calvin-Cook, the British Ambassador), as the new President basically guaranteed to all the continuation of their 'privileged relationships' (pillaging the mineral wealth of the substratum) in the tranquillity of 'enduring civil peace' (the total submission of the surface, i.e. the general population).

With a glass of champagne in his hand, the double received the congratulations intended for Pereira who, a little later in his study, negotiated the new percentages for gold, nickel, oil and akmadon. Pereira insisted on more for himself than the late General, but he managed to be forgiven for it by opening an account in each of the banks where there worked a relative of the person he was dealing with.

'Take it as a personal tribute to your family, Your Excellency.' Then to extinguish any lingering doubts, he added, 'A tribute which gives you the right to a commission.'

With Sir Anthony he even allowed himself to make a little joke.

'Our Marxist friends are right: the family is the basic cell of capitalism, especially when it is formed as a board of directors.'

So, assured of his power within the country, provided with well-endowed accounts in foreign banks, Pereira can treat his local agoraphobia by indulging in his second passion: being elsewhere.

Before making his escape (for he couldn't ignore the fact that it was an escape), he had a meeting with his double. He announced that he was going on a journey and he was leaving the speeches his double would have to give during his absence, in the desk. 'Do you see it? The roll-top desk over there.' There was one for every occasion. The double couldn't go wrong: they were in a pile in date order.

'I want you to learn them by heart. When you're standing in front of the crowd, I want my words to flow like a fountain of truth from your mouth. I'm not one of those European politicos who read their speeches to the public. When I speak, I'm a president possessed. The voice of the people is heard through my mouth – a last vestige of the primitive in me! Do you see, it's all in the *tone*?'

The double indicated that he did.

'In other situations, just hold your tongue. I am, above all, a silent president.'

The double made a vow of silence.

'And another thing, don't forget your origins: don't touch a woman of my class. If you do, I'll have your balls. Let's say that I'm a chaste president. I'm married to my people, so I have no time for women.'

The double made a vow of chastity.

'You will only lay a hand on a woman to open a ball on ceremonial occasions.'

Pereira had taught his double to tango.

'On our continent, a president worthy of the name should dance the tango better than anyone else!'

The double had become a *tanguista* beyond compare.

'Right. Now, just one detail.'

Here, Pereira explained to the double in substance that if, after this total immersion in his President's prose, the idea ever came to his mind, the double's, to take his place, the dictator's, well, he, the double, would perish as suddenly as if he had taken a cyanide pill.

'Try, just to see. Standing there in front of me, try just for a moment to seriously believe you are me. Go on. Make a effort. Are you the President? Are you my father's son? Do you think you are me, even a little? Come on. I'm waiting. I'm waiting!'

Not only was it impossible for the double to imagine himself President in the President's place or the son of Pereira da Ponte or godson of the Bishop, or even the friend of Eduardo Rist, or having the slightest power over the snake seller in Teresina, but simply attemping to do so filled him with such terror that he was already half dead when he stammered, 'I can't. You are you . . . and I'm me.'

You're right, Pereira thought, you're nothing like me. The body is just shit before the thaw.

But all he said to him was: 'And don't you forget it.'

5

AS FOR WHAT Pereira did in Europe, how many years he spent there, the countries he visited, the towns he lived in, the women he loved, we have nothing but a blank chapter. There's no doubt, however, that he left his mark wherever he went. Two examples: the winning system called 'the Pereira', which was all the rage in the casinos on the Riviera a few months after he arrived in Monaco; and in the world of chess, 'the da Ponte opening' with which the Indian Mìr slowly but surely overpowered Grand Master Turali at the Championship of the Two Flanders in Amsterdam. (Wondering how Mìr got wind of 'the da Ponte opening' will reveal the link between

Pereira and Kathleen Lockridge the dancer and the Indian champion's muse.)

Colonel Eduardo Rist's account of that would be rather interesting:

'This opening with the black bishop's pawn would ensure that Pereira won, but it made the game go on for ever. We spent whole nights on it at boarding school. Pereira loved drawing things out interminably like this and witnessing the slow exhaustion of his opponent's strength. I have never known a man who was so impulsive and so patient at the same time. Whether it was chess, politics, love or silence, he was like an anaconda. If Manuel taught his opening move to Grand Master Mîr, it was probably to do his love life a favour: while the Indian was busy winning games that lasted for ever, thanks to his new friend, Manuel and the dancer spent the time together in bed. I swear it!'

As for the blank chapter, the more you look into it, the more you're convinced that an inventory of the traces Pereira left behind him during his stay in Europe would take volume upon volume. You find his mark in activities as vain and varied as gaming, dancing (a sliding tango sidestep is named after him), fashion, numismatics, bullfighting, the art of cocktail-making. (Cocktails, my God, all that endless variety ... only to achieve the same coppery aftertaste, every last one!) And there were the love affairs – adulteries, abductions, pursuits, duels, desertion, depression, suicide – which established his reputation as the last of the neo-romantics and (according to Kathleen Lockridge) made him the model of Rudolph Valentino, the film star who dominated the cinema of this frivolous era and who (once more according to

Kathleen Lockridge) looked as much like Pereira 'as two drops of cloudy water in a Murano glass'.

Limiting ourselves to concrete examples only: take the uniform worn by the head porter at the Hôtel Negresco in Nice during those years. There's no doubt about it: someone dressed him up like the General, the late President. No, no, no, not dressed him up *like*. Take a good look at the photos: dressed him *in* the dead man's musical-comedy uniform – the very one the dictator was wearing when Pereira killed him!

It's reported that Manuel Callado Crespo, Chief Interpreter and Pereira's biographer, was of the same opinion. 'I'm not surprised to hear that Pereira should have unloaded the bastard's uniform on to that luxury hotel flunkey. Seeing crowned heads, ambassadors, ministers, the rich and famous greeted on the Promenade des Anglais by a porter dressed like a dead clown must have given him great pleasure. It's the unavoidable anarchic side of petty tyrants who think of themselves as "self-made men". And besides, Pereira was a da Ponte boy. Up there, they don't forgive the people they kill.'

Another track that's easy to follow is the debts Pereira left in his wake. Gambling debts, bills from luxury hotels and fine restaurants, accounts from tailors, jewellers, gunsmiths, florists, shoemakers, train and ship companies, the claims came pouring in to Teresina. The double had the task of answering them, sending off letters written by Pereira himself. The young President deplored the fact that someone should be passing himself off as him in Europe and leading a life that was far more diverting than his, here in Teresina, which was 'entirely given over to affairs of State and the care of its people'. He added that he would be willing to pay off the debts of this unscrupulous double 'if a reprehensible feeling of envy did not stand in my way'.

'Ah, the high moral standards of the Jesuits,' Pereira's godfather the Bishop would have remarked, had he been told the story.

One evening in Paris, Pereira repairs to the Restaurant Lapérouse with a lady friend. The member of staff with a good memory for faces recognises him and tries to stop him from entering. Instead of killing him on the spot, as he is momentarily tempted to do (the man will never know that he was nearly the third victim of Manuel Pereira da Ponte Martins, an agoraphobic and instinctual dictator), Pereira draws him close and speaks directly in his ear: No, he is not the double of President Pereira da Ponte, he is President Pereira da Ponte in person, come to Europe for the very purpose of putting an end to the misdemeanours of that double. Will this man with the good memory for faces agree to work for him? He will be extremely well paid – and handsomely rewarded if the double is captured.

The most telling document in the Teresina archives on Pereira's stay in Europe is, without any doubt, the letter in which this man respectfully claims his wages, not knowing of course that his name will be added to those of the creditors, of whom he has supplied a complete list to underpin the validity of his claim. (The name of this man with such a good memory for faces was Félicien Ponce.)

To cut a long story short, Pereira was having a good time.

Not a very happy kind of good time, all the same . . .

Was he suffering from the effects of being an exile or from the untranslatable *saudade*?* Did he curse the agoraphobic nightmares that prevented him from going back to Teresina? No longer blinded by love, was he finding that in the end Europe 'was not his thing'? Or did he hate it with the possessive kind of hatred of a North American? Whatever, he amused himself without ever laughing, which is never a good sign.

Perhaps these joyless tricks were part of his nature.

One can form a fairly accurate idea of the said nature by closely studying the origins of the *bacalhau do menino* ('the kid's cod'). You can still order this dish today at the best tables of the Estoril: a layer of chilli, a layer of black beans, a layer of white rice, a layer of egg yolk, a layer of brown onions, a layer of cod, and so forth seven times, chilli, beans, rice, egg, onions, cod, dusting the whole thing with manioc† flour before cooking it in the embers (nowadays it's usually done in the oven) until it has the discouraging density of a building block. According to legend, it was Pereira's 'charity dish', invented by him when he was a child, to feed the poor. His mother cooked it every day and old da Ponte served it with his own hands to the queue of starving peasants that lined up daily in front of the family kitchens, etc.

Saudade: an intense longing for a person, time or place; a profound yearning and sense of loss.
†The root of manioc provides cassava, from which tapioca and flour are made.

This has been checked and it's all true.

But with cookery as with the finest works of art, you don't understand anything about a dish if you don't know the *purpose* behind its creation. To find out the ulterior motives behind the *bacalhau do menino*, you have to go beyond restaurant gossip ('"Charity dish", you must be joking, how much was it, darling?') and listen to those who came to really know Pereira, like women, for example – great purveyors of mythology in happy times and tireless seekers after truth when the skies cloud over – and pick out just one, Kathleen Lockridge, the Scottish dancer. If you could read the four thousand or so handwritten pages of her unprocurable Memoirs, you would come across the description of a dinner, at the Estoril in fact, when she was served the *bacalhau do menino* under Pereira's watchful eye.

'Well?' he asked, before she had scarcely swallowed the first mouthful.

'Exquisite,' she replied.

'Exquisite,' he repeated after her.

He didn't say another word. She ate everything on her plate and the two that followed.

Late at night, when she was still awake with indigestion, he said it once again: 'Exquisite . . .'

He smiled at her. 'It's my recipe.' He added, 'A combination of shame, hate, disgust, scorn and nothingness.'

He was still smiling as he recited: 'The chilli is only there to mask the poor ingredients; it's the worst element of our cuisine. The beans have a black skin – food for slaves; and rice is hardly a substance at all – paper paste. Egg yolk smells like a fart – a hypocrite's insides. And the onions? Raw they're girls' tears; cooked, bits of dead skin. As for the cod . . .' (He got up and looked at the sea through the open window.) '. . . all the stupidity of Portugal: sailing so far from their shores to fish for the worst fish in the world!'

He turned round.

'And you sit there and simper, "Exquisite." '

'You've forgotten the manioc flour,' she pointed out, quite offended.

'There you have it! That is the nothingness! Manioc flour is nothing. No colour, no flavour, no substance.'

He was silent for a moment, no longer smiling.

'It's nothing and it's all we have in our part of the world. Just a ruse to fill our nothingness: that's what the flour is.'

As she was showing signs of becoming emotional, he sat on the edge of the bed and leaned over her.

'Child, I invented the horrible thing so that the poor wouldn't be tempted to take a second helping. When I became President, I made it our national dish.'

You can imagine the silence before Kathleen Lockridge replied in an unsteady voice: 'Well, I took another helping.'

'Because you're rich, European, vacuous and sentimental. You make it a point to like anything that's unthreatening . . . It's your search for "authenticity". In two hundred years, if the poor in your country haven't eaten you, the stuck-up women of your class will still be licking their plates . . . "Exquisite".'

Whereupon, he began to dance around the room improvising a poem in the nasal, metallic tone of the 'duettists', those guitar players in the Teresina markets, who challenge each other to sing verses turn and turn about.

Na França, Henrique quatro
Rei queridinho do povo
Inventou a 'pulopo'
Nosso Pereira criou

O mata-fome supremo
O Bacalhau do Menino!

Henry the Fourth of France
The people's king and able,
Invented Chicken in a Pot
For every Sunday table
But the stomach-filler of all time
Is our Pereira's own creation
The Kid's Cod, it is called
The great dish of our nation!

He leaped around the room as he sang, in ferocious good
humour, like a child taking it out on other children.

6

So, it would be the story of Manuel Pereira da Ponte
Martins, an agoraphobic and nomadic dictator, who left
no mark worth remembering in the countries he travelled
through.

Yes, but what of the double?

Actually, how *does* the double get on in Teresina?

He gets on by following his orders to the letter. He is the
double of a man who will knock off a president with no more
conpunction than killing an ox in the marketplace. Before his

departure, Pereira left a threat hanging in the air that would make your hair stand on end: 'I'll never be far away.' The double avoids thinking. Thinking is a tricky operation for someone in his situation. He has been ordered to pass himself off as someone else without ever being tempted to think he *is* that person, despite all the tributes paid to him, the decorum that accompanies him, the respect given to him, the fear he inspires and the love he is shown. (Or else, cyanide. He hasn't forgotten the lesson.) Pereira's portrait hanging everywhere is not his portrait, but he sees himself everywhere in him. The double is reduced to nothingness, but this nothingness had taken on the mantle of a demigod. He feels dizzy as soon as he thinks of it. And since he lies to everyone, he doubts everyone. Do they really believe me? Do they really take me for Pereira? The people, perhaps. The people only worship and destroy images, but Eduardo Rist, the friend since childhood, or the Bishop, or the father, who do they take me for? Could a father – and a da Ponte! – really say to someone who is not his son, 'You are the pride of my flesh and blood'? Is that possible? Even if we look alike? No, no, those three are in the know. Pereira is in the eyes of the father, the friend, the godfather, and maybe also the snake seller. Pereira isn't far away; Pereira is everywhere, including in me, hidden deep inside, waiting for me to make my first mistake! That's what the double thinks, as soon as he starts thinking. Hence his decision not to think any more and just to stick to his role, so that the spectators do not depart from theirs.

'Politics is the paradox of the spectator,' Pereira had told him.

The double wasn't sure that he had really understood, but he felt that somewhere in that sentence lay a truth his life depended upon.

Consequently, he plays his role to perfection.

It is a role with a written text and a great deal of silence. When the double is not busy learning Pereira's innumerable speeches, he's giving them, and when he's not busy speaking to the people, he forces himself to listen to them.

Every evening when the sun comes down like a verdict, the double is to be found sitting under a flame tree listening to the poor and lowly.

'Do as my father did,' Pereira told him. 'Listen to them at the appointed time. Look at them in silence with the appropriate humane expression. To indicate that the conversation is over, simply state, "I have heard what you say," and go on to the next.'

'Is that all?' the double asked.

'Yes, and it's quite revolutionary,' Pereira added. 'No one has ever listened to them before. It will take three generations for them to think of asking for anything more. By that time, you and I will no longer be in a position to listen to anyone.'

The double loves delivering Pereira's speeches to the crowd and seeing their eyes light up in response to his passionate sincerity, but he hates these long evening sessions of miserable complaints. It's hard to look as if you're listening when you aren't really paying attention; hard not to nod off, lose patience, count how many more there are in the queue, think of what's for dinner, give in to the urge for just a small glass of banana beer, resist the women's charms ('I'm a chaste president!'); hard not to scratch yourself; hard to control your bladder, to give the impression of being totally there when you would like to be . . . But where exactly? Where would he rather be than there? You mustn't even think of that question. Listen,

listen to every individual as if he were the only one with a grievance – Mother of God, how many of them are there in that bloody queue? – and listen to him as if yours were the only possible ears to hear him, more receptive than a mother's womb, more attentive than the Eternal Father at the hour of judgement.

'Go on! Listen to me as though your ears were all I had in the world.'

Pereira had trained the double long and hard to be a good listener, with himself role-playing the various parts of the worn-out peasant, the worried shopkeeper, the starving widow, the privileged son and his stifling existence. Yes, he, quiet Manuel who had never unburdened himself to anyone, had taken the opportunity to confide to those hired ears the endless boredom of his childhood, his father's sanctimonious inflexibility, his mother's passive stupidity, the mindless adoration of the peasants, their spineless resignation and their idiotic superstitions. He even went so far as to tell him about the terror the da Ponte house inspired in him, with its silence and shadows, its total isolation in the vast expanse of the family estates. Whenever the double's attention wavered, Pereira would stick the barrel of his automatic pistol into his side.

'This is training with live ammunition,' he warned. 'Being a double is a sought-after occupation! And a double is very easily replaced! All that's needed is for people to believe in the resemblance.'

(It's odd how things work themselves out. Everything that

followed, right to the tragic end, is probably contained in that one sentence.)

And so the double has learned to listen. However unbearable he may find these twilight confessions, they have shown him his real gift for acting: he really is a good listener. He reads it in the eyes of the man and the woman as they leave him, heads gently bowed, with the grace of a bird turning in flight.

'I have heard what you say.'

He is thinking: 'Next, next! . . .' but he never gives to the least of them the impression that he is waiting for the next man or woman. He is exhilarated by the discovery of his talent: he is no longer an ordinary double, he's a great actor. Pereira's speeches gain added strength and sincerity when he delivers them. The reason Pereira's words ring so true – everyone in the region says so – is because he listens to what people say. The reason why he touches everyone's heart is because each of us has a place in his. The image of the dictator becomes infused with saintliness. In every home, his picture has pride of place next to the one of Christ the King with the blond curls. The double plays the part of the young monarch receiving communion in the form of 'the people', which is the tyrant's Eucharist. He even begins to detect a kind of respect in the eyes of the father, the Bishop and the friend, where until now he thought he saw nothing but amused admiration.

Not once, however, did the double give way to the intoxication of his role. Cool-headed, eloquently silent and word-perfect, he will never be tempted to think he is Manuel Pereira da Ponte Martins, the hallowed dictator. But it is no longer because he is afraid; it is because he is persuaded of his own genius.

1

WHAT FOLLOWS IS self-evident. As time went by, the double tired, not of play-acting, but of always performing the same play, and in a theatre that he finally found too small. Always the same script, the same production, the same rounds in the same towns, the same audiences, the same applause . . . Other parts on other stages under other skies beckon . . . Americky, to be sure! North America – so close, so full of promise!

The cinematograph, perhaps.

Of course, the cinematograph!

The double emigrated to the United States.

Before leaving, he chose a double who was as much like him as one man can resemble another, to the nth degree, of course. No one noticed that nth degree, as the new double had followed exactly the same programming as the first one had received from Pereira; he thought he had been hired by the dictator in person, underwent the same terrifying training, played his role as the pseudo-President with the same apprehension at first, the same enthusiasm later, finally felt the same boredom and had himself replaced in turn by a double who, after experiencing the self-same soul-searching, passed the baton to the next double.

And so on.

8

T HEN CAME THE day when Pereira went home.
For what reason?

A *coup d'état*? If that had been the case, with the fortune he had in the European bank accounts yielding a good profit, Pereira would never have gone back there. Homesickness? No more likely. The story of the *bacalhau* shows well enough that the *menino* could do without his roots. Just as he could do without power. The fun had been in seizing it. And putting a bullet in the General's neck – that was a sensation as short-lived as it was intense. The job, in the theatrical sense of the word, did not thrill him. He was no longer the child who dreamed of being President. Pereira even found it 'interesting' that a double could do that job perfectly well. (In addition, the idea that Manuel Callado Crespo could prepare his funeral oration while watching someone quite other amused him.)

And then, as we've said already, the ghost of Mãe Branca was still with him when he slept. His agoraphobic nightmares did not induce him to go back and mingle with the crowds of peasants in Teresina. Every night when he was sleeping, the big empty plaza would fill up, the peasants would surround him. He had just enough time to notice the white light at the foot of the lamp-post in front of the two men leaning on a bicycle, laughing; just enough time to say to himself, 'That's real life,' before waking up certain he had died.

So what could it be? The demands of the narrative? Naturally Pereira had to go back so that his destiny could be realised, in the way the author described it at the end of Chapter 3. But that's not a good enough reason; there's no margin of freedom which means that, if the Good Lord sets a precise time and place when we are to meet Him, He has a lot of fun in the meantime with the paths we think we have chosen and our reasons for choosing them.

Pereira decided to go back to Teresina after a game of bridge, in the shadow of the Jungfrau at the Interlaken Victoria Hotel in Switzerland. The cards had just been dealt and bids made. Pereira had a nice hand in spades, and for a partner, a dummy with a lisp. He was a French manufacturer in 'de luxe luggage', (his own expression, which he pronounced 'de lukth luggeth'). With his cards laid out before him the dummy was gossiping away with no regard for the conventions of the game of bridge, which require silence while the hand is being played. The manufacturer had come back from Latin America, where he had gone to stock up on rare skins – snake, armadillo, lizard, iguana, crocodile, etc. – and on the basis of that 'enriththing ekthperienth' felt entitled to deliver a thorough-going critique of European and other constitutional monarchies. Down there 'in the tropicth', he said, the way to deserve power is to take it.

'That means you have dictatorthipth which are no more or leth rethpectable than our governmenth. At leatht you know who you're dealing with: it'th alwayth with the both and he talkth in realitht termth: i.e. wisely sharing the wealth.'

Among other capital cities and 'bothes' he had visited, the manufacturer had been to Teresina, where he had done business with the local potentate, a certain Pereira da Ponte.

Pereira, the real one, was unhurriedly playing his good spades. He knew the whole file. The double had telegraphed him the essentials and Pereira had replied with the percentages.

'There's no quibbling with thome underling in the Minithtry of Commerth,' the Frenchman continued, oblivious to the disapproving silence. 'From the very beginning, it'th the Prethident himthelf, who ith very informed about inter-nathional currenthy, and definite about perthentageth! A quick deal, a dothile workforth, cuthtomth' fathilitieth . . .'

Pereira arranged his tricks in small, neat, alternating piles. He was playing incognito, perhaps under an assumed name, having had his fingers burned in the episode of the man with the memory for faces. He did not avoid looking at his partner, who addressed him each time Pereira picked up his cards and their eyes met.

'Thith Pereira ith thertainly an ekthtraordinary character! When he wath young, he did in a thwordthman who knew nothing about commerth and took hith plathe, jutht like that. A perfect *coup d'état*! To thay that the people trutht Pereira would be to vathtly underthtate the truth: they jutht love him from the bottom to the top of the thocial thcale which, by the way, hath only a top and a bottom, and that'th altho thomething we should learn from! He'th more than the Prethident: he'th the head of the family and they worthip him like a thaint . . . A quiet man with it. He lithtened to me, talked figureth, and that'th all. I only had to thign on the dotted line. An exthtraordinary character, really! Hith interpreter thpoke French amazingly well,' he added, like someone awarding a diploma.

When Pereira returned to his room and his bed, he went over what he had seen and heard. The Frenchman had made no mention of any resemblance between the double and himself. Not the slightest allusion. Well, he was certainly the importer to whom he had granted the monopoly on 'the reptilian skin trade' ('the reptilian thkin trade' – here again the expression comes from the manufacturer . . .) for an appreciable commission and percentage – through the intermediary of the double, of course. The Frenchman could not possibly have forgotten the face of the person with whom he had been dealing, and who, in his own words, had made such an impression on him. So? Was he being discreet? No, he was too anxious to describe his 'enriththing ekthperienth'; if he had recognised Pereira, the businessman would have said so, with a comment like, 'Don't tell me . . . !' Was he pretending to be someone he wasn't? A spy in the pay of heaven knows who? Why would a spy draw attention to himself by *not recognising* a man whose double he said – to his face – that he'd seen? Pereira didn't close his eyes all night. There he was, someone who avoided people with good memories for faces, and now he was alarmed at not being recognised! He gave a wry smile. He decided to go and sit at the manufacturer's table for lunch to put his mind at rest.

The next day at noon, the regular guests of the Hotel Victoria were celebrating the anniversary of a dramatic event that had taken place a few years earlier in that dining room, at the very table at which Pereira and the French businessman had just sat down.

'I wath there,' the Frenchman said. 'Well, I arrived at the end. Poor Müller wath already dead.'

'Dead? Good Lord! How did he die?' a woman's voice asked.

'A bullet in the knee, one in the thigh, one in the kidney, one in the spleen, one in the pancreas and a sixth – pardon me, ladies – in the lower abdomen,' replied Hofweber, the maître d'hôtel who had subdued the murderess.

'The murderess!' another voice exclaimed.

'Indeed, a young, inoffensive-seeming woman who offered

no resistance when Hofweber caught her under the hotel veranda with her Browning hanging from her finger, gazing at the snows on the Jungfrau.

'No need to use force. You can see that I'm not resisting or thinking of trying to escape.'

The Browning was empty; the seventh bullet had lodged in the table top.

'A thertain Mitheth Thtratford,' said the French manufacturer.

'If I may be permitted,' Hofweber intervened to correct him, 'that's the name she gave when she registered. Her real name was Tatiana Leontiev.'

'A crime of passion?' someone asked.

'A political athathination,' the French businessman replied.

Although Pereira had other worries on his mind, he was caught up for a moment by the story of this young Russian zealot, Tatiana Leontiev, who had come here and killed an unfortunate gentleman she took for Piotr Nikolaievitch Dournovo, Tsar Nicholas II's Minister of Police. The white dress crossing the vast dining room, the woman's pistol suddenly produced in a gloved hand, the wild emotion (a whole magazine for one victim!), the last look at the pristine peaks of the Jungfrau . . . Pereira regretted not having been there, to get the confused beauty into his bed and to be able to put a face to so much idealism. The man's life would have been spared and the lady would have had a broken heart, a much better reason for ending her days in the Müsingen asylum, wherein she had been incarcerated.

'And do you know the betht of it? She had never theen Minithter Dournovo. Never! Not wunth, not even a photo!'

34

The French manufacturer with the lisp looked at Pereira, wide-eyed with amazement just thinking about it.

'All she knew wath hith caricature in the newthpaperth!'

Then, with the most innocent sincerity, he exclaimed: 'Would *you* recognithe a man you had only theen in *caricature*?'

. . .

So, it would be the story of Manuel Pereira da Ponte Martins, a nomadic and agoraphobic dictator, who could have ended his life as an unimportant predator in Europe, like so many others, but who rushed to meet his fate, haunted by the certainty that back in Teresina, where he had left a double who resembled him in every respect, the man who reigned now was not a double but a caricature.

9

AND IT WAS his caricature that Pereira killed six weeks later with a single bullet to the middle of the forehead. That took place in the central plaza of Teresina – a circular open plaza bordered with adobe houses, which on that day was crowded with peasants.

It was a public holiday. The anniversary of the day when the sainted President came to power was celebrated throughout the country with a free, general distribution of *bacalhau do menino*, the national dish. About thirty metres from Pereira, an almost hunch-backed figure dressed in full-dress uniform (the same one Pereira wore to Mãe Branca's funeral) stood on the steps of the presidential palace, filling with a ceremonial ladle the bowls and dishes held out to him. Pereira could not have said whether this man was a crude sketch of himself or, on the contrary, a portrait that was too perfect and had gone beyond the point of precise resemblance into the uncontrollable proliferation of any possible version. The differences in their appearance were all the more obvious because the impostor was officiating under a huge portrait in which the original Pereira was shown in all his radiant, unchanging beauty.

But it was not the sight of this dwarfish figure which most surprised Pereira (when one is drifting towards the idea of caricature, one more or less expects this kind of vision), nor the ceremony in itself (it followed to the letter the ritual that he himself had perfected), nor the fervour of the people (on that score, the aim had been predictably realised). No, what froze his heart was seeing this caricature flanked by his father, old da Ponte, his godfather the Bishop, and Eduardo Rist, his friend since childhood. God in Heaven! The expressions on their faces: paternal love, episcopal devotion, fraternal fervour . . . These people who knew him so well were looking fondly at the impostor as if he were really the son, the godson, the friend!

Standing slightly further back among the ministers and representatives of the foreign delegations, Manuel Callado Crespo, the Chief Interpreter, was looking about him, mentally taking notes. And all around, the worshipful crowd converged on the white steps that had become an altar in front of the presidential palace. Pereira, who had made up his face to mingle incognito with the people, a tin dish in his hand, realised that even without make-up, no one in that plaza would have recognised him. Had he gazed deep into the eyes of the snake seller, she would have smiled at him as she would at a stranger, pointing to the impostor saying, 'Isn't our Pereira handsome?' Then she would have added, like a concerned mother, 'But good Lord, how tired he is!' Which would have inspired a series of comments: 'Yes, our Ear is ageing before our eyes. Being President is no easy task!' 'Devotion like that will cost him his life . . .' 'No, a da Ponte doesn't die of overwork!'

Pereira must certainly have wondered about the identity of this stranger who was so good at passing himself off as him in the people's minds and a father's heart that he did not even take the trouble to get the resemblance right.

'That question's unimportant,' Manuel Callado Crespo would have replied, had Pereira put it to him.

And the Chief Interpreter would probably have added: 'Even if they had reached the end of the line, going from nth degree to nth degree of difference, and they'd lumbered the population with a last double who was a one-eyed old biddy, hairy as a goat, and if the creature had played her part reasonably well, they would still have called her "my ear", "my son", "my friend" and "my godson".'

'But you, Callado' (Pereira would have exclaimed, finally beginning to wonder), 'did you realise from the first double that it wasn't me?'

'Oh, I'm an interpreter and translator,' Manuel Callado Crespo would have replied. 'In the seven or eight languages I can find my way around in fluently, I have never met two words that mean exactly the same thing. I can take no particular credit for recognising the doubles: I earn my living hunting down that nth degree of difference.'

But this conversation would never take place. Pereira was in too much of a hurry to punish the impostor. Actually, the impostor was already dead. Pereira had lined him up at first glance. ('Aim before your take out your gun,' the General and ex-President had taught him. 'You only squeeze the trigger as confirmation.') Pereira held in his sights something of himself that had escaped and should disappear.

'Beauty like that,' said a young woman in the crowd, 'is the beauty that comes from goodness.'

Pereira dropped his bowl and fired.

When the palace guards had cleared the plaza by firing volleys at the feet and over the heads of the crowd, all that was found of Manuel Pereira da Ponte Martins, the real one, the dictator torn to pieces by the crowd, was an unrecognisable mass of flesh and bone. He was thrown into the fertiliser pit, and the approximate double he had killed was given a funeral at which the people, the government, the family and friends all shed the same tears. The Bishop applied to the Vatican for beatification, old da Ponte died of paternal grief, and the friend, Eduardo Rist, inherited the seat of power that had become vacant.

That's it. That's the story that should have been told.

II

WHAT I KNOW ABOUT TERESINA

1

WHAT I KNOW about Teresina is contained in a night memory: that soft white light flickering at the base of a street lamp, watched by the two laughing men leaning on a bicycle.

'That's real life,' Manuel Pereira da Ponte Martins said to himself before the crowd closed in on him.

'That's real life,' he thinks fleetingly in his dream.

Well, that vision, or more exactly my memory of it – the street lamp enclosed by the darkness of the Teresina night, the two men seen from the back, the silent laughter, their shoulders shaking, the bicycle they were leaning on, and that dancing light hiding their feet from view – that is the reason for this book, that is what gave birth to it.

It's recorded in a letter I wrote to a friend in November 1979.

At that time I was living with Irene in the North-East region of Brazil, in Maraponga, a suburb of Fortaleza, the capital of Ceará. Irene was teaching. I spent the greater part of my time hanging between earth and sky in my hammock, dreaming up novels I never wrote.

The rest I spent looking around. My letters reported all this to my friend.

2

IT'S TRUE THAT the Brazilian dictator at the time had publicly declared that he preferred the smell of horses to the smell of people. It's true that the dictionary joke about him was doing the rounds: 'There's been another attack on the President: someone threw a dictionary at him!' It's true that there was no lack of Pereiras and Martinses on the South American continent. It's also true that at Fortaleza I saw a white witch tell a group of ecstatic anthropologists their future, sprinkling them with perfume and spinning around like a top, while I looked on bored stiff. It's true that in the same region of the Brazilian North-East, a *fazendeiro** doctor we knew gave free treatment to the peasants he starved on his lands, and that if he is dead today, this gentle supporter of slavery is probably looked on as a saint. It's just as true that in the Hotel Victoria at Interlaken in Switzerland, the radical revolutionary socialist Tatiana Leontiev (the historian Jacques Baynac devoted a book to her: *The Novel of Tatiana*) killed a gentleman she thought was Minister Dournovo, whom she had only seen in caricature. It took place on 1 September 1906, at 12.45 precisely. In the course of the inquiry, Ernst Hofweber, the maître d'hôtel, uttered these words: 'A caricature can easily look like anyone at all.'

It is also true that Yasmina Melaouah, Manuel Serrat Crespo, Évelyne Passet and a few other of my translator friends doubt whether 'la fenêtre', 'la janela', 'das Fenster', 'the window' or 'la finestra' refer to exactly the same thing, since

*Owner of large farming estates.

none of them opens to the same sounds or closes to the same music.

But the starting point of this story, the window that led me into it, is still that soft white light in the night, in Teresina, the capital of Piauí, at the base of that street lamp, watched by two men leaning on a bicycle, silently laughing.

3

WE WERE COMING back to Fortaleza from Brasilia, Irene, Gouvan and I, in a plane that was losing oil in mid-flight. The passengers were not aware of this detail. They were all lost in their own particular night worlds, except for the man next to me, a famous chemist, who sat there with pen in hand, never raising his eyes from his formulae.

At that time Brasilia was still in the course of construction. It was generally agreed that this town served no useful purpose: a fictitious capital, a dormitory deserted by members of the government after every Cabinet meeting, some sleeping in Rio, others in São Paulo. As for the workers, they were shut up for the night in huts on the outskirts, which soon created a ring of poverty around the town. Brasilia was nothing but the recording chamber of Brazilian federal laws. But it was magnificent, a monument town, a kind of newborn millennium child placed on the world's back, at an altitude of 1,200 metres, to impress the Martians.

I was composing the letter to my friend in my head, sitting in the plane leaking oil. How could I describe to him the *physical* sensation of living on a planet such as one felt in Brasilia? The town was almost empty, the trees had not yet grown, everywhere you looked the horizon was curved under a perfectly clear sky. These light, soaring structures of glass and concrete, all these graceful, useless birdlike forms seemed to spring up there solely to commune with the stars. Hence the feeling of cosmic solitude, always a feeding ground for superstition.

The word was going round that Brasilia would one day be the capital city for sects. The dream peddlers were already selling little squares of land carved out around the town, for the extraterrestrials would come to Brasilia to save those who would escape a cataclysm predicted for 1984 – after Orwell, it had to happen.

'The earth is round; Brasilia proves it.' I must have been thinking of an expression like this for my letter when the voice of the man next to me, the chemist, broke into my thoughts.

'Are you an excitable person, Pennac?'

'. . .'

'Because we're losing oil,' he added after a swift glance through the porthole.

4

I'VE ALWAYS LOVED silence. I love it with the same passion as some people love music. What bothers me most about the tinnitus I've had for a few years now is not the sound it makes, but the fact that it deprives me of silence. There's a definite high-pitched hissing noise in my head. Is it the sound of gas, steam, the dentist's drill, or a mad cicada that robs me of the qualities of silence? When everything is quiet, this one note leaves me hanging in space. But at the time I'm talking about, oh, there were such wonderful moments of silence. I collected them. The one that settled on our plane after the captain confirmed the chemist's diagnosis rates very highly.

Sorry.

Damage.

Forced to change course.

The nearest airport.

If possible.

Don't panic.

Dead silence; the human body and mind at its most elemental; my fear building within it. One of the finest silences in my collection.

. . .

(To find one as 'preoccupied' as that, in any category, I would have to go back to my father's silence when he was immersed in his books: the armchair, the glasses, the old woolly jumper, the cone of light, the pipe smoke, the second and third finger moving over his temple, the crossed legs, the slight swinging left foot, the regular, recurrent punctuations of a page turning . . . He was never so much a presence as when he deserted us into that silence.)

. . .

We were losing oil . . .

So, has oil got into the jets?

You couldn't see anything out of the portholes, only the thin plume of white smoke coming from between two plates on the jet engine and disappearing into the blackness. It left a phosphorescent trail we all thought could catch fire at any moment.

'Where are we?' I asked the chemist.

He glanced at his watch.

'Somewhere over Pernambouc, or Piauí. Somewhere in the interior.'

5

THE INTERIOR ...

What was her name again, the poor soul who died a few months later? She was a student at the Alliance Française in Fortaleza. With her cooks, her housemaids, her nannies, her gardeners, her husband's chauffeur and her own, she had nine *empregados* in her service. On the subject of these employees, all from the interior, she would say with a perfectly straight face: 'They made my emancipation possible.'

Despite her wealth, she was left-wing. She had read Beauvoir. She knew Dom Hélder Câmara, the 'Red Bishop'. She asked charming questions in grammatical French. She always used the polite 'vous'.

'When you are in France, do you occasionally travel in the interior?'

Soledad, with all of her twenty years and many fewer teeth, thanks to the extraordinary gap between rich and poor, asked the same thing.

'When you're back home, do you go to the interior?'

This is because Brazilians live crowded up against the ocean as the interior is so vast. They turn their backs on the land, gazing out to the empty sea. Hence Brasilia: the necessity to set up a capital city in the middle of nowhere to ward off the demons of the interior.

And these demons are no creatures of fable, if you believe what the *cordel* poets* sing in the town squares of the interior. It seems that soldiers – a platoon of them – are sent to settle a problem with the peasants in the sertão; the soldiers disappear. They send a company; the company comes back cut to pieces. (This happens in 1896, in the North-East near Juazeiro do Norte. Euclides da Cunha, a contemporary journalist, relates the tragedy in a large book entitled simply *Os Sertaoes*.) They send a battalion; the batallion is swallowed up in the sertão. They send a regiment; their uniforms are found hanging from the caatinga trees,† the soldiers' severed heads lined up facing each other on either side of the road where they were overwhelmed, and the Colonel's body empaled (despite the fact that he was called César). (Eighty years later, Vargas Llosa also writes a solid thousand pages on the same subject, *The War of the End of the World*.) They call on a brigade of the federal army which distinguished itself in its victory over Paraguay; the brigade is defeated. It takes a third of the Brazilian army, infantry, cavalry, artillery, an unheard of deployment of forces, finally to crush these peasants under the stones of their village: Canudos. A few hundred men, women and children, led by a chief who was

---

Literatura de cordel (string literature) are cheap booklets of narrative poems with woodcuts on the covers sold in street markets in the North-East of Brazil. They are displayed hanging side by side from a string across the stall. They represent the lives and traditions of the people, and are often used in song tournaments where the singers accompany themselves on guitars.

† Caatinga is a type of semi-arid scrub forest found principally in the Brazilian North-East. The area is also called by that name.

chaste, a cuckold and a mystic, a man with a limp who will be a legendary figure for ever: Antonio Concelheiro.

'How could that possibly happen?' people asked each other in their drawing rooms overlooking the sea.

In the interior, the guitar duettists of *cordel* literature still sing the Canudos epic accompanied on their battered old guitars.

6

THE DEMONS OF the interior . . . Things that are suddenly there but seem to come out of nowhere.

They appeared to us on the day that Gouvan took Irene and myself to see the Concha Acústica on the outskirts of Brasilia.

In fact, for someone who loves silence . . .

The Concha was an open-air opera theatre, where the Pavarottis of the day were supposed to come and do their stuff. But where was the audience? There was nothing, as far as the eye could see, but *mato* scrub outlined by that empty curved horizon which didn't look any more promising. In fact, the Concha was more like a monument glorifying solitude and silence than a theatre. We had come in a hired car and stood for a while beside its open doors.

All that was real, that was what was out of kilter.

Not a bird to be seen.

No breath of air.

A few insects.

And the opera theatre.

The empty rows sloping down to the wordless well of the stage.

Just the three of us standing above that huge hole, vaguely Greek, all concrete, devised as a sanctuary for man's noise until the end of time.

You could hear the bonnet of the car cooling down.

An opera just for us on an uninhabited planet, now that was tempting. The next thing, we were going down the central aisle, standing on the stage and declaiming into the void. We were three young idiots writing our graffiti in the sky, no more, no less. I can remember Irene and Gouvan sitting in the one of the tiers of seats, arms loosely entwined, playing to a full house. What did I recite? Probably some lines from *Le Cid* in de Gaulle's voice, an old party piece from my youth. Or maybe a variation on the Quebec speech, adapted to the Brazilian agrarian problem: 'Long live *sertão libre!*' And long de Gaullean periphrases on the redistribution of land to the peasants of the North-East . . .

Until I noticed a presence out of the corner of my eye, on one of the high tiers to my right.

Someone is looking at us.

Someone is listening to us.

We're not alone.

The Concha Acústica had not been excavated in vain.

It was a big, yellowish dog with grey spots. It was standing still and very attentive up there with its head bent towards us in the depths. Hello, dog. All it did was raise one eye towards the other side of the steps. I turned round: there was another dog. It was as big as the first, but with a black curly coat like a Briard. They were both very thin, very wiry and very interested in our presence at the bottom of the pit. It's one thing to try to be clever for a familiar audience, but these newcomers looked more demanding. I went over to Irene and Gouvan, pointed out the dogs to them, and the nature of the show suddenly changed. The two big dogs were not alone. To tell you the truth, it was like the Apaches in a John Ford film suddenly appearing on the skyline. There were about thirty of them above the stage, all with their heads lowered, noses pointing towards us, and their thin shoulders outlined against the sky. Gouvan turned pale.

'Let's go.'

'Don't run,' I added.

'And keep on acting the fool,' Irene advised.

The dogs also started to move. They spread out in two semicircles behind their leaders following the curve of the shell, backs hollowed and eyes trained on us. Where did they come from? We had to go up the central aisle and reach the car before these apparitions could block our path . . . Slowly, step by step, and in a clear voice if possible. There was every imaginable combination of guard dogs and mongrels, mutts which had recently found themselves without masters or old bruisers that had been feral for several generations. Every breed, every colour, every type, every mixture, but all with wounds, all with ribs sticking out, unwavering eyes and a silent tread. I counted sixteen of them on my left alone. People who like dogs are still wary of a dog in the manger. I am like that. If one of them decided to take a short cut through the tiers, they would all come at us at the same time.

There is no point in prolonging this artificial suspense. The fact that I remember it today means that we got away. We didn't hold out until the end, though; we ran the last few metres. As expected, they threw themselves at the big game. They bounced off the car doors as we slammed them shut and shot off in a cloud of dust.

7

ANOTHER WEIRD IMAGE of the interior: the trapdoor spider that burns without being consumed by the fire, while Soledad watches. People kill them to avoid being bitten. They burn them with methylated spirits so that the eggs don't hatch after the spider is dead. And there's the black body still blazing, its legs in the air, burning without shrivelling, taking an age to go out . . . It's dead, but it still seems alive; it's an authentic image of hell: indestructible.

Once you get rid of the trapdoor spider, you get bitten by the mosquitoes it used to eat.

You learn to prefer the spiders.

They don't bite.

8

THE DEMONS OF the interior . . . Even before Brasilia was complete, six psychoanalysts had already set up practice there.

9

THAT'S THE KIND of thing I was writing to my friend. Stories about the interior. The one about the short-lived railway track, for example, on which were brought all the materials needed to build a new town for loggers deep into Amazonia; a whole town complete with swimming pool, police station and airstrip. The train made its way through a 2,000-kilometre tunnel of vegetation, dug out by workers from the North-East who laid the rails in front of the engine as it advanced. When the town was built, the train went back, swallowing its track as it went. The workers took up the rails, loaded them on to the wagons, and the forest closed back over what was not even the memory of a railway track.

Was it Gouvan who took this photograph of the abandoned locomotive a few weeks later? Couch grass had gripped the wheels, and a vine had twined its way right up to the controls.

10

SO, THERE I am stuck in that plane; yesterday it was fear, today it's hunting a memory and choosing the right words.

Anyway, that was the night I heard the name Teresina for the first time. It came from the intercom with the captain's voice announcing that we were going to attempt a landing.

Teresina . . .

'The capital of Piauí,' my neighbour the chemist explained. 'I doubt that the aerodrome will be big enough for the plane,' he added before immersing himself once more in his work.

The silence of the chemist is also part of my collection – in the British category, subset ostentatious. As for the other passengers, theirs was the silence of desperate prayer. In situations like these, the soul bargains with every available deity. There could be no shortage of them on that plane, given the length of time that the angels of the sertão had been copulating with the spirits of the Caribbean, blessed by Christ, the Virgin and all their saints. There must have been plenty of promises to make pilgrimages during our descent into Teresina! And small fortunes spent on offerings of thanks for vows fulfilled! And great investment in repentance! Just as the attendance of a doctor is urgently requested when someone falls ill, I would not have been surprised to hear the intercom ask for a Mother of the Saints to make a prediction as to our immediate future.

In situations like these, one does not scorn superstition. You grip the edge of the seat and think of whatever you can. In a plane that's going down, there's a very thin line separating a spirit that claims to be free and one that thinks it's in other hands. Both refuse this unique opportunity to rise above their predicament. They just want to live a bit longer, to have a soft landing.

It's not impossible that I thought of our friend Geraldo Markan while Irene and I placed all our faith in our seat belts. Geraldo was not with us in the plane, but he believed in all those things about the hereafter . . . he believed in them completely, but he was – how can I put it? – completely relaxed about it. Grace with grace . . . It was Geraldo who told me the story of the professor who went to consult a white witch to know if he would get the Chair of Religious Anthropology at some great university, then went straight to a black witch to dispose of his rivals. Geraldo told it with a smile that curled his whiskers. The fact that an anthropologist could subscribe to the superstitions he was supposed to study didn't scandalise him any more than discovering that a historian had political beliefs. Perhaps he thought that, all things considered, this duality is the only subject worth studying. If he'd been with us in the plane which was losing its oil, and if we'd taken the opportunity to talk about superstition, Geraldo would probably have said to me: 'Only one of two things can happen: either we crash and the debate about superstition is closed, or we land and in twenty years' time you find out that the socialist president you'd like to see in charge of your country had consulted your local Mãe Branca to gain this secular throne.'

We landed, twenty-three years have passed, the President reigned, then died, and at the time of writing these lines (Tuesday, 10 April 2001), the astrologer he did indeed visit has just been awarded a doctorate in sociology by the University of the Sorbonne.

No less.

A study of the epistemological position of astrology through the ambivalence of fascination/rejection in postmodern societies . . .

No kidding.

If I'd taken exception to it in that plane, Geraldo would probably have replied: 'Why not? Wouldn't Al Capone be best placed to defend a sociology thesis on organised crime, *Myth and Reality in Contemporary Tribality*?'

*

Whereupon Geraldo, having indulged in the little pleasures of these mind games, would have taken out the tiny ivory comb he used to straighten his moustache.

11

OF COURSE I did not think of Geraldo Markan in the plane losing oil, but Irene has just told me that he has died. They found him in his house at Fortaleza. Was it still the house with the whispering fountain at the entrance?

Whether we believe in it or not, we picture the hereafter as a revised and corrected version of life here on earth. Our personal heaven is made up of people who have made our lives bearable. Chosen by our perception of them, they sit enthroned at the right hand of our absence, for the years we have still to get through (with a few who were a pain in the neck, by way of variation). The question of knowing whether we'll meet them again when our own time comes is only interesting if one is discussing it with a delightful friend, in a hammock if possible, and, if possible, in a house designed for Corto Maltese.

That was the situation on the afternoon in November 1980, when Geraldo Markan and I were chatting, each of us lying in a hammock under the veranda at Maraponga. (What were we talking about? All I can recall is Geraldo's face and voice, the languid progression of his thought, the benevolent look in his eyes, the impression of wisdom that radiated from the feeblest of his jokes, his looked-for smile. Most of the subjects we spoke of have been lost in time; what Geraldo has left with me is the music of his unique personality.)

All that aside, it was on the same afternoon at Maraponga that a drunk interrupted us, appearing suddenly from under the trees. Thin, ragged and extremely agitated, his eyes bulging from the *cachaça*[*] he had been drinking, he rushed towards us, zigzagging through the coconut trees. With cries of terror, he told us that he was being chased by a ghost. He absolutely had to have twenty *cruzeiros* to burn a candle to St Rita, so that she could make the ghost rise up again and go back to where it came from. If we were good Christians, we would . . .

Geraldo coughed up without a word.

Surprised, Cachaça stopped yelling and began bargaining for more. With fifty *cruzeiros* the candle would be bigger and the ghost's ascension would assuredly be quicker.

Geraldo refused.

'I know your ghost. He was a neighbour, a good man with very few sins on his conscience. He's not heavy; twenty *cruzeiros* will be enough for St Rita to raise him up to heaven again.'

Cachaça bristled with suspicion for a moment.

'If you know him, why didn't you burn the candle yourself?'

'Because I'm mean. If you burn that twenty *cruzeiros*' worth, it's your money you'll be spending.'

And then out it came. His little moustache comb.

---

[*]*Cachaça*: a cheap, highly intoxicating drink made from sugar cane, containing between 70 and 80 per cent of alcohol. It is the most popular alcoholic drink of the poorest people in Brazil.

12

ONE MORNING WHEN I was writing to my friend (perhaps I was telling him the story about the drunk), a young woman appeared under the veranda at Maraponga. I got up from my table to greet her. She asked if she could wait there until the rain stopped.

But it wasn't raining.

Indeed, it was a glorious day.

She was a girl of about thirty, grey eyes, hair pulled back, a plain dress and flat-heeled shoes. I had never seen her before. She came neither from the *favela* nor from the houses round about. Soledad offered her a cup of tea. She would prefer fresh coconut milk. When we came back with the coconut, she was lying in the hammock looking at the sky.

I went back to writing my letter, very pleased to have this unexpected story to tell. From time to time I glanced at our visitor through the blinds across my study window. Although Soledad thought she had a *cabeça fraca* (she was not quite right in the head), she was very calmly sipping her coconut milk. Her attitude expressed nothing but the wise patience of a woman waiting for a shower to end before going on her way again.

When I told Geraldo Markan about it, he replied in all seriousness: 'That's because it must have been raining somewhere else.'

13

GERALDO SITS ENTHRONED in my heaven, along with my father, Dinko, Soulat, Mounier, Jean and Germaine, Aymé, Little Louis and Patrick, my wild rabbit, my poor, radiant Cécile who used to laugh so much at the play on words in Tardieu's plays, my beautiful, lively cousin Monette, always putting her foot in it, now with Mathilde, Thildou, so affectionate, and Thierry our builder, all taken one after the other while I was writing one of these pages, never suspecting the worst; also Chief Thomas from my childhood, dear old Philou who dreamed of Amazonia, with Annie, yesterday, Annie de Sylvère, such a gracious lady in her old age, and with all the others who would be very surprised to learn, in their hypothetical eternity, that every day their memory gives me an acceptable reason to exist. It's my Olympus, my academy, my tribe, it's me – at any rate, one of the few worthwhile versions of me.

14

ALL THAT HAPPENED a long time ago: a whole life in the twinkling of an eye. The plane landed, Geraldo died; Alice, Tiago, Janou, Roland, Gilles, Louna, Laetitia, Antoine, Élise, Aurélie, Rémy, Victor and many others were born; Soledad, Emmanuelle, Loïc, Jérôme, Vincent and Charlotte,

Mélanie, Christophe and Carole, Alban and Sophie are now men and women. With these tides of time, Brazil has acquired a semblance of democracy, the *cruzeiro* has become the *real*, the *real* has been tied to the dollar, the coast still attracts the hungry people of the interior, Fortaleza has become a well-known beach resort, a few large buildings have finally grown up in Teresina, empires have crumbled, Europe has moved right and left, merging and cracking, Africa is dying from every evil, while global commercialism claims to eradicate 'isms', some two thousand students have been through my classes, some couples and friendships have broken up, others have been formed. Minne and I met, Irene and I separated and, in the Vercors, in the house that Christophe renovated, I've written books, but never anything about Brazil.

My reluctance is due to the Sleeper in the Sertão.

Yet another story of the interior.

15

THE SLEEPER IN the Sertão was a university lecturer who had come travelling in Brazil with the firm intention of publishing something. Physically, he was a Tartarin from Saint-Germain,* with a battery of pens stuck in the cartridge belt of a seasoned traveller's safari jacket. Mentally, he was a big baby safely curled up in a womb of theories. Socially, he

---

*A reference to Alphonse Daudet's novel *Tartarin de Tarascon* (1872), which relates the comic exploits of a naive adventurer.

was a university teacher living on a staple diet of theses here, a column there, obviously an author, occasionally an editor, a collector of committees and judging panels, favoured by one person, not badly thought of by another, a pawn on each square of the chess board, a man for every off chance, a subject in search of importance: one of these days a government minister, a diplomat or adviser to a prince.

Naturally, he wanted to 'go into the interior'. For one thing, he wanted to see the priest he had been told about who was fighting for peasant rights. As it happened, this priest was virtually invisible – even for an observer from Europe. Two hired killers sent by some *fazendeiro* had tried to shoot him. The *sertanejos** claimed that they had come into his church on horseback. Another priest had died, but he got away, protected by his flock. He was in hiding somewhere in the caatinga.

But the Sleeper in the Sertão wanted to 'witness' it, on the spot, with his own eyes.

The priest, the priest! He had to see the priest!

Following up various leads to his hideout, it took us several days to find him. He was an old Belgian Jesuit (or was he Dutch, or maybe Canadian?), tough as old boots and thin with it. The first thing he showed us in the house where he was living was one of those hand mincers made of red cast iron, used by butchers when I was a child to mince the horsemeat my mother used to put on slices of bread for us. 'Meet my dentures,' he said to us with a gummy smile. The few teeth he'd had left, he'd pulled out himself. It was a matter of 'settling the problem once and for all'.

He offered us some fresh coconut milk and then suggested

*Peasants living in the sertão.

we make use of the hammocks. Our observer took out his notebook and asked his first question. It was to do with agrarian problems; this was certainly the place. The Jesuit gave an answer that was both technical and detailed. It turned out that he wanted to be less an evangelist and more of a legal adviser. He taught law to the peasants so that they themselves could see to the proper application of the '64 laws passed in Brasilia, which none of the landowners in the North-East obeyed: sharecropping quotas in relation to levels of production, the right to sell in markets, etc. He needed to teach these *sertanejos* to read and write well and to understand the legal weight of a contract, then persuade them that this law was real . . . For the moment, the Jesuit was more specifically engaged with sixty families expropriated by a *fazendeiro* against all kinds of laws. He had to find shelter for this little crowd thrown out into the sertão, so that it would not go and bump up the population in some *favela* . . .

That sort of thing . . .

Yes.

Yes, yes . . .

But our witness to the historic moment had fallen asleep.

In his hammock.

His notebook resting on his stomach.

The Sleeper in the Sertão.

The Jesuit asked us not to wake him, and the conversation continued between us. When we came to the subject of the drought, just when the Jesuit was talking about irrigation, his voice was drowned out by the premonitory rumblings of a storm. It wasn't water from heaven, it was the Sleeper in the Sertão snoring.

16

I STILL HAVE A glowing memory of that Jesuit. Literally. It's a story that took place in the sun. He had built a system of guttering that wound its way around the village, converging on a tank where every last drop of every last rainfall was collected, from the first day of the year to the last.

'In short, enough to make gardens grow, if the *fazendeiros* would install water tanks everywhere!'

In his opinion, part of the problem depended on just that: the large landowners refusing to invest in water tanks. They put up with the dryness of the sertão. The vastness of their estates guaranteed their profits and the lack of water kept the *sertanejos* in a state of dependency. The owners were free to send tanker trucks to them or not, as they wished.

When we took the shower the Jesuit offered us, frogs tumbled down with the water. Born in the darkness of the reservoir, they fell on our heads before sticking to the cement walls. Tiny, translucent frogs, like little startled, palpitating puddles.

'And they would have us believe that drought is inevitable!'

17

NOW COMES A memory of shadows: the family home of the *fazendeiro* who, for the purposes of fiction, became the father of Manuel Pereira da Ponte Martins, the dictator with the silent childhood. He was one of the biggest land-owners in the North-East. But he did not live it up on the coast like most of his kind, who were happy to leave the running of their lands to overseers. He lived there, in the heart of his empire, with his own little world. He was a small, gentle doctor, who reigned over a territory as vast as one of our *départements*.* He could go from his house to Fortaleza by rail. His Land-Rover travelled on the rails: 'It's much faster than the road.' Trains just had to be stopped to let him pass.

He greeted us, speaking quietly, in a monumental room where peasant women were embroidering. The *doutor*'s daughter was being married in six months' time; these women were preparing her trousseau. They worked by the light coming through the windows, which lit only their work. The centre of the room where the *doutor* (he never took off his white coat) was talking to us remained in shadow. The *doutor* told us in a whisper about the hard life there, the drought in the sertão, the harsh laws of the marketplace, the long days he would spend in the hospital where he treated the peasants for nothing (offering courses of treatment with Coca-Cola for dehydrated children), the afflictions of all and sundry. 'Above all, I listen to them; they talk to me and I listen to them.' The smell of a poor man's soup rises from the kitchen next door. Apart from a few extra embellishments, this was the normal family fare. Women and children were waiting on the doorstep with bowls in their hands. 'We're a big family, and everyone must be fed.' And the family got on very well together: there was the paternal love of the *fazendeiro* for his *sertanejos*, the filial love of the *sertanejos* for the *doutor*, shining love of one and all for the girl who was getting married,

*The administrative divisions of France, run by a *préfet*.

unquestionable love of the sons for their father, charming love of the sister for the brothers, everyone's love for Christ, crucified in every room . . . If I have no memory of the mother, it's because she must have been nowhere and everywhere, the invisible thickener in this rich sauce of love.

I can say it ironically today, but I remember very well being charmed by this feudal tranquillity. The atmosphere was such a contrast to the blatant brutality of those in power: the grinning arrogance of the dictator, the governors' unsmiling militia, police roadblocks that ripped off travellers close to cities, the killing of trade union leaders or Amazonian ecologists, massacres of natives, torture of students, exile of opponents, demonstrators in São Paulo ripped to pieces by dogs, children killed on the hills in Rio . . . All that was absolutely unimaginable in the *doutor*'s house. No violence in that haven, no swear words. Actually, few words of any kind.

What kind of a son would I have been, what kind of man would I have become, had I been born in that cocoon? What path could a child conceived in the *doutor*'s house follow, to go from that cosy love nest to the strange lands of the law? Looking through the window, how could he imagine that this happiness could *share the same nature* as that violence? How could he accept the fact that the foster-father could also be starving his foster-children, and that his paternal charity was the halo of deadly paternalism?

No. If the demons of the interior wake up one day and decide to tear the *doutor* to shreds, his sons will never understand it. If, three or four generations later, the history books give legitimacy to this massacre, his great-grandchildren won't understand it either. He was such a good man . . .

*

When the sun went down, the embroiderers left and the *doutor* turned on the light. It was a naked 60-watt globe hanging from a long wire. It lit only the centre of the room; the walls and ceiling vanished in the gloom. The globe was turned on by giving it a quarter-turn in its socket. A quarter-turn to the right, you have light; a quarter-turn to the left, time for bed.

Did the Jesuit hunters receive their orders under this globe? Or under a very similar one?

Whatever the answer to that, if one day the story of Manuel Pereira da Ponte Martins, the dictator who lost his way, ever gets told, I could quite easily see him being born into this kind of paradise.

18

TWO MONTHS LATER, we received the book of the Sleeper in the Sertão through the post. It was a complete tour of Brazil in which João Pessoa, the harbour capital of Paraíba, became 'a small township in the interior' (you might as well describe Toulon as a large village in the Cantal), Gilberto Freyre, the most famous Brazilian sociologist, became a 'novelist' (as the dramatist Auguste Comte would say . . .) and our Jesuit delivered a long monologue to the Sleeper, who claimed to have listened attentively.

'A real fieldworker,' Irene commented.

Then she added, 'Provided it's his own.'

I owe my vocation as a novelist to this champion 'on-the-spot eyewitness'.

19

A LL SORTS OF people came to visit us. The pleasantly hippy architect, for one. After going to Brasilia to meditate before Niemeyer's immense work, he too wanted to go up to Ceará and be taken around 'in the interior'.

There we were, the two of us, under a torrid sun, driving on the road to Canindé, perhaps . . .

As we came round a bend, a huge field suddenly appeared in the monotonous grey-ochre landscape. It was like an explosion of green.

'Stop!' my passenger shouted. 'Stop, stop!'

He looked as if he might jump out as we were moving.

'Look at that *grass!*'

He was yelling, with his eyes practically sticking out on stalks.

'Christ! That *graaaaass!*'

I didn't stop. He would still be there smoking a field of manioc.

20

I F IT HAD been up to him, my friend Gouvan (the one who had escaped the wild dogs in the Concha Acústica) would have cut the balls off the lot of them: the Sleeper in the Sertão, the Jesuit, the *doutor* and the hippie. He would have sent the middle classes on the coast and the industrialists of the South to fertilise the caatinga with their repentant tears. He would have confiscated the intellectuals' glasses and shoved reality under their noses. He would have eradicated religion, rooted out superstition, re-educated the subjugated peasants, driven the traitor out even from people's minds, flushed out the class enemy even from children's hearts . . .

When I put it to him that Pol Pot's Cambodia had just lost two million lives out of five with this very prescription, he replied that this was the price that had to be paid and I felt, in the most heated moments of our discussions, that my own balls could very well be added to his avenging skewer when the time came.

Fortunately he was with us in the plane that was going to crash.

More fortunate still, if we got out of it alive, our friend Gouvan had another priority: to do a doctoral thesis in organic chemistry in Paris.

History hangs on such things . . .

However, when he was not considering the possibility of redeeming humanity through extermination, Gouvan was the most cheerful fellow alive. His healthy laugh echoed through the vast spaces of the caatinga.

As for the old chemist (was he so old, now that I come to think of it, or was I still so young? What was his name again? Was Gouvan one of his students? Was the chemist supervising his thesis? What were we all doing there in that plane? We were coming back from Brasilia, yes, but why were the four of us there together? Oh! my hopeless memory . . .), anyway, when he was not affecting the stoicism of the noble soul, the chemist sitting next to me was a delightful travelling companion, giving as much attention to the smallest molecule as to the whole of the tangible world. He was curiosity itself.

21

THE QUESTION OF memory.
The impressions that people leave with us . . .

A warning to any authorities that might summon me as a witness in a court case: I do not easily recall things. My memory seems to hatch scrambled eggs. My most recent memories are shadows. Many times in my life I have seen the same picture again in the same art gallery, the same landscape around the same bend, and it's as if I'd never seen them. I have scarcely experienced an event before it disappears from my screen, and the same thing applies to pages read, most films seen, glasses of good wine tasted. It's enough to make you think that there's an attentive forgetfulness making sure that my lack of culture is maintained at the same level. Names and faces dissolve and disappear too quickly from my mind; my contemporaries make impressions on me that are both vague and deep, like tattoos done with diluted ink. The most sensitive among them are obviously hurt by this, and accuse me of being indifferent or selfish . . . What can I say? So let them help me to work out where I've parked my car, or find the forgotten PIN number of my credit card somewhere in the folds of my brain.

I have a poor memory, therefore an unreliable presence in the world, which prohibits me from giving testimony or being a witness. Hence my enthusiasm for writing novels, no doubt: the imagination starved of memories works furiously at recomposing life from sketches.

22

IT REMAINS THAT the essentials here – the people, events, circumstances, conversations – are certified as genuine by the letters to my friend, which are on the table in front of me. Do you want proof? The visit of John-Paul II to Fortaleza: *Over here it's the invasion of the pontifical Pole, the Attila of the TV channels. They speak of nothing but him, show nothing but him, hear nothing but him. Some advertising firm in Rio has found a double for him, someone who touts for a few of the big stores. Which means that, even when it's not him, it's still him* (Fortaleza, 14 July 1980).

Thinking about it today, the almost miraculous ubiquity of the Pope on television screens (which did not give rise to the miracle of the loaves) and, more generally, the unrelenting duplication that our cult of the image forces on us certainly count for something in this story about doubles of doubles. A world like the one on the Vache Qui Rit label, that's the ideal of our 'communications' people. Every one of us as endless mirror images of each other . . .

23

THE PLANE WAS coming down now as though we were falling. The sound of my heartbeats was blocking my ears. All Irene and I could see through the porthole was that white smoke in the blackness of the night.

'If he gets us down, it'll be a Brazilian-style landing,' my imperturbable neighbour had warned me.

And he did indeed land us Brazilian style.

Which is to say that he closed the throttle two or three metres above the runway, so that the plane fell vertically on to it with all the weight of a building. I really did think that the landing gear would come through the cabin. At the very same second he engaged the retro thrust and the jet engines screamed with tonsil-ripping intensity. My seat belt almost cut me in two, my nose smacked into the stowed tray table; overhead lockers opened, luggage rained down; there was an interminable sensation of braking, as if the plane was swallowing us row by row . . .

We came to a stop at the very end of the runway.

For a while we all just sat there, stunned.

Then the body finally relaxed.

Applause.

Welcome to Teresina, the capital of Piauí.

'It's a bit startling,' my neighbour the chemist conceded, as he put away his little notebooks into a school satchel. 'But when the runways are short, the Brazilian-style landing is more prudent than your asymptotic approach.'

24

WE WERE HELD up for a good two hours at the airport. They were looking for a hose connection.

That's what the breakdown was: a burnt-out hose connection. All that was needed was to replace it.

I concentrated my mind, wishing they wouldn't find one in the clobber they had in their tool kits. The idea of taking to the air again in the middle of the night with a patched-up plane didn't thrill me. I told myself that *all* the planes in the world are probably patched up, that the whole world flies night and day in patched-up aeroplanes, but it was no good: I just didn't want them to find a hose connection, and that was that.

Wish granted. Instead of a hose, they found us a hotel in Teresina.

In his nightmare, Pereira imagines his hotel in the centre of a round, open space. (In dreams everything takes place in the centre.) Pereira goes out, the plaza is empty; he hears someone calling his name, the plaza is full; the hotel has disappeared and he, Pereira, has become the centre and the peasants are rushing towards him. He will never again trust open spaces: he has become agoraphobic.

In real life, the hotel was a concrete cube standing on the edge of a plaza in the hot Teresina night. Giant cockroaches awaited us on the flaking walls of our rooms, and the taps spat spurts of metallic water from temperamental pipes.

The kitchens were closed, so they warmed up for us a mixture of white rice and black beans dusted with *farofa*, browned manioc flour. I recognised this dish: it was the one

Mãe Martins, Soledad's mother, served us when we visited her in the interior. Rice and *feijão* were the everyday fare of Latin America, when the beans or the rice were available. It was a mixture for the hungry that had to give ballast to the featherweight peasants of the caatinga, to stop them from flying away. On high days and holidays, Mãe Martins would add some chicken blood.

I can imagine how the son of a *fazendeiro*, brought up in a large, silent house dreaming of faraway places, could hate this subsistence food from the interior. And I can understand how he could come to see *farofa* as nothingness; but in this case, it's Kathleen Lockridge, the Scottish dancer, who is right: beans and rice go well together, the whole continent of South American will corroborate that. As for *farofa*, with that delicate hint of grilled broad beans, the very thought of it brings on my *saudade*.

. . .

Here, we jump forward a few months: Irene and I are in a chic drawing room in Rio. I'm standing, trying to balance a cocktail of something or other and a complicated canapé (what the hell were we doing there?). Replying to a question, I hear myself saying the name Piauí.

'Piauí? Where's that?' someone asks.

'Somewhere in our prehistory,' replies our host, a smart guy from the South, a *carioca** brought up on the fat of the land.

But I prefer Irene's reply to that sophisticated one:

'Piauí is the interior of the Interior.'

. . .

Yes, and Teresina is its centre, and our hotel the heart of

*A native or inhabitant of Rio.

that centre, and our table, the centre of that heart, and each of us bending over our plates . . . (There is no end to the possibilities of the concept 'interior'.)

In short, a chance mechanical hitch had sent each of us into the heart of himself. Irene, the old chemist, Gouvan and I.

Someone suggested we go out.

To take a look at Teresina.

But one doesn't 'go out' in Teresina. Outside is still inside. The square was surrounded by low houses with corrugated-iron roofs. By the light from the hotel, we could make out that they were washed in those greens and ochres that make every town in the interior a tempting subject for a watercolourist. A few yards further on and the colour of the houses was lost in the darkness. Not a peep of light on the horizon. Nor the slightest sound in the vicinity.

'The bottom of the barrel,' Irene murmured. 'If I'm still here in twenty-four hours, I'll have forgotten my own name.'

Teresina was sleeping. How many stomachs had had their fill of rice and *feijão* behind those mud walls? And when was the last time that water had fallen from the sky on to the Teresina earth crunching under our feet? Teresina went to sleep with hungry bellies and dry throats. It suddenly occurred to me that the architectural unreality of Brasilia – its tall glass buildings, its artificial lake, its sweeping bird's wings – had been thought up only to blot out the reality of Teresina. I knew nothing about the town and never would, but on that night, although I did not know it yet, Teresina became the capital of this story.

Back home in Fortaleza, Irene hastened to look at a map to

be sure that Teresina actually existed, and that our enforced stop hadn't been the result of a 'shared hallucination'.

We had now left the plaza in front of the hotel. We were wandering aimlessly from one narrow street to another. We weren't talking, or if we were it was very quietly. What were the sleepers in Teresina dreaming of in their hammocks? The bright lights of the coast, according to Irene, everything that attracted them to the coast: 'The brilliant shop windows, the magic of the merchandise, the tourists and the money, gaiety, work, excitement . . . to experience the mirages of the coast that you pay to see.' Yes, and end up in the outer circle of some *favela*, drowning our *saudade* in *cachaça*, busking in Rio or singing about the glories of the sertão on the markets of São Paulo with a guitar across our shoulders with the other exiles from the caatinga, counting how many *reals* it will take to satisfy the new dream: return to Teresina, Canindé, Juàzeiro, Sobral Campina Grande, get back to the sertão and that priceless part of ourselves patiently waiting for us there under the flame trees: our solitude.

It was then that we came out into the round, open space – the one in Pereira's dream – and saw the light of the street lamp over on the other side, the only one in the town as far as I can remember. It was a real surprise, and the two silhouetted figures standing at the base of it, a real revelation of life. Our isolation and our need for light sent us towards that company. Once we reached the centre of the open space, we could make out the scene more clearly: they were two *sertanejos* leaning on a bicycle. Their tattered trousers hung loosely around their skinny legs, and their shoulders were shaking with laughter we could not hear. They were looking at something on the ground at their feet which gave out a dull gleam. We entered the ring of light from the street lamp. There was no doubt about it: the pale glow at the *sertanejos'* feet was making them laugh heartily, but not out loud. This wordless hilarity also attracted us, together with the dancing light, now hidden by their bare feet and the frayed bottoms of their trousers. It was an old television set. They had somehow connected a small black-and-white TV to the town electricity supply, and it worked. They were watching *The Gold Rush* with Charlie Chaplin. The first man had his elbows leaning on the seat, and the other had his hands crossed on the rusty handlebars of the bike. Both of them were laughing silently at a film without words. They laughed as they watched Charlie struggle against the wind and the snow; they laughed as they watched Charlie eat his boot and suck the laces; they laughed as they watched Charlie transformed into a tasty chicken chased by his hungry friend; they laughed as they watched Charlie woo Georgia. And now we were there laughing with them because Charlie had stuck forks into two bread rolls and was making them dance for Georgia. But Georgia never arrives: it's a dream. Charlie has fallen asleep at the table he set so festively for her, but in vain. Georgia is dancing with others in a saloon and Charlie, asleep in his lonely cabin, is *dreaming* the dance of the bread rolls, and we keep laughing: the two of them who have never seen bread rolls, let alone ballet shoes, and the four of us who have never been hungry, we were laughing the same silent laugh, at the same parts of the film, looking at the same pictures, laughing at the same gags of that inexhaustible comedy of the starving, that humour of loneliness. We were laughing together in the darkness of Teresina, which we knew nothing about, and where we would never return – Teresina, which had suddenly become the capital of the world.

'That's real life,' Manuel Pereira da Ponte Martins thought fleetingly, in his own dream.

And that's where the window of my story opened.

III

LA FENÊTRE
THE WINDOW
LA VENTANA
EL-TAKA
LA JANELA
DAS FENSTER
LA FINESTRA

1

IF I WERE going to write the story of this agoraphobic dictator, Pereira's first double would make his escape through this window.

Discovering a Chaplin film . . .

Like a visitation by the archangel.

That would turn his life upside down.

But would leave his fate unchanged.

2

WHO IS THIS double? Where does he come from?

An anonymous person from the interior, like all the others (servants, policemen, henchmen, prostitutes, gardeners, charwomen), recruited into silent service. When Pereira hired him, he was working as a barber in a little town near Teresina, three days' journey from the village where he was born. Until this meeting, his life story was a simple one: a child intelligent enough for the inevitable passing Jesuit to spot, take to town, teach reading and writing to, plus a little Latin so that he could serve Mass, three words of foreign languages, a few notions of mathematics, and good manners. But the Jesuit was killed by a priest-hunter, and the local barber took the boy, teaching him the art of sabre and scissors before dying of *vomito negro*, leaving him the shop. (Ah! He taught him Italian too. This barber was an old Italian who fought for Garibaldi and was exiled way back in the dim, dark ages – a Red Shirt flung into the furthest reaches of the world.)

Once he has reached manhood, our apprentice barber lets his facial hair grow so that he can practise his trade by shaving himself, as bearded men are few and far between in the interior. Forked, square-cut, pointed, imperial, bushy or curled *à la* Garibaldi, every month he has a different beard with moustache to match. He cuts a fine figure, whatever the style of face he adopts. And he's a good hairdresser to boot.

It so happens that on the day of a presidential visit, a man who looks rather like Falstaff rushes into his shop. It's Manuel Callado Crespo, the Chief Interpreter. Callado wanted the Amazonian vegetation on his face tidied up a bit. Our barber hacks away at the Chief Interpreter's beard, thins the brushwood of his hair, removes the brambles from his nostrils and the ferns from his ears, clips the wild hedges of his eyebrows, then styles his hair, gives him a spray of perfume and completes the civilising process by applying the hot towel and talc. In short, he makes him such a presentable fellow that an hour later President Pereira himself comes into the shop and immediately sits down in the chair.

'I want to be as handsome as that one, over there.'

Pereira points his thumb over his shoulder at Callado standing behind him, completely transformed.

'But don't forget that I'm an image,' Pereira stipulates. 'You mustn't change it in any way.'

There's not much for the barber to do: trim the President's hair, emphasise his fine features. He knows that presidential head very well: it's posted up everywhere, including in his own shop. He has the impression of copying a drawing.

The President's eyes never leave the young man as he goes

about his work. This is unusual. Customers generally look at themselves when they're having their hair done. This one stares at the barber, who continues to ply his scissors and comb without embarrassment.

But the President suddenly springs out of the chair, pulls off his towel and points to the door.

'Callado, I want to be alone with this man.'

Exit Manuel Callado Crespo.

'Sit down.'

Pereira hands the barber the shaving brush and soap bowl.

'Shave off that ridiculous beard and moustache, do your hair like mine and tell me what you see.'

And that's how the young barber discovers that his face and head resemble the young dictator's to the nth degree, the sort of face that is so clean-cut it looks to be drawn with a single line, and which, for the same reason, never ages as one would wish. ('To think that he was so handsome when he was young . . .')

We know what happens after that. Pereira employs the double with great secrecy ('You'll tell your mother that you've taken a job as barber on an ocean liner'), teaches him how to mimic and forget himself, in short gives him the role of his life, so that he can go and live his own life in Europe, far from murderous crowds of peasants.

3

RIGHT. AT THIS stage of the story, the double (he has already been playing the President for a while now) still knows nothing of the cinematograph. He was born in the same year as the moving pictures, but twenty-five years later they have yet to reach Teresina, this lost heart of a continent.

Pereira himself prefers the theatre. Actually, prefer is not the word; the cinematograph just doesn't interest him. No, that's not it either. It's rather . . .

Surprising as it may seem, the first time Pereira saw pictures move, he was frightened; and that's the truth. It was at the very beginning of his stay in Europe. Pereira happened to be in London, part of an audience looking at a stupid piece of pantomime with the actions accompanied by an out-of-tune piano. The people around him were roaring with laughter as they smoked their pipes and cigars. (The film being projected is of little importance; something like *The Hoser Hosed* . . .*) Once again Pereira felt the childhood terror that gripped him when the moon and the wind made the dark shadows in his mosquito net begin to dance. When that happened he could scarcely breathe, and his bed suddenly seemed lost in the vastness of the continent. The black and white frightened him. The silence of the pictures frightened him, those wordless mouths frightened him, that mute speech emphasised by the din in the hall . . . the insubstantial figures on the screen . . . those ethereal bodies . . . their trembling, precarious existence . . . the livid beam of light

---

*The Hoser Hosed (L'Arroseur arrosé), one of the Lumière brothers' earliest attempts at moving pictures, a film lasting only a few minutes.

from the projector . . . death floating in the air, all of it . . . the vague feeling that if the machine conked out, those visions would take the light and the audience with them, leaving them alone in the dark for ever.

But with Pereira, the statesman quickly came to the fore once again. The cinematograph is a ghost factory, he decided. Our peasants have enough superstitions of their own without adding these intangible fantasies. There would be no cinematograph in the land of simple-minded peasants, and that was that. Therefore, it would not be permitted in Teresina. The health of the people was at stake.

The theatre on the other hand . . . Pereira swore by the theatre.

'The theatre is a metaphor for politics.'

He would often elaborate on this theme, chatting with Kathleen Lockridge.

'Onstage one plays at being a king without ever forgetting to be oneself; in the audience, one pretends to forget oneself without ever leaving the auditorium . . .'

He was fond of delivering truths of this kind.

'A fool's game?' the Scottish dancer replied, venturing an opinion.

'But they know they're being fooled, my dear. That's the whole fascination of politics.'

It was a subject on which he could hold forth indefinitely.

'In politics,' she objected one day, 'the dead don't come back to take a bow.'

'While bad actors always do, it's true,' he admitted. 'Which goes to prove that there is morality in politics – mine included.'

One day when she had cornered him, stoutly defending the modern benefits of the cinematograph, Pereira delivered a sledgehammer argument.

'Cinemas smell of sweat, theatres smell of women; which I prefer. That's all there is to it.'

Cultural policy is sometimes decided on nothing more substantial than that.

And so the cinematograph was forbidden in Teresina, where the young President, as compensation, had a theatre built and named after himself. It was an eight-sided rotunda of metal girders and beams. The commission was given to the French engineer Gustave Eiffel, but the designs were by Pereira himself. Pereira wanted it to look like a 'tropical glade'. He ordered veins on the surface of the iron beams, which were to be twisted like branches with every rivet like a knot in the wood. The roof had been covered in lead leaves; creepers of twisted cable tumbled down around it; the whole thing was given an undercoat of red lead, then painted green – like the greenest green vegetation. The total effect was of a piece of stainless Amazonia set in the dry heart of Teresina: the Manuel Pereira da Ponte Martins Theatre.

4

A S CHANCE WOULD have it, the double discovered the cinematograph on the very evening he was to open the Manuel Pereira da Ponte Martins Theatre. A Parisian company was presenting a comedy, *La Cagnotte* by Eugène Labiche.*

*Eugène Labiche (1815–88), a prolific author of light comedies. *La Cagnotte* dates from 1864.

The double makes his entrance into the presidential box with its fringe of golden leaves. Ah! There's the President! The audience stands; the swish of evening dresses, the soft applause of gloved hands. God, he's handsome! Thank you, thank you, greetings to you all, pray be seated, say the hands, the beautiful pastoral hands of the pseudo-President. The lights go out, the three knocks ring out indicating the play is about to begin; the curtain rises. Manuel Callado Crespo, the Chief Interpreter, slips into his seat behind the double – 'I'm here, Mr President' – and from the actors' first lines, boredom once again descends on the box. The double has been playing Pereira's role for a long time now. He is, you might say, at the peak of his profession. The actor in him judges the other actors: those people onstage don't know how to play their parts. The words come out of their mouths without having first come from their bodies. They speak through their noses and shout at the top of their voices, as if they're talking to deaf people or children. And they're in such a hurry to say their own lines! Get off, and let me be heard . . . They have no idea of how to listen. They're so impatient. How long would they last faced with the queue of unfortunates whose confessions I have to hear every evening? And how would they say that 'I hear what you say', which sends them away consoled? The double has lost the thread of the play. What's happening? It's all going at such a speed . . . The double doesn't know the French language well enough to follow the rhythm of the dialogue, but the bits that Callado translates in his ear confirm his opinion: the characters are not really *speaking*, there's no serious *import* in those words, the person doesn't really *exist* on that stage. The double glances idly at the boxes around him. The diplomatic corps certainly seems to be enjoying itself. One can even make out a half-smile on the profile of Sir Anthony Calvin-Cook, the British Ambassador.

'Make no mistake, Mr President,' Callado whispers, 'the Englishman is saying to himself that Shaw is decidedly superior to Labiche.'

The double smiles in the darkness. 'The diplomats are happy: they realise that there are worse play-actors than they are . . .' But his smile suddenly disappears. He's not the one making the joke; it's Pereira's voice. The obsession returns. Pereira is thinking in me! Pereira is talking in my head! Cold sweat. It's possession pure and simple! Snap out of it, the voice of Pereira sneers within him, get out of yourself, don't think about me, the action's onstage . . . The double obeys; the double makes a superhuman effort to once again take an interest in *La Cagnotte* by Eugène Labiche.

By happy chance, the door to the presidential box opens and there appears Captain Guerrilho Martins, an intelligence officer. The Captain has come to inform Mr President that his officers have arrested a person who had committed a serious infringement of the rule about posting bills.

'I've had the man arrested and his equipment confiscated,' Captain Guerrilho Martins reports, adding, 'He's being questioned.'

'That doesn't concern me,' the double replies. 'Go and see Colonel Rist.'

But, just as the door is closing: 'No, Guerrilho, wait. I'm coming!'

And to Manuel Callado Crespo, whom he leaves behind, he says: 'Tell me how it ends, Callado, so that I don't look foolish when I have to congratulate those idiots.'

The words that the double has to say to the actors later are all written down in the cable Pereira sent him specially for the occasion: *You will say to them:* 'La Cagnotte *is a comic masterpiece. The only playwright I find as amusing as Labiche is George Bernard Shaw, but in a different register.*'

5

B<small>Y LEAVING THE</small> presidential box to escape Pereira's voice, the double knows that he has departed from his role. He knows that he should have stayed at his post and let Captain Guerrilho Martins report to Colonel Eduardo Rist, as the chain of command requires. It's nothing much, a tiny bending of the rules, and the very first time he has done it, but it will radically change the course of his life – but without changing his fate – and on that subject, he will say later, 'I did not know it yet.'

In Pereira's office (the office in which Pereira taught him to dance the tango, among other things), the double takes a few minutes to relax. As he smokes a leisurely cigarette, he looks at the equipment confiscated by Guerrilho Martins' men: a kind of photographic chamber with a crank handle, mounted on a tripod (a projector – he has never seen one before), and four round, flat metal tins. The double opens one, splitting a fingernail in the process (a film – he has never seen one of those either). There is also a roll of the notices that the stranger was putting up on the walls of Teresina.

'Ah, that's the mortal sin . . .'

The poster unrolled on the desk shows the face of a man

who is neither Christ the King nor President Pereira da Ponte. A head with curly hair under a bowler hat that is too small for it and worn at an angle. It only takes one glance for the double to understand Guerrilho Martins' reaction. It would take real cheek to put up a head so obviously seditious on a wall in Teresina. Everything in that face is poking fun. The crooked smile is mocking: 'Do you really believe it?' The other corner of the mouth, which goes down, is mocking: 'So much the worse for you!' The wide-open right eye is mocking: 'Are you so easily fooled?' The left, drooping eyebrow is mocking: 'You poor souls . . .' The light in the eyes is mocking, the two dimples like quotation marks are mocking, the moustache (false?) is mocking . . .

And all this mockery proclaims his name:

Charlie Chaplin

Comedy, subversion, resolve . . .
More than a clown, an ironist.
A troublemaker.
Determined to make the whole country laugh.
At whose expense?
That's what Guerrilho Martins' men must have asked him.
What does this Chaplin look like in real life?

'Bring in the prisoner.'

6

CHARLIE CHAPLIN, IF it is he, no longer looks like anything at all. He raises his head, revealing a black eye like a baboon's behind (Alex, the baboon in the Teresina zoo). The other eye is closed. They have broken his nose and perhaps his jaw as well. The guards drag him rather than bring him in. God Almighty! They certainly didn't pull their punches when they questioned him! Colonel Eduardo Rist won't be happy about that. Peasant guards, he'll say, man-handling is all they know. As far as they're concerned, information is man juice: you get it by crushing.

The double points to a chair.

'Sit him down and leave us.'

Once he is alone with the prisoner, the double shows him the poster.

'Is that you?'

A shake of the head.

No, he's not the one on the poster; the one on the poster is Charlie Chaplin, an Englishman who works as an actor for the gringos, in America, an immigrant who's become famous . . .

He, the prisoner, is a nobody, an ex-employee of the Mutual Film Corporation, a projectionist returning illegally, a Latino who fled Hollywood with the machine and a few films, to go home to his country, his family and his house.

'Did you steal them?'

Yes, it was a few years ago. It was a stupid idea. He thought he could provide for his wife and children by showing films at home, where the cinematograph was unknown, but he hadn't thought about the question of electricity. Electricity had not yet reached his village. He had to take to the road again to work the biggest towns on the coast. Unfortunately, the first cinemas were being built and the competition was fierce. He had been threatened, beaten up and driven out everywhere. Most of his films had been stolen. (He had only two left, *The Immigrant* and another with the title missing after a foul-up with the projector, but Chaplin plays a soldier in it.) He must have crossed many frontiers, travelling deep into the continent. Teresina was the furthest capital he had reached. He humbly begged Mr President to pardon him, as he knew nothing of the local law about billposting. Honest to God! He didn't know that the cinema was banned either. That's the truth! No, they weren't propaganda films. No, there was nothing to fear, just innocent fun, a mime show projected on hammock canvas or on saltpetre walls, something like *Guignol*, as harmless as the *bumba-meu-boi* dance of the Brazilian sertão, that's all. Pictures for children! Just something to make the working class laugh and amuse the peasants. Charlie Chaplin? A clown, nothing more, just a good clown: hits, kicks and custard pies. No, absolutely no attempt to undermine the dignity of the President, not the slightest allusion to local politics. He swears it on the heads of his children! What's more, he has organised screenings in the barracks of the *guardia civil* in Argentina. Need he say more! And also in Uruguay, for President Battle y Ordóñez, 'your colleague over there'.

'Show me,' says the double, amused by his story. He points to the projector and the reels.

'Go on, show me! If Don José has seen it, I can see it too.'

That was the moment when his life turned upside down.

The moment when the projector threw the first pictures on the wall in a dazzling rectangle of light just above the roll-top desk where Pereira kept his speeches, and the pictures *came to life*!

Considering the upheavals that followed, one might well think that the double experienced what his mentor the Jesuit called 'ecstasy': that moment when souls are on fire and become one with Truth; the 'rapt amazement', the Jesuit also said; the sudden illumination of 'the longed-for Light', he explained; 'Revelation'! It certainly was a revelation: the pictures were moving before his very eyes! The double felt that he had been hoping for this miracle all his life. At last! At last! Amazement and ecstasy . . . Someone had come and liberated images from the confining coffin of photography and thrown them live into a rectangle of light. 'Wake up and move!' Resurrection! The vitality of that Charlie Chaplin splashing over the wall! And the walls would continue to dance long after the death of Charlie Chaplin! The walls would dance as long as the projectors kept clicking around and around! The cinematograph was a machine that kept you eternally alive, that's what it was! And Charlie Chaplin was the archangel of this Annunciation! Its archangel of light! What an actor! Really, what an actor when you compare him with the wooden puppets playing in *La Cagnotte*! What grace! What precision! What energy! What realism! What freedom!

An absolute revelation.

The double did not waste time marvelling at it.

He made up his mind immediately.

He too would become a living picture! He too would act for the cinematograph! He would pass on his second-hand pseudo-President's mantle to another double, and leave to make his own bid for immortality over there, in Americky, home of the cinematograph! Yes, yes! That's what he would do! He would get rid of the projectionist ('death' was the order contained in Pereira's telegram, when the double reported the offender's case to him), secretly keep the projector (a 1908 Motiograph, which he would have nearly all his life), look at the Chaplin films again and again until he had unlocked the secrets of his art (so often that the films crumble into dust . . .). He would leave Teresina for Los Angeles; not the Los Ángeles of the Bio-Bio in Chile, no, Los Angeles in California, the real one – Hollywood! – where, according to the projectionist, angels took flight on the beams from the projector . . .

That's what he would do!

7

A FEW MONTHS LATER, on the day of his escape, the double finds himself in a mining province of the North, a gunshot from the border. He gives a final speech on the steps outside the residence of the Governor, Cesare Elpidio de Menezes Martins. Above him, covering most of the palace façade, is an enormous portrait of Pereira. At his feet, the central square of the small town is black with the dark heads of the crowd. Beside him stand Governor Cesare Elpidio in his white uniform, the three biggest landowners of the district, a few officers of the guard, village headmen, and Manuel Callado Crespo, who is always there on official trips. Ten or so trucks form a semicircle around the Governor's palace. They are covered with white tarpaulins, like tabernacles promising hidden marvels. And there he is, the double, standing on the steps, above the trucks, facing the crowd, playing the part of the President, which never occurs without gifts. It's his final performance. He is giving his last presidential speech. He'll be leaving that evening. He in turn will be replaced by a double.

For a month he has given the same speech, wherever he has been: written by Pereira, it defends the need for the peasants to become miners. Giving priority to mining the substratum is the chief preoccupation of the moment. Progress depends on it, the President maintains from the steps. A necessary development, the President maintains, as inevitable, the President maintains, as electricity 'which weaves its web of light in our darkness'. Whereupon the President points to the electric lamp-posts recently installed around the square. The President also makes his audience laugh. For example, he asks if a mother of the saints, just one in the whole of the country, and even here in this crowd, could have predicted that 'you would have day and night in your bedroom simply by pressing your thumb on a little banana'? Although they all live in the same room, all sleep in hammocks, all are lit by flickering oil lamps; although none of them can exactly picture that magic banana, all of them laugh happily, as if the little banana was really hanging above them at the head of a conjugal bed. They have such confidence in the President's words! Didn't he kill the Butcher of the North? So many have come to listen to him! So many will come this evening and sit at the foot of the flame tree in old Cesare Elpidio's garden to confide in the Ear! The President speaks to them like a picture book. He convinces them to exchange their peasants' shovels for the miner's pick. Do they know the difference between an aubergine and a gold nugget? It's a riddle. The President asks them this riddle. The difference between the aubergine and the nugget. Yes? No? Well, do they know? Don't they know? The President enjoys waiting for the reply. And they make sure they don't give it to him, even those who have heard the speech elsewhere, because they like it when the President pretends to be waiting. He seems so close to you then, like a friend standing at the bar with his elbow next to yours, about to come out with a really good joke.

'The aubergine makes you wait, while the nugget waits only for you, you bunch of nitwits, that's the difference!'

That's when he begins to imitate a peasant waiting for an aubergine to appear, and the whole plaza bursts out laughing at the same time. And the officials on the steps burst out laughing with them. A peasant waiting for an aubergine to grow is really funny!

'Gold isn't affected by drought,' the President continues, becoming serious again. 'Gold is sheltered from time and weather. Gold, silver, copper, nickel, oil and akmadon are where God has hidden them, so that man can find them and share them with his brothers.'

The President allows several seconds to pass between each of his sentences. Suddenly, a question:

'Do you want foreigners to come and take out the gold that God has hidden under your land?'

(He didn't say 'our', he said 'your' land . . .)

No, shouts the crowd, not foreign miners. No!

Thus speaks the President. It's a trickier speech than it appears. He's talking to the peasants of the North, the very same ones that the late General and President massacred a while ago, precisely because they refused to leave their fields to go down the mine.

'Of course there have to be peasants! The joke about the

aubergine was to make you laugh, but there have to be peasants, and *vaqueiros* and hunters. Life itself depends on them; the full bellies of your brother miners depend on them! And when the miners are tired, they will take their turn at being peasants, and the peasants will take up the miner's pick, and the miner the peasant's shovel, for the peasant should make money and the miner should breathe fresh air; and that's called brotherhood, and it's the very strength of our homeland, this brotherhood of yours, the mighty strength of our homeland!'

(This time he said 'our', 'our homeland'.)

An ovation. Obviously.

Thus speaks the President. In the next flight of eloquence, he emphasises the advantages of regular wages compared with the uncertainty of crops. The miner's wages are like good rain, and they come at the end of every week. You can open your hands on Saturday night in a dry season, and do they fill up? No! But perhaps they've heard that the mine kills more than it feeds, that they'll be treated like slaves by armed overseers, that not one gram of gold will go back into their pockets. You've heard it said, haven't you? You've even heard it directly! You've heard it from the mouths of people who've come back, people you know looking more dead than alive, people who have seen their cousins crushed under badly shored-up galleries, washed away by torrents of mud, murdered when they discovered their first nugget, consumed by miners' fever, died of gold madness. Haven't you? Well, it's the truth! the President exclaims. Those people told the truth! He sees the word 'truth' imprinted on all their faces. The real truth! he repeats. Before adding, much more quietly but seething with anger, rather as if he were swearing an oath on his own head: 'But that was before I came.'

Thus speaks the President.

'Look me in the eye! Come on, all of you, look me in the eye!'

And all of them, right down to those standing furthest away from the steps at the back of the square, focus on the President's eyes, and each and every one of them becomes immersed in those eyes.

'Do you think that I would lie to you like the late President?'

Think hard! Did he rid them of that murderer just to deceive them himself – here, him, them? Me? Me! He sees them shaking their heads; he hears their voices saying no.

'It's your dead who send me to you: your father, who I avenged! Your brother, who I avenged!'

The President points his finger vigorously here and there in the crowd, and all those who have lost someone close to them during that dreadful campaign of repression feel that the avenger's finger is directed at them.

Thus speaks the President.

And then he announces a surprise.

'Remove the tarpaulins from the trucks!'

The trucks are crammed full of brand new equipment: sieves, pickaxes, acetylene lamps, the complete miner's panoply, the gold-seeker's chance, and the whole thing given free by the three biggest landowners in the region. 'Don Mercucio Martins has given the lamps, Don Theobaldo de Menezes Pereira the sieves, Dona Cunha da Ponte, my own aunt, has provided the rest . . .'

Thus speaks the blessed President, who will personally watch over the miners' health and the peasants' prosperity . . .

'Personally!'

But deep inside, the double is thinking something very different.

The double has already taken his leave.

The play-acting is over. This is my last speech. It is not me who will be listening to your complaints or your thanks, this evening, under the flame tree in Cesare Elpidio's garden; it'll be another me who isn't me.

8

BY THAT VERY evening, he has indeed crossed the border and is galloping towards the sea. The sea is some distance away. He has to cross half the continent to reach it. He's holding the halter of the mule carrying his gear, his weapons, his water, his munitions, the projector and the cans of film. He's galloping as fast as a mule can follow a galloping horse. He too, like the Pereira in our tale, is a man trying to escape his fate. He too will fail, but he too makes an attempt that is a story worth telling. He has no other preoccupation for the moment than to put as much distance as possible between himself and the border. By the time he has crossed the continent, he will have built up enough impetus to hop over the ocean. Ah, yes! If he had his own way, he'd flap his wings and fly over to Americky in an instant!

Luckily there was a moon that night. The pebbles on the track, stretching to the horizon, form a white perspective dotted with regularly spaced electricity pylons. When wires are eventually strung between the pylons, rails laid at their base, and trains sent out on the rails, the gentle swell of the undulating electric line will give a rhythm to the journey.

And so he gallops and gallops, following the future path of electricity.

But the hours go by.

The pylons disappear.

The track peters out into the thorny bushes of the caatinga.

The horse baulks.

The mule tires.

The moon clouds over . . .

And there he is, lighting a fire in the very heart of the continent.

He takes the pack off the mule, puts the projector and the cans of film by the fire so that they don't get damp with dew. He has loaded his gun and now he is thinking, as he stares into the flames.

He is thinking of his double who has been sitting under Governor Cesare Elpidio's flame tree all evening, listening to the grievances of the whole population. At that time, he should still have a long line of penitents to hear. Hours of human misery to get through, with nothing more to offer than the obligatory 'I have heard what you say', as a form of absolution. You raise your hand, you put it on a shoulder and you say, 'I have heard what you say.' No, no! Don't squeeze my shoulder. For heaven's sake, are you trying to make love to me, or what? How many times do I have to tell you: the hand isn't there for consolation alone. It's a paternal hand, yes, but it's already reaching for the next in line. It's a big family, you see! Your hand must console *and* dismiss. Now start again! It lightly enfolds and it pushes away. I've told you a hundred times. Once again. Tell me, 'I have heard what you say.' No, you haven't heard what I said, you idiot! I couldn't feel it in your voice, or in your eyes or under your hand. This time your hand has no warmth; it's like a dead fish! How can I feel soothed by this limp thing on my shoulder smelling of cold piss? I may as well confide in a chamber pot. What is it? Are you thinking of your bed? Retiring? Dinner? Have I just been confiding in a belly? Start again. I don't confide in a stomach. I'm one of the wretched of the earth! A greedy belly that tries to pass itself off as a bleeding heart will soon feel the blade of my knife! What do you take them for? You can't deceive them like that. You can only deceive them if they want to be deceived! It's up to you to awaken their desire to be deceived! It's up to you to keep it alive! Politics is the paradox of the spectator. They don't actually like the *bacalhau do menino*; they *want* to like it. Do you understand? If you don't do this properly, you'll make it food for revolution. They'll believe someone else, and fall on you with their machetes. Do you think that I'd allow you to put my government at risk? Start again, you imbecile! Find the right note or I'll slit your belly. I'll spill your guts, believe me!

During one training session, he had slipped the blade of a knife under his double's last rib. A flick of the wrist would have done it. And he *would* have done it. On another occasion, he had pressed the barrel of his pistol against his temple, as Pereira had done. His finger was on the trigger. He would have pressed it.

'Training with live ammo: to be a double, you've got to want it! And a double is easily replaced! People only have to believe in the resemblance.'

He has just said Pereira's words aloud, alone there in the middle of the caatinga. The horse shivers, woken from a doze. The mule stamps its back legs as if it has been bitten by a tarantula. He gets up slowly, holding his gun. He listens to the thorn bushes. Silence. He thinks that he should have taken a dog. Dogs are good barometers for leopards.

They are so afraid of pumas that they can smell them miles away.

Nothing moves in the night.

He sits down again slowly.

He's no longer afraid of anything.

Not wild animals, snakes, spiders, wild dogs, bandits nor even the silence of the continent hold any fears for him. He used up his stock of terror during his Pereira years. All the same, it's incredible how Pereira scared him! He realised the extent of that fear while preparing his own double to take over from him. The fury he put into his training sessions rose out of his own terror.

'Look at me! Are you the President? Are you my father's son? And if you ever think you are me, be it ever so slightly, I'll be waiting. I'll be waiting!'

Now he's smiling. With his head against his pack, just about to fall asleep, he's smiling. It was stupid. Pereira never seriously threatened him. Pereira terrorised him so that he wouldn't have to worry about him in the future. Pereira made sure that he was always present in his double's head so that he could live peacefully in his own. Pereira cleared out, just as he had, with no intention of coming back. Pereira has actually done him nothing but good. This Pereira, whom he feared like his own death, is responsible for the revelation of his life: his gift for acting. And, in a way, Pereira also made possible his discovery of the cinematograph, which will give him glory, wealth and eternal life, over there in Americky!

Say thank you to Pereira.

'Thank you, Pereira.'

Lying on his back with his rifle in his arms, he invites sleep by humming what Guerrilho Martins' men encourage people to sing on market days in the squares of Teresina:

Dentro da nossa pobreza
É grande nossa riqueza
O povo de Terezina
Por uma graça divina
Recebeu um soberano
Melhor dito sobre-humano!

Tho' poor in all but health
Yet still we have great wealth
The people of Teresina
Have by a grace divine
As leader such a true man
More superman than human!

He drifts off to sleep with a long, silent laugh.

9

THERE'S NO NEED to linger over the details of how he crossed the continent. He tells it himself during the last years of his life, to anyone who'll listen. He'll describe the day when the puma killed his mule after luring him far from his campsite, shitting here, pissing there, leaving tracks so fresh that it always seemed within rifle range. It even showed itself from time to time (the man had time to get the animal in his sights twice; it wasn't a puma, it was a *suçuarana*, a big cat the size of a tiger with leopard spots like rusty scars in its black coat), but the animal immediately disappeared, drawing him ever further, deliberately getting him lost until it decided to leave him in the middle of the thorn bushes, while it went back and killed the mule, sharing it with the rest of its family. All that was left were the jawbone, the hooves, the cans of film and the projector.

The horse died next, stung on the nose by a horned viper when it bent to drink from the mud pool where the snake was hiding. How long had the filthy thing been waiting coiled up in that pool for his horse's velvety kiss? It weighed fully seven kilos for its 1.60 metres. Then it was almost his turn: when he was cutting off the reptile's head with his machete, he must have pierced the venom sack. A drop of poison spurted on to his cheek, infecting a mosquito bite, and then he started swelling up like a balloon and raving like someone possessed. He'll tell about the nightmares he had, how he dreamed of fauna that had acquired intelligence: wild animals, birds, reptiles, insects, all united against humans, and he was the only one left in the world. He'll tell how he walked, delirious as he was, without horse or mule, with the projector across his shoulders and the cans cradled like newborn babes in the hammock tied across his chest.

'Christ crucified and Virgin and Child all in one! Yes, I was an apostle of the cinematograph.'

Finally he sank into a deep coma and woke up in a mud-brick room with his face covered in astringent leaves. He had been picked up by a family of Native Indian peasants and fed like a bird by the grandmother.

'That old woman chewed up coconut meat and slipped it between my lips with the tip of her tongue. As she also chewed tobacco, I swallowed her tobacco juice as well. I got better really fast so that she would stop.'

Of course the Indians had no electricity and did not even

know that the cinematograph existed. When the villagers asked him about the machine – the projector – and what useful purpose it 'performed' (for years afterwards he was still amazed at these simple folk using that prescient verb), and what the two wheels without an axle did – the cans of film – he replied that it was a machine for showing dreams, and that the dreams in question slept all rolled up in the round tins. They wanted to know whether these dreams were their dreams. For the sake of convenience, he said yes. And what kind of dreams were they? Well, for example, the dream of leaving, or, for example, the dream of eating as much as you want. When they asked to see the dreams in question, he hadn't the heart to tell them that they would have to wait until they had electricity. He got them to string up a white hammock between the trunks of two *umbuzeiros*, then he set up the projector at the appropriate distance, threaded the film, asked who in the village dreamed of leaving, placed a lad who replied 'yes' behind the projector, and when he gave the signal to start turning the handle, he began to act Charlie Chaplin's *The Immigrant* for them by miming in front of the white canvas.

'And that was my first public screening.'

He will describe all that at the end of his life, staggering from bar to bar, trying on trembling legs to act out again the roles of *The Immigrant* he had performed for the laughing villagers: not only Charlie, the girl and her mother, but also the crowd of immigrants, the members of the crew, the heaving boat and the plates sliding from one end of the table to the other.

'I even played the plates and the table! When the kid stopped turning the handle because he was laughing so much, I stopped too. And if he turned it backwards to play a trick on me, I rewound myself, if you get what I mean . . .'

That's the story he will tell, going from bar to bar, in the last years of his life.

Nobody's listening . . .

The other customers staring into their glasses . . .

On the rare occasions when someone asks him why he drinks so much, he will never mention any kind of despair, his collapse, a life wasted trying to find himself; no, he always comes back to that period of his life – crossing the continent – when the sun, he says, turned him into a dried-out cuttlefish.

'You know. One of those white things you give budgerigars to peck.'

The fact is that he was caught by the drought. He left the village on 14 March, and it hadn't rained since Christmas Day. When the peasants told him that it was a sign of drought and that there wouldn't be a drop of rain before the next birth of Christ, he didn't believe them. He set out again with his equipment strapped to two very small donkeys, one of which had a weeping right eye, as if it already knew that the earth was going to become as hard as an anvil, and that it too would dry out and die where it stood.

The donkey was right: two months later, he and his companion expired a few kilometres from each other, nothing but skin and bone.

'Go and see for yourself, if you don't believe me. Nothing rots in that part of the world. The donkeys are still there.'

He swore to God that he had crossed plateaus so dry that the trees grow upside down, burying their branches in the earth as protection from the sun, and that plants with nothing in common join forces against the sky by twining their roots in the depths of the earth to share their water.

'That's what it's like. Under our continents there exists a

society of plants that show more solidarity than we do on the surface! I know. I've dug the ground!'

Come off it . . .

He couldn't get anyone to believe him. That's because no one in the bars he frequented knew Humboldt's *Table of Social Plants* or had read the botanist Saint-Hilaire, or even glanced through *The High Countries* by Euclides da Cunha, which were used as documentation for these pages . . . Nor would they believe him when he described his worst memory: rain that never reaches the ground. The long-awaited clouds gather at last above his head, the skies open like a slit wine skin; the rain falls then, but the drops explode as they near the scorching earth. 'They explode just above your outstretched hands, your open mouth, your peeling lips; the drops explode before they reach you, as if the earth has become the sun itself, and then they shoot up again as little bursts of steam to form clouds that the wind blows away to somewhere else. It's then, yes, it's then you really know what hell is . . .

'And that's why I drink.'

10

IT WAS A miracle that he reached the coast alive. Lindbergh will be fêted for crossing the Atlantic; he crossed the sun, and what did he get? Nothing. No one will ever believe him. He arrived at the edge of the continent almost naked and certainly penniless, as he also had to contend with bandits, who took everything except the projector and the films, which were of no use to them. Then one day he came up over the top of a dune, starving, his kidneys dry and his intestines stuck together. Recognising the sea, which he had only ever seen in Chaplin's *The Immigrant*, he vomited, just like Charlie in *The Immigrant*. The mere sight of the surf immediately made him sick with spasms that doubled him up, but while producing spurts of burning bile ('I was head down, arse up like Charlie'), he was smiling with happiness. This was not just because he had reached the sea; it was the realisation that he could be so completely bewitched by the magic of the cinematograph.

'I know you, you old ocean, I know you better than you know yourself. I've seen you alive and heaving in a film, so of course I vomit!'

He had to find something to eat and drink quickly, very quickly. In the first *tasca* he came across he struck a bargain to give a screening for a plate of fried octopus washed down with fresh coconut milk The innkeeper had him show the films as many times as the laughing clientele wanted to see them.

That was how he got back on his feet again as he went down the coast: he showed his films for food, shelter and even clothes. Then, when he was decently fed and dressed, he asked for money. Forewarned by the experiences of the late travelling projectionist, he avoided hanging up his canvas screen in the centre of large towns, where the owners of cinemas held sway. He preferred to put on his show in certain closed establishments along his route. Some of these places (Doña Taïssa's brothels, for example, or the convents of St Apollina) reminded him of Teresina. They were so self-enclosed that reality only penetrated them through whatever stories people might bring from the outside world. He held screenings in barracks, boarding schools, border posts, but also in society salons and in those hospices where charitable ladies earn their salvation by opening the doors of death to old men they would never have allowed through the doors of their own homes. The cinematograph brought laughter to bed-ridden invalids and even tears to teenage girls who had sworn not to be moved by anything. Almost as soon as the handle began to turn, forgotten feelings revived, sudden cries of surprise surfaced in lives that had seemed inert: 'Oh' and 'Ah', 'Gosh . . .', 'Did you see that?' and 'Look, look!' The dying revived; their faces lit up. They'd had eyes, but now the cinematograph allowed them to see!

For the whole of his journey down the coast, travelling from country to country, he considered himself a dealer in resurrection. He had just crossed a desert, and now there were dead people coming to life as he passed!

'That's what it was like, when the cinema was just beginning. Everywhere I set down my projector, Lazarus arose from his grave.'

He was mistaken. This was not the beginning of the cinematograph. ('That's true. In fact it was *my* beginning, and I was screening in places where moving pictures had never been seen before, hence the mistake.') He learned much more about it by going to see other films in real cinemas. He read movie magazines, talked with film fans until he was talked out. He learned that Charlie Chaplin was not the only one to make films: from France to Argentina, plus Japan, Italy, newly formed Soviet Russia, even tiny Finland and far-off Australia, the whole world was already speaking the unique, silent language of the cinematograph. The magazine *Photoplay* confirmed the fact that Hollywood was indeed the sun in that galaxy: 80 per cent of films made on this planet were made there, almost a thousand a year. ('In fact Teresina was a prehistoric exception; our diplomats must have been the last *Homo sapiens* to show any interest in Eugène Labiche's *La Cagnotte*.') *Motion Pictures* and *Picture Goer*, *Photoplay*, *Screenland*, *Moving Picture News*, *Motography*, *Variety* and the *New York Dramatic Mirror* taught him all he needed to know about the Hollywood Olympus: Mary Pickford and Douglas Fairbanks were the world's No. 1 couple, Peggy Hopkins Joyce was on to her fifth husband, and Gloria Swanson wanted to eat Pola Negri alive. As for Charlie Chaplin, he was returning from an absolutely triumphal tour of Europe. He had left the First National to found United Artists with a group of friends, spearheaded by Mary Pickford: it was a *coup d'état* against the all-powerful empire of producers and bankers. The little man who raised the dead by walking like a duck was worth five million dollars! Ten years earlier he was a music-hall clown earning five pounds a week.

'All that encouraged me enormously.'

One day, as he was leaving an orphanage still ringing with laughter inspired by Chaplin, he had the idea of adding to the magic by dressing and making himself up like Charlie in the films: the bowler hat a size too small, the frock coat that was too tight, the trousers too big, huge boots, flexible cane and false moustache. The effect was immediate: seeing him turning the handle here and acting on the white sheet there, the audience (prisoners in this instance – thieves and murderers) looked on him like a god who could be in several places at once.

'Some of them pulled at my sleeve to make sure whether I was the picture or the picture was me.'

He had never seen such enthusiasm in people's eyes; not when he was a boy accompanying the Jesuit to the dying, nor as an adolescent when his master barber, full of the hope he had for him, recited the revolutionary poetry of Garibaldi, nor even in Teresina when the most wretched came to speak in his ear. He thought that Charlie Chaplin must experience every day the unutterable happiness of being both the image and the man at the same time. That was fame! That was glory! He swore that this happiness would be his and his alone, and as soon as possible! Like all those who have a passionate desire for it, he had a very clear idea of what that fame was like, relishing it in anticipation: every time he met someone's astonished, admiring gaze, he would experience the mystery of his own incarnation! Beatified in his own lifetime! To be both oneself and that 'glorious body' which his mentor the Jesuit promised to the blessed at the moment of the resurrection. Glory! Pure joy! He would at last have the honour of his own company.

Let's go! Let's go! Sail as soon as possible!

Cross the ocean once and for all.

Hollywood! Hollywood!

He wasn't going to hang about for long dressed up as Charlie. He would throw the old clothes away so that he could be both himself and the image of himself. Fame! At last!

'Tell your mother that you've taken a job as a barber on an ocean liner.'

How soon can I start?!

He scoured the ports, offering his services as barber to dozens of captains. He really would have liked to find a berth as a barber. Fate (or whatever passes for it: chance or bad luck – which of course appears as a stroke of unexpected good luck) decided otherwise.

11

W HERE EXACTLY DID he set sail? From Montevideo? Buenos Aires? Strangely enough, he won't remember. From the other side of the continent?

'Not from the Brazilian coast, at any rate; they spoke English and Spanish in the cheap eating house where I found myself at the time. The only thing I can recall is the name of the boat, which would seem to have wiped out all my other memories.'

The *Cleveland*.

'That's right. The *Cleveland*, a steamship of the Hamburg America Line.'

And the name of the Captain.

'An Italian, Captain Polcinelli.'

A name for a character in a comedy . . .

'That's no consolation, believe me.'

He had given up trying to get a job as a barber. Apparently it was much sought-after. He decided to pay for his passage. He would earn enough money for the crossing with his projections – he almost had enough already – and would travel steerage with the immigrants. Isn't that what he was, after all? If he started at the very bottom, he would be all the prouder once he reached the top. He could hear himself already praising the advantages of American democracy from a great height; America, where 'anything is achievable', as Mr Chaplin maintained in his interviews, 'himself an immigrant, if I'm not mistaken'.

So there he is pushing open the door of that tavern. ('Now what port was it in, for God's sake?') The crew of the *Cleveland* is busy getting full on beer. They're all drinking, smoking, shouting, and couldn't be in a better mood for a bit of fun. As soon as they see his silhouette, the sailors raise their glasses.

'Hey there! Charlie!'

Right, they're Americans. American sailors prefer port lights to dim town centres. He has never run into them anywhere but on the docks. It's certainly not the first time he has been hailed by his character's name. He greets them like Charlie, raising his bowler hat with the tip of his cane, which he's slipped behind his back.

'Charlie! Come over here!'

He puts the projector down in a corner and navigates his way between the tables with his duck's waddle walk. They laugh. Without saying a word he holds out his hat and points at it insistently, eyebrows arched, lips pursed. The first coins drop into it. He bites one to make sure it's not fake. He disdainfully flicks another one away – a very small one – so that it lands in a spittoon. He does it all very well. He's practised it for hours in Pereira's office. And twirling his cane, and turning round on one heel, and pretending to lose his balance, and smiling with fake embarrassment, and the sideways glances, and the hiccups . . . He knows his role as Charlie inside out. They all laugh. The hat fills up. Pocketing his takings, he then screens *The Immigrant* on a tablecloth tacked up between two windows. Some of the sailors have already seen the film but everyone laughs heartily. They ask for more, and he obliges. He mustn't stay too long all the same, he has other inns to visit and that rather smart restaurant he noticed on the sunny heights of the town.

As it happens, he won't visit any inn or any restaurant. He will go directly from that tavern to the deck of the *Cleveland*.

'Rather like the time when they used to get boys drunk and

drag them off to sea. The kids woke up as cabin boys on some old whaler way out on the ocean.'

(Except for the fact that they didn't get him drunk, and that the *Cleveland* is a luxury ship of the Hamburg America Line and he'll make the crossing in the best cabin.)

'Mr Chaplin?'

He has just given the last turn of the handle.

'Mr Chaplin?'

He turns round. The light goes on. He finds himself looking at the beaming face of Captain Polcinelli. After the tiniest moment's hesitation, the Captain looks amazed and murmurs in Italian, 'Charlie Chaplin . . . *Non posso crederci!* (Charlie Chaplin . . . I can't believe it!)'

Captain Polcinelli has just come in, still fresh from the world outside. He takes a step backwards and shouts through the open door, 'Tommaso, come in here. Look who's here!'

Another officer appears in the doorway. It's the Purser from the *Cleveland*, Tommaso Morasecchi. Morasecchi's face lights up with a childlike smile.

'Chaplin? *Charlie* Chaplin? *Ma non è vero!*'

'*Guarda, guarda!*' the Captain urges. 'Look! Go on, look!'

12

THEN, THERE WAS a pause.

A sudden halt, even.

Years later, staring into one of his innumerable empty glasses, the fake Chaplin reflected, 'If I'd taken into account the tone of those *"guarda"*, especially the second, maybe I'd have realised what those jokers intended, and I wouldn't have sailed on that bloody boat.' He added, 'One can never say that one wasn't warned . . .'

Yes . . . Yes, it's true. If he had been more attentive to the tone, and no doubt to the expressions of the two officers, he would never have gone on board the *Cleveland* and the rest of his life would not have turned up in these pages.

The tone of the first *guarda* should have conveyed the meaning: 'Morasecchi, take a good look at this fellow trying to pass himself off as Charlie Chaplin.' And the second *guarda* added: 'Well then, if he wants to be taken for Chaplin, let's oblige him. It'll give us a laugh.'

In other words, neither Polcinelli nor Morasecchi believed for a moment that they were looking at the real Chaplin. Their exclamations, *'Non è vero, non posso crederci'* (said in a tone of astonishment and delight to fool the usurper), were to be taken literally.

A question of tone . . .

Words are not mere words: in fact, they are almost nothing without the intention, the purpose for which they are used. This is entrusted to the tone and transcends the meaning, which is always a prisoner of the dictionary. You have to have been a boarder for the whole of your youth to understand this sort of thing, or a prisoner in the presence of suspicious guards, or brother and sister boxed in with a stifling family, or a doctor who has to give unbearable news every day, or else two diplomats, or even two seamen on ocean-going ships, Polcinelli and Morasecchi for example, used to the shared boredom of endless days and nights in lounges or on the vast and empty sea.

That being said, let's not exaggerate the powers of

observation shown by the Captain and his Purser. The reason why they didn't believe that the double was Charlie Chaplin is that they immediately took him for someone else. When Captain Polcinelli exclaimed, 'Tommaso, come in here. Look who's here!', the relative pronoun 'who' – the *tone* Polcinelli gave to the pronoun – clearly indicated to Morasecchi's understanding ear that both of them knew the newcomer and that the Captain was delighted to see him again. The Purser instantly reacted with the same pleasure when he too thought he recognised the man hiding himself behind Charlie's disguise. (The tone of his *Ma non è vero* was immediately tinged with affection, which the double took as a particular manifestation of the universal affection in which Charlie Chaplin was held.)

A veritable imbroglio of misunderstandings.

And, in the case of the two seamen, a mutual mistake. (Sharing the same mistakes is one of the disadvantages of friendship.)

Who then did Polcinelli and Morasecchi think they recognised in the person of the double?

To understand that, we have to go back nine years into their shared history, to the month of May 1913, when the *Cleveland* was crawling along on a glassy sea under a leaden sky (a machine fault had reduced its speed by half), and the first-class passengers were bordering on depression, so much so that Captain Polcinelli had to say a few words to his Purser.

'Find something to entertain them, for God's sake. They don't even want to sleep around any more. Can't you see that they'll start jumping overboard if you don't do something?'

As a last resort, Morasecchi (does the maritime profession

of purser, the amphitryon of the high seas, still exist?) went to find inspiration among the immigrants in steerage. And there, in the midst of fermenting bodies and the smell of stinking latrines, greasy metal and bad meat, all stewed by an infernal heat, a magical sight awaited him.

A couple were dancing the tango.

Useless to try to describe the indescribable.

There's no phrase light enough.

As far as choreography was concerned, the girl wasn't wonderful, but he, . . . he, the boy . . . thought Morasecchi, struck by the silent fascination of all the types of spectators that humanity had packed into that hold . . .

The wonder in their eyes!

The common happiness shared by people who were so different!

No, they had never seen such a dancer, and an artist never had a more appreciative manager that that ragged crowd . . .

'It was as if he had been chosen by the whole world,' Morasecchi said to Polcinelli years later, one evening when boredom once more reduced the two men to rake through their small store of sea memories.

To cut a long story short, the purser hires the young *tanguista* at six dollars a week, slaps a dinner jacket on him (what grace, even in a penguin suit!) and releases him on to the first-class dance floor.

There's no shortage of partners; the cruise becomes an unforgettable experience.

Unforgettable, what am I saying? . . .

Historic!

. . .

For in the following decade the handsome young man, after rapidly gliding through a career as a society dancer, reached the heights of Hollywood, and made a name for himself throughout the world as Rudolph Valentino.

Rudolph Valentino! *The Sheik*! The No. 1 star of the day. That was the man the two friends thought they recognised in the features of the double disguised at Charlie.

Chance, you might say, chance . . .

Fate, more like it.

Improbable?

No. Not if you go back to pages 18–19 of this tale, and listen to Kathleen Lockridge, the Scottish dancer, declare that Manuel Pereira da Ponte Martins (and consequently his double, although she did not know that he existed) and Rudolph Valentino were as alike as 'two drops of cloudy water in a Murano glass'.

13

How was i supposed to know that? (This will be one of the double's longest monologues, a tirade people will ask to him to repeat; it even happens sometimes that they fill his glass several times to get him going again.) How could I suspect that at first glance the moron Polcinelli had mistaken me for Rudolph Valentino? Because Pereira looked like him? But I had no idea about that! I had never seen a film of Valentino – it was shop girls' stuff – and after *The Sheik* came out, all his photographs show him swathed in Arab clothes! How could I have recognised Pereira under all those luxury tea towels? No, I couldn't really know that those two idiots had recognised Rudy, the toast of Hollywood, under my Charlie wig, or that the tone of the two *guarda* meant: *Take a look, Morasecchi, watch out, Tommaso mio, do you see that fellow who's trying to put one over on us? Well, look closely, it's not Charlie Chaplin, it's even better, it's Valentino! Don't you recognise him? Rodolfo! Rodolfo Pietro Filiberto Raffaello Guglielmi di Valentina d'Antonguolla, alias Valentino! It's just as I tell you, Rudy in person! The kid in steerage ten years ago, the tanguista who climbed the Hollywood hills on his white horse, the star we discovered, you and I, down in the immigrant pit: Valentino, the Sheik! Now do you see? Have you placed him now, Purser? He's in the right pigeonhole?* Pick up all that in the tone of two *guarda*? Come on . . . What's more, I didn't even know that Rudy had immigrated on the *Cleveland*! I didn't know that the *Cleveland* was the tub he came in on! I'd have to have known that too!

14

A ND BESIDES, HE was too caught up in the excitement of his act to be on his guard, too thrilled to be taken for Chaplin by these two officers, educated men who were used to first class, to men of the world you don't try to fool. Their enthusiasm confirmed his great talent as an actor, that's what he was thinking! He was also too happy hearing the Italian of his childhood. All the more so because Purser Morasecchi, with his beard, curly hair and round glasses, reminded him of his old Garibaldian barber.

So, without lingering over the tone of the two *guarda*, he had extended a friendly hand to Purser Morasecchi, and said in his best Italian: '*Guarda e toca, Tommaso, uomo di poca fede.* (Look and touch, oh man of little faith.)'

And Tommaso shook his hand for ages.

'Mr Chaplin! And you speak Italian into the bargain!'

'Italian, Spanish, Portuguese, British English, and even a little French when I really have to appear intelligent.'

15

IT'S TRUE. I started speaking Italian to them into the bargain! *Tommaso, uomo di poca fede . . .* When I think of it . . . The look they must have exchanged at that moment! 'Shit, you're right, Polcinelli, it's Valentino, he speaks Italian and he hasn't lost his Puglia accent!' That's right, I have an accent when I speak Italian, seeing as my barber, the Garibaldian, was from Puglia, like Valentino, and like Purser Morasecchi's mother, who grew up in Taranto. 'He speaks the Italian of our region, it's Rudy! His father was from Castellaneta!' 'And his mother was French, wasn't she?' 'Yes, an Alsatian.' What mad ideas they must have got as soon as I turned my back! 'But what's he doing here disguised as Chaplin?' 'Who knows . . . To prove to himself that he can play something else besides a romantic lead whispering sweet nothings in the desert . . .' 'Yes, but why Chaplin?' 'Because he's a comedian! Because there's no one more different from him! And because Chaplin's the best! Because if you can bring that off, be taken for Chaplin when you're Valentino, you can play anything!' . . .

With hindsight I can imagine the wild speculations those two bloody idiots must have indulged in . . . 'Disappointed in love too. He's just been dumped by Rambova, although she's his second wife! Heaven knows how an idol like Valentino would react to that?' 'Hang on . . . just a minute. What about Pola Negri? Hasn't Pola Negri been mentioned recently? I thought that he was consoling himself with Pola Negri . . .' 'Pola Negri, Pola Negri . . . I say, isn't she one of Chaplin's exes, Pola Negri?' 'Yes, yes! *The most deadly boring comedian of them all,* she called him.' 'Taking the mickey out of Chaplin then? Does Valentino want to get his own back on Chaplin?' . . . God Almighty, I can just hear them . . . all that juicy magazine gossip . . . It's because sailors get bored. Have you ever seen the ocean? A field of cotton covering two-thirds of the globe! Just think of it. Ploughing your way across that, back and forth, all your life. As a result, anything becomes possible on a boat. Anyway, I can't really blame Morasecchi too much: it was a good chance to play to the gallery. No purser could have resisted the temptation: *Ladies and Gentlemen, may I have your full attention, please. I have an important announcement to make. Rudolph Valentino is on board this ship, but for personal reasons he wants to pass himself off as Charlie Chaplin. I'm counting on you to have the courtesy and discretion to respect his wishes to remain anonymous. Just act normally; it will make the crossing all the more exciting!*

16

So, FROM THE very beginning in the tavern they pretend to think he's Chaplin. They ask him to take a seat. The leading seaman and the engineer join in. Sly winks. They remain impassive. They ask him what he's doing in this eating house, in this port, so far from your home, Mr Chaplin. He replies that after his recent triumph in Europe – that 'surfeit of fame' – he felt the need 'to restore his image' by allowing himself a little South American escape incognito, and that he went deep into the interior, where he was still unknown, where the cinematograph still did not exist, and that he has just relived the original, magical emotion of that first encounter with the 'moving pictures'. Did they know Teresina? No? He tells the story of his return journey, how he navigated his 'inland trading voyage', his visits to hospices, barracks, orphanages, prisons, the reactions in those closed establishments, the cinematograph as it was at its birth! But now the holiday is over, he must go home, there's a series of important films to be made, for United Artists. Really? He's going home? On what ship? He hasn't decided yet. In that case, why not ours? We're going to New York, it would be such an honour, don't say no, Mr Chaplin, it would all be free plus the royal stateroom, of course . . . Well, it would be a pleasure, but . . . Yes, yes, you must! Come on, Signor Chaplin, *venga con noi, la prego*! The *Cleveland* proposition is naturally tempting, very tempting; however, he makes one condition, sine qua non. And what's that? Secrecy, of course! Absolute secrecy. What would happen to the double I left in the USA if it was being said everywhere that Chaplin, the real one, was lounging on an ocean liner of the Hamburg America Line when he was supposed to be shut up at home putting the finishing touches to his plans, tell me that? What would my friends in United Artists and the bank investors think? A broken contract, lawsuit, damages! It's out of the question for this to go any further than the ship's rail; even the fish should know nothing about it! It must stay a secret between the *Cleveland* and myself. My brother Sydney is the only person who knows that I've run off like this, no one but Sydney, and even he doesn't know when I'm coming back. I want to surprise him.

Don't worry about any indiscretion, Signor Chaplin, you're at no risk on that score, there's no danger of that at all! Count on us, maestro. You see to it personally, Tommaso. Not a word, our lips are sealed, all right? Your Purser's stripes depend on it!

. . .

That's it.

More or less.

17

THE CROSSING WAS much the same. The same stories in the evening at Purser Morasecchi's table, told in more detail, naturally, as dinners go on for a long time at sea, and the women's perfume stimulates the narrative glands. Morasecchi, acting the perfect gentleman, got the double going again when he saw the story was flagging. For example, how many times did he get him to describe the time he projected the film without electricity in the Indian village?

'Ah, yes. They had a wonderful time!'

He naturally kept on embroidering the story of the Indians: 'They had no idea who I was, but I can't tell you how much pleasure the simple laughter of these half-savages gave me: it was their *recognition* of me as an actor! I felt as if I had been born again. I was dubbed an actor by Primitive Man!'

To the end of his days, he'll hear himself holding forth at that round table.

'Talk about travelling deep into the interior! Did I ever travel deep into the interior!'

That's what the evenings on the *Cleveland* were: embroidery at sea. He gave spontaneous answers to the countless questions the ladies asked him. But that spontaneity was nothing to be particularly proud of, as he was with people who politely slip into the questions what they want to hear in the replies . . . (He got these answers from the magazines he'd been reading to learn all he needed to know about the film world.) 'Is it true, Mr Chaplin, that you were in an orphanage?' 'Yes, in London, when my mother was ill . . .' Sometimes the husbands became irritated, 'Being English, as you are, how is it that you escaped the war?' He began with a candid laugh and a sad expression: 'Declared unfit for service! Too short! I didn't have the fine physique that no doubt makes you a hero.' He got people laughing with him rather than at him, especially the ladies, with his streams of sophisticated nonsense. Sometimes he pretended to fight back a tear and, at these emotional moments, there was always a gracious hand to press his.

'God . . . when I think of it now . . . dear, oh dear . . .'

The days were divided into three periods: morning in his cabin, a leisurely awakening, a light meal, but fit for a prince;

screenings in the afternoon in steerage class where the candidates for immigration were crammed in like cattle.

'And believe me, despite everything that's happened since then, showing *The Immigrant* to immigrants still remains in my mind as a fantastic memory!'

Then came the evening. Dinner suit, martini, dinner, brandy and, during the first half of the night, tango. The couples moved back to watch him dance. He blessed Pereira for having made him an incomparable *tanguista*. And he himself did not regret having nearly broken his own double's back until he could follow his steps. He was king of the dance.

'Their great admiration for my tango, that was also a sign. But there you are . . . There's no shortage of signs in this life; it's the code that's missing.'

The couples quickly moved back to the edge of the dance floor as soon as he swept on to it with a woman in his arms. He thought that they were admiring him as a dancer, and the illusion gave him wings. ('Besides, I was *also* admired as a dancer, *I* was the one who was dancing anyway, not Valentino!') 'The music launches the *tanguista*,' Pereira explained to him, 'but it's the look from those watching that really makes him. One always dances in that look,' Pereira claimed, 'especially the tango!' (He had trained for months on end under Pereira's gaze.) 'You can do without music, but not without that look. Start again!' (And he would start again.) 'The real dance floor is the eyes of those not dancing, the staring eyes of all those who feel inferior just by looking at you. Start again, you moron, you couldn't make a legless cripple feel inferior!' (Ah! Pereira . . .) 'I want them to be glued to their chairs when they see you, do you understand me!' And glued to their chairs or rooted to the spot, they certainly were! Without any doubt, Pereira had made him the viceroy of the tango. He danced alone on the ocean, with a woman in his arms, and every time it seemed to him that she was the most beautiful woman in the world!

The beauty of the women – now that was another side of the question. He was no longer a pseudo-president married to his people. The vow of chastity was over. He no longer had to content himself with opening a ball then going to bed, lying alone between his presidential sheets. During the Pereira years, he had breathed his fill of perfume but had not touched a single woman – at least not those he called 'real women'. As for the others, he had used them unreservedly: in brothels all over the country, in the most remote villages; they were 'necessary physical workouts' as Manuel Callado Crespo used to call them. But of those he called 'real women', women who wear perfume and dance, women who wear evening dresses and jewellery, women with white arms, rounded shoulders, supple backs, women with satin thighs and taut bellies, women radiant in their low-necked gowns, lithe, silky women, women with soft white skin, full lips, rose-petal cheeks, smooth foreheads and pure, cultivated gaze, all those who communicate even when silent, who never raise their voices, women of the presidential caste, of those, no, not one. He had followed Pereira's instructions to the letter. He had been intoxicated by their perfume, his dancer's hands had felt the promise of their hips all night. Looking down from his presidential box he had let his eyes plunge between their breasts and slide over their curves, but nothing more. And that's the truth!

Well, those times were past.

Finished.

This was confirmed on the first evening when, quite late at night, he heard a tap at his door and his first dancing partner slipped into his cabin, into his bed, silk slithered to the floor, they lay naked in the cool air from the open porthole . . .

But shock. . .

he thought,

perhaps surprise,

it was so unexpected . . .

In short, that night he could not respond.

. . .

He pleaded fatigue after his long journey into the interior, time needed to readapt . . . But really, she shouldn't worry; it was nothing to do with her. It was him, it was exhaustion. Gently he saw her out of his cabin and, when she turned round sadly at the end of the gangway, he gave her final, delicate little wave *au revoir*.

. . .

He woke up with a feeling of masculine shame, and spent the day avoiding his partner's eyes. Fortunately it was not she who tapped at his cabin door the following night, but another. Unfortunately the result was the same. And so it went on, night after night, always a new, desirable woman, followed by fiasco after fiasco. He took out his frustration during the day with the immigrants. After greasing the palm of someone to stand guard, he had rough sex in dark corners with the aggression and speed of a cat. As a result, almost every day he left a weeping girl in steerage raped by a predatory god. Once night had fallen, it was his turn to weep at his own humiliation.

'Pereira had me by the balls!'

'Don't touch women of my caste, or I'll cut off your balls.'

With that kind of threat, you only have to believe it once.

The more he turned these thoughts over in his mind as he

lay in the bare arms of 'real women', the more the life went out of him at the moment of incarnation. Result: a wet rag.

'It's Pereira who's made me go limp! There's no other explanation. I've never got over it.'

To each of his conquests he gave a different but always pitiable explanation: tiredness, agitation, awe at her beauty, fidelity to his own wife, brandy, a drop in energy levels, the untimely memory of his mother . . .

Nonetheless, he still continued to play the ladykiller on the dance floor and the show-off at the round table. Encouraged by Morasecchi, he claimed that after his experience of South America, Africa was the next place he would visit. Yes, one day he would make another escape. With his Motiograph projector on his back and his films under his arm, he would go to Africa, incognito! He would show his films to the Kaffirs and the Zulus! 'I may as well take the opportunity to civilise one or two Boers . . .'

'I was really . . . you could say that I was . . . well . . .'

But, what can you expect, he moved them. The 'real women' dissolved into tears as they listened to his nonsense. They opened their hearts to him through their eyes – their secret selves that were quivering, moist and warm, in silken shade, as deep and full of promise as Eden. Not once could he enter.

'I was always like one of the damned before the gates of heaven.'

At those times, when the life force was ebbing within him . . . All the more devastating for him, so preoccupied with the desire to become someone!

'I no longer existed at all.'

One of the 'real women' was moved by his plight one evening when he burst into sobs. She took his head in her hands and rested it between her breasts (and they were so white, and so firm, and so tender, and so warm between, so like the breasts of his dreams!). She ran her fingers through his hair, stroked him during this noisy outpouring of despair, then, when he had calmed down a little so that he could hear her, she said, 'It's nothing, Rudy. It happens to the best of men . . .'

18

'RUDY . . .'
He will soliloquise to the end of his days about that name, as if it were lying in the bottom of his glass.

'I paid no attention to it the first time someone called me Rudy. I thought it was a Rudy she knew, or that she'd made a slip of the tongue.'

. . .

'And then it happened a second time: "Don't worry, Rudy, I'm here."

'I must have said "Rudy?" with a question mark to her. She gave me that look they sometimes have when you hardly know each other and they want to make up the time you haven't spent together. She put her finger to my lips and murmured, "I know, I know, I won't say a word . . ."'

. . .

'If I'd only known who this Rudy was, I'd have jumped into a lifeboat and taken to the open sea.'

19

WHEN I THINK of it . . . When I think that I actually believed I was bedding them . . . It's they who were picking me! Yes! Picked, peeled and shared around! Like a nice piece of fruit! Don't shove, there'll be enough Rudy for one and all! Like a kind of raffle. They must have drawn numbers. Those women adored raffles; there was one almost every evening in aid of the people in steerage class. Thanks to friend Morasecchi, the real women thought they were getting Rudolph Valentino when they slipped into my bed! Valentino! First it was fascination, but then it was verification. Medical examinations, that's what they were giving the star of stars. To think that even this didn't make me suspect! Because, well, a good tango dancer, even if he's passing himself off as Charlie Chaplin, can draw, let's say . . . two or three first-class women to his cabin. A dozen at the very most. But not all of them! No, not all! For all of them, the husbands would have to consent! And at the time, Valentino was the only one who could bring off something like that. He was the archangel of Hollywood, Rudolph Valentino, the star of stars! They'd seen him dance on every screen: in *Alimony*, in *The Four Horsemen of the Apocalypse*, in *Camille*. Rudy, the tango personified! And a heart for the taking as well! Because they all knew that Rudy had been the unhappy husband of Jean Acker, who took off just one day after their wedding, and that his second wife, Rambova, had also thrown in the towel after the first round. They were all ready to console him, as you can imagine!

You should have heard the way people spoke of Valentino at that time. They said about Fairbanks, 'Oh, how handsome he is, how bright, how strong, what vitality!' Those who knew him better added, 'And what a decent chap, if you only knew!' They said of Chaplin, 'What intelligence! What a business-man! And what a humanist, with it!' No one said anything about Valentino; seeing his photo they just whispered, 'Look, it's him.' And there wasn't a woman in the world – in the world, you hear what I'm saying – who would ask, 'Who do you mean?'

Were they ever primed to recognise him! And recognise him they did. In me! Bloody hell, in me!

Oh! Rudy . . .

They thought they'd won the sun, and they found themselves in bed with a dead star . . .

At the end of the day, that's what makes me most ashamed. Because, if you really think about it, it's not the two crappy marriages that gave Rudy his reputation as a cockless wonder, it's me!

As soon as we reached shore, his reputation spread.

Because of me.

On a worldwide scale.

The Hollywood effect . . .

And it ruined his life.

But what could I have done about it?

. . .

And if I couldn't have done anything, why do I get the feeling of not having done what I could?

20

'**O**H, RUDY...'

But eventually the patrons grow tired of his stories. The years pass and no one encourages his monologues any longer in the bars where he still rehashes his memories, even though Rudolph Valentino is long dead, and he himself is sliding towards the exit ... They catch odd bits and pieces ... A crazy old man who thinks he's Chaplin or the late Sheik Valentino ... Or who doesn't actually want to be taken for either of them ... You can't really say he's complaining: he's brooding over the past, that's all, like a person who has been so surprised by something that he's never got over it. And when he cries, it's not for himself, it's for Rudolph Valentino's lost honour.

He ponders.

'All that happened because Valentino looked like Pereira, so-called...'

The ice in his glass has melted to warm water.

21

CONVINCED THAT EVERYONE thought he was Chaplin, and determined to perfect his act, he suspected nothing right up to the end of the voyage. He was too occupied in suffering with his 'real women', taking out his frustration in steerage, shining on the dance floor, and picturing the magnificent future ahead of him. He thought that after such a wonderful acting performance (the Pereira years and a whole voyage as Chaplin without the slightest suspicion!), he could interpret any role imaginable. Hollywood couldn't do without so universal a talent. He would play everything because he could play everything! At last things were going to change; he would become the actor he had always been! He would *become* it and restore his ridiculed virility. He would become it and finally attain the erection he deserved! It was a duel between Pereira and himself. To the point that one night he dreamed about it as a film. ('Oh, Christ, yes, I remember that dream.') He dreamed that he was filming his own story; the story of an insignificant barber ('me'), the unsuspecting double of a mad dictator ('Pereira'), who escaped his domination by turning out to be a great actor. The double became a star in the Hollywood firmament, and the dictator was lynched by the people in the dazzling dust of a public place that was round like an arena.

After he woke up, the dream became a resolution: he would make that film! He would write the scenario, direct it himself, take the two main roles and, for good measure, he'd produce and distribute it throughout the world. Where would the money come from? Why, from the fortune he'd amass as an actor, performing for the greatest directors: Griffith, Walsh, Fleming, Lubitsch, perhaps Chaplin himself, the cream of Hollywood!

His film would be not only a worldwide success, but also a masterpiece of the cinematograph for ever. He had to find a title as soon as possible.

Let me see . . .

A title . . .

Why not something to do with that 'becoming', with that change, that transformation?

Becoming? No. *Transformation*? No. What about *Metamorphosis*?

Perhaps . . .

What do you mean, perhaps? *Metamorphosis*? It's splendid! Could you find a title more typical of the American ethos than that? More typical of Hollywood?

METAMORPHOSIS.

That's settled.

Metamorphosis, the film that would smash box-office records and make President Manuel Pereira da Ponte Martins lose *his* erection!

'My greatest success at Morasecchi's table was the scenario for this film! I gave them an episode every evening before sending them off to bed. It was the story of my life, and they all exclaimed, "What an imagination! Honestly, what an imagination! How on earth did you dream up all of that?" '

22

AND SO, WITH the firm intention of realising this metamorphosis, one morning he saw Manhattan open its misty arms to him and the Statue of Liberty rise from the waves to welcome him in person.

'To tell the truth, what struck me most was the silence. You would think the ship was gliding along on the general astonishment.'

Then you heard cries of 'New York!' rising up from steerage, mixed with blaring sirens, the loud hurrah of hopes fulfilled, much kissing and hugging, much activity preparing to land, the *Cleveland*'s slow progress into dock, and the endless procession of the now silent passengers leaving the ship. The double spent the day in his cabin. Captain Polcinelli had advised him to wait until the evening before making a discreet exit, as the ship would be completely empty and the limousine that Morasecchi had insisted on obtaining for him would be waiting.

'Just tell the driver where you want to go. We guarantee his discretion.'

And so at nightfall, he is the last to go down the accommodation ladder. Morasecchi and Polcinelli, leaning on the rail, keep waving him goodbye. They have already thanked him again and again: an unforgettable voyage, thanks to him, thank you, thank you. The Captain and the Purser don't know how to express their gratitude. He gives them a friendly tap on the shoulder.

'Say no more, please. There's no need for profuse thanks . . . Besides, we'll see each other again. I won't forget to recommend the *Cleveland* to the Fairbankses.'

Now he leaves . . . Looking down the long perspective of the gangway leading to the car with the shiny roof, he descends into the hum of the city. He wonders what destination he'll give to the chauffeur, who has already put his bags away and is now standing on the dock by the car door, cap in hand. He goes down, with his heart beating fast, into an atmosphere smelling of oil, still sea water, sheet iron and greasy rope, wet stone and nature newly come to life. New York! He's arrived! Americky, the home of the cinematograph! He's made it! He's foiled the immigration process! He turns round, looks up, and gives a last wave to the Captain and the Purser, who are just shadows against a pale ink sky, as the chauffeur bids him good evening and the door opens silently to a whiff of expensive leather and French tobacco.

He gets in, still wondering (almost tempted to giggle) what destination to give the driver, when he realises that he's not alone in the back seat of the limousine.

Pereira is there, and Charlie Chaplin . . . the real one this time.

Sitting in the back seat of the car.

Which moves off.

23

THE SHOCK WAS so great that he dreamed about it for the rest of his life. Pereira and Chaplin! Right up to his last night on earth, he will be roused suddenly from his sleep by the torments of that nightmare: Pereira and Chaplin waiting for him in that car on the evening of his arrival in New York!

The car has left the port. Manuel Pereira da Ponte Martins and Charlie Chaplin are conversing without taking the slightest notice of him, 'as if I were dead'. The car is going along a park that looks as dark as a fearful child's imagination. He wants to get out. He wants to jump out while the car is still moving. But he can't, the door is locked, of course.

Later, even when he's lost everything, even when the street is his only refuge, he'll wake up with his mind and heart pounding, immensely relieved to find himself back in poverty, the packing cases that protect him from the sky, the old newspapers that keep out the cold, the cul-de-sac where he has found refuge and his final solitude . . . Calm down, it wasn't Pereira, remember, it wasn't Pereira! And that's true. It wasn't Pereira. Right, it wasn't Pereira. Nevertheless, the dream will return night after night.

'What do you expect? When you've really lost the game, when all you have left is nightmares, in the end you get attached to them. I have that one just for the pleasure of waking up.'

'So it wasn't Pereira?'

'No, it was Valentino, of course.'

'. . .'

'. . .'

'No kidding?'

24

'IT'S THE TRUTH, for Christ's sake! Chaplin and Valentino were waiting for me when I got off the ship! I've got a heap of details, I can . . .' The make of the car, 'fitted out like an old madam's salon', the make of the hats, Valentino's French cigarettes, Chaplin's English shoes, the pigskin gloves worn by both of them, the subject of their conversation, 'they were talking cinema; Valentino wanted to try directing', the name of the chauffeur, his white coat with the black velvet collar . . .

(It sounds like the list of a chief set designer going around the stage, notebook in hand, making sure that everything is in its right place and of the right period.)

He'll spend hours at it, raising the status of these details to that of irrefutable proof! No one will even try to believe him. They'll titillate him, for a laugh.

'Go on. Tell us some more about Chaplin and Valentino!'

For the price of another glass.

'When I realised that it wasn't Pereira but Valentino, the thing that struck me first was how different Valentino looked from Pereira. Although, God knows, he was like him! Down to the way he held his cigarette holder. But Valentino was a Pereira with a soul, and that made a huge difference! Nature does come up with these strange things now and again . . . Do you know he was a saint, Valentino? Did you know that?'

At this stage, no one understands what he's saying. The idea of this *dissimilar resemblance* goes right over their heads.

'It's not very clear what you're saying.'

'That's because it's true.'

25

INSIDE THE CAR that has left the docks ('And this time it's not a dream!'), Chaplin is gently lecturing Valentino. He talks to him like an elder brother. The two stars are talking cinema. Apparently Valentino wants to take up directing. He must have been describing a scenario to Chaplin and become rather excited: his eyes are still shining. He asks Charlie what he thinks of his subject: 'Gordon is very enthusiastic about it, you know!' 'That's not the question,' Chaplin replies patiently. 'Every banker in the world will think your subjects are wonderful, Rudy.' The big brother is giving the learner a lesson about the real world. 'By moving to the other side of the camera, you're coming down from Olympus; you're really entering the arena.' Chaplin is speaking in a soft but clipped voice that's slightly nasal. 'Here on the ground the attorneys are lying in wait for us, Rudy.' He's speaking from experience. 'Beware of bankers, especially Gordon. I saw a lot of him when I was making *The Kid*.' Chaplin is quite categorical. 'Films aren't made on Wall Street.' And again: 'Investors will always listen favourably, especially to you, Rudy, but in the end they'll persuade you that good ideas are fished exclusively out of their cash register. That's rubbish!' Chaplin is quivering. 'Don't let them force anything on you: not your subjects, nor your actors, or even the most menial hand in your technical team.' A moment's silence. 'Nevertheless, if you want to do a serious work, of course . . . Tell me, Rodolfo, do you really want to do a *serious work*?'

It's quite dark now. The car is driving beside Battery Park. 'And what about Pola?' Chaplin is asking Valentino what Pola Negri thinks of him wanting to become a director. 'What does Pola think about it?' Valentino sidesteps the question. 'Who knows what women think?'

26

IN ANOTHER VERSION, he tells a slightly different story.
He gets off the ship, into the car, Chaplin and Valentino are
there, they continue their conversation as if nothing has
happened; the difference is the subject of their conversation.
As the car drives along (it has left the docks and is passing
Battery Park in this version too), Chaplin is talking about a
competition held a few years before, a nationwide competition to find the best Charlie double. Dozens of candidates
came from all the states in America with the suit, the cane, the
shoes, the false moustache . . . The preliminary rounds took
place in Santa Monica and the finals here, on Broadway.

And Chaplin finishes by saying, with no sign of a laugh: 'I
came third.'

. . .

('The last time you told us that, Chaplin said he came sixth.'
'Sixth, third, what does it matter? Doesn't anyone ever get the
real point of a story?')

27

THE CAR WAS driving beside Battery Park. A strong whiff
of rich grass made him choke. Teresina had not taught
him that nature could produce such lush vegetation. He
decided to escape while Chaplin and Valentino were talking.

Americky was big; it would take them for ever to find him if he dashed into the darkness of that park. He surreptitiously slid his hand over the chrome of the handle. He waited for the car to slow down or stop at a crossing.

But no, the door was locked, well and truly.

It was then that Chaplin spoke to him.

'Well?'

'...'

'Who are you?'

'...'

'Since you're neither Valentino nor me, who are you? Or rather,' (the question of his identity being of secondary importance after all), 'who's paying you?'

Without giving him time to reply, Chaplin went through the names of all those he thought likely to hire a clown to get at Valentino and himself: frustrated bankers, rival producers, rejected women, jealous actors, people of all kinds bent on revenge, columnists looking for copy, also friends who liked practical jokes (in Hollywood, you could never tell with Douglas, for example, or mad Fatty, what kind of joke they might be hatching). Who? Who had taken advantage of Rudy's retreat to Falcon Lair to make people believe he was on board the *Cleveland* disguised as Chaplin? Who had decided to employ a mercenary clown? And who had tipped off the *Chicago Tribune*?

'Who?'

28

'Because – and i didn't know this either – also on board the *Cleveland* was a writer for the *Chicago Tribune*, the one who later tried to blacken Rudy when *The Son of the Sheik* came out. You remember that article, don't you? *Why didn't someone drown Rudolph Valentino a few years ago? Then he wouldn't have been imported into the United States.* That's it, word for word. *Rodolfo Guglielmi, alias Rudolph Valentino, who never goes out without his powder compact.* Homo americanus, *my dear!* . . . That kind of nasty anti-Italian garbage. They went as far as handing out the paper as the audience came out of the Mark Strand Theater, on the evening of the premiere! Well, that fellow, that journalist was on board the *Cleveland*. Valentino disguised as Chaplin! You bet he leaped at the chance!'

(At this stage of the story, he holds out his glass. Of course they fill it for him.)

'Especially since they also had their eye on Chaplin, the Englishman who refused to become an American citizen. You can just imagine! So this muckraker cables the news to his office. The chief editor contacts Chaplin immediately, partly to find out if it's true, partly to needle him. "I'm told that Valentino is taking the mickey out of you on one of the Hamburg America Line boats." Naturally Chaplin grabs a telephone and calls George Ullmann, Valentino's manager. Ullmann is flabbergasted. "Rudy at sea? But Rudy's at Falcon Lair! Charlie, you know how he needs to go off on his own now and then!" "George, I'll only believe it when I see it." "Where are you, Charlie? I'll tell him to call you." "That's not good enough. I want to see him with my own eyes."

'To cut a long story short, Valentino and Chaplin meet and send a joint telegram to the *Chicago Tribune*, so that they can muzzle the little squirt on the *Cleveland*. Once that's done, they cable Polcinelli, asking him to keep me on ice. If Morasecchi and he want to keep their stripes, they'd better stop any leaks by explaining to their passengers that I'm neither Valentino nor Chaplin; and that everyone had better keep their traps shut, as there could be court cases in the offing. As for me, they should let me carry on playing the fool, and on arrival hand me over without notifying the police. A car will be waiting for me.'

29

AND NOW, IN the back of that car, Chaplin's eyes nail him to the back of his seat.

'Well, who's paying you?'

'Nobody.'

'Meaning?'

'. . .'

'. . .'

He had to explain to them that not only had nobody paid him, but that he himself was nobody. To his great surprise, he found himself plunging headlong into 'the description of a scenario that should have fired the cinematic imaginations of Chaplin and Valentino'. He found himself relating the tragedy of the travelling projectionist who had been arrested and executed in Teresina. This time the story came out as an exciting fusion of fiction and historical fact. It was a good idea: Chaplin remembered the young man who had deserted the Mutual Film Corporation, borrowing a 1908 Motiograph and a dozen of his films. What was his name again? Yes, an excellent projectionist; yes, a Latino. He disappeared one morning to the great consternation of Caulfield, who alerted all the sheriffs in the region. ('The Motiograph cost $216, after all!')

'It was just before I left for First National,' Chaplin recalled. 'So he decided to do a tour in Latin America, did he? He was right: "It will be mailed to you absolutely free," according to the Motiograph advertisement . . . Where did you say you met him?'

'In Teresina.'

He told them that the projectionist had landed in his little shop and died there, pursued by the political police who thought he was a dangerous propagandist.

'I was nobody, just an ordinary barber, which I would have remained if that man, the projectionist, tortured beyond words, hadn't arrived and died at my place.'

He hadn't had the heart to turn him over to his executioners. But it wasn't an act of political courage. Oh no. In Teresina, if you didn't want to end up nailed by your feet to the centre of the sun, you didn't meddle in politics. Yet, well, when the dying man showed him *The Immigrant*, 'the first film I'd ever seen, I was converted on the spot!' In his youth, the Jesuit had intended him for God, and in his teens the Garibaldian barber destined him for revolution, yet it was the cinematograph that claimed him, bursting with faith. And then the projectionist – the angel of my Annunciation! – begged me before he died to go to his native village, find his wife and children, and give them the small amount of money he had earned for them . . .

And indeed, that is what he did. He packed away his barber's instruments, closed the shop, took up his pilgrim's staff, crossed a burning continent, found the projectionist's village, the adobe hut, the woman and her children, including one at the breast (he realised *in extremis* that this child could not have belonged to the projectionist, 'a question of dates', but Chaplin and Valentino seemed moved by the picture of the starving little thing clinging to that withered breast, 'so I quickly corrected this, saying that the baby was the last-born child of Dolores, the projectionist's sister, who had been carried off the day before by typhus'). He took pains to describe the swollen bellies of the other children, the nursing mother's prominent ribs, the dirt floor, the silence under the burning sun. Then he began on 'the peals of laughter' he still drew from all these unfortunate people when he screened *The Immigrant* for them, and how he had become aware of the cinematograph's great magic and Señor Chaplin's great genius in being able to overcome starving people's hunger just by 'making plates dance before their eyes!' Yes, Señor Chaplin's cinema proved to be 'a food for the soul, which could even satisfy the appetites of the body!'

'I've never been so inspired! Really! Even with the passengers around Morasecchi's table!'

And so he was astounded to hear Chaplin interrupt him point-blank.

'After all,' Chaplin remarked to Valentino, 'instead of taking the *Cleveland*, our friend here could just as easily have travelled on the *Olympic*, where I was an immigrant!'

'In which case,' Valentino replied, 'he would have passed himself off as me, and they would have thought he was you.'

'And a writer from the *Morning Telegraph* or the *United News* would have given the alarm,' Chaplin replied. 'They didn't leave my side for a moment on my tour of Europe.'

They shared a clubby laugh, then Chaplin decided to bring the matter to a close.

'You have done serious damage to our image, sir.'

'. . .'

'Have you any idea what the word "image" means in Hollywood?'

Valentino came to his aid.

'It's something like *honour*. Do you understand?'

'. . .'

'It's priceless,' Chaplin explained.

30

THE MOMENT HAS come to close the window on the double. At this stage of the story, it seems fairly obvious that his situation cannot improve.

When he suggested making up for his wrongs by offering Chaplin and Valentino a large percentage of his future fees as an actor, they looked at him with such astonishment that he doubted he had even spoken. Fees? Actor? Him? What kind of actor did he think he was? All the passengers on a transatlantic steamer had taken him for Valentino when he was trying to pass himself off as Chaplin. What producer would risk a single dollar on a genius like that? It was like a bucket of cold water thrown over rutting dogs. They were right. They were right. They were right. They had sized up just what a nonentity he was. An actor? Never. Not during the voyage nor before it. To attain the high level of an actor, it was not enough to pull faces for indulgent diplomats or to trick a people blinded by the desire to be loved. Him, an actor? He suddenly remembered the laughing faces of the villagers and the sailors at the inn. He thought he had made them laugh, while in fact they had quite simply been laughing at him, like the passengers on the *Cleveland*, and like the cream of Teresina. Of course, old da Ponte, the Bishop and Colonel Eduardo Rist had not been deceived for an instant. Not for one instant had they taken him for their son, godson or friend; they had always known he was Pereira's double, Pereira's 'good idea'! How could he have doubted it? Taken for Valentino when he thought he was imitating Charlie!

'No, no,' muttered Chaplin. 'The damage has been done and the guilty party is insolvent.' 'Insolvent and illegal,' Valentino pointed out. 'Yes, he entered American territory illegally,' Chaplin agreed. For a moment they were tempted to hand him over to the immigration authorities. The consequences were obvious:

Ellis Island,

Questioning,

Prison,

Return to Teresina,

Firing squad,

The end.

Luckily (if one can talk of luck in that situation), Valentino had an immigrant's instinctive reaction. He turned his gentle, short-sighted gaze on to the trespasser, looked him slowly up and down, admitted that there was a 'vague resemblance', and offered to employ him as his lighting double at $10 a week, no contract of course, and on a trial basis.

A double's job in fact.

'I jumped at the chance, as you can imagine. I accepted right away.'

As for Chaplin, he showed that he too was magnanimous by giving him the projector and the films. 'Keep them. The statute of limitations has run out, Caulfield won't know anything about it, and besides, today the Motiograph's an antique.'

That was it. From Pereira to Valentino, a double he had been and a double he would stay. He had tried to escape, but through a window that opened on to the same room. It was the story of his life. However surprising it may seem, this conclusion was not even original, as was proved to him when he arrived in Hollywood and was shown his quarters by Valentino ('a white caravan in the grounds of the Pickford-Fairbanks studios'). He opened the door and discovered two other Valentinos lying one above the other on bunk beds, idly leafing through magazines: they were the riding double and the tango double.

31

THE LONGEST TIME in man's life is the end.

For three years he worked in Valentino's shadow, as lighting double, until that fatal year 1926, when Rudy played *The Son of the Sheik* (the sequel to *The Sheik*, made in 1923).

Once again Hollywood went Saharan. Tons of sand were poured into the California studios. Tents were erected. People sat cross-legged on Saracen carpets. Whiskey was poured in thin streams from teapots held high, as is the custom with Bedouin. He, 'the lighting double', moved here and there, waited patiently at each break, as they trained the projectors that would light Valentino on him. He did his job conscientiously. A little more to the right? He moved a little more to the right. Your left profile! He gave them his left profile. Fitzmaurice was directing and Barnes was behind the camera. Their attention to detail went as far as dressing him like a musical-comedy Arab. 'It's not you we're lighting, it's the costume.' They also made him up as an old sheik, as Valentino was acting the parts of both father and son.

'Move half a yard forward.'

He moved forward.

'Lift your head a little . . .'

They lit his make-up. Then they washed his face.

In Yuma, Arizona, in the scenes where Ahmed Ben Hassan, the son of the sheik, gallops full speed towards the beautiful Yasmin, the riding double takes his place. And it wasn't he who was strung up by the wrists and whipped by the thieves after the ambush scene, but the tango double – for the curve of the back.

He went out a little in the evening. It was strictly forbidden to go as Valentino – he would lose his job if he did. 'Recognised once, deported for ever,' Ullmann had warned him. 'Is that clear?' He found it both clear and reasonable. Therefore it was wig, glasses and false beard for him. 'And no tango. Is that understood?' He did not complain. Relieved of the burden of becoming someone, he was now the shadow of a star, and satisfied with that. As for Hollywood – Hollywood, the centre of the world – as he never stopped saying, 'it's the home of ghosts'. He existed in a state of heavenly weightlessness, where at last there was no need for his dreams to be realised.

During all this time, he saw very little of Valentino. Two or three times in the distance or quickly passing through. One afternoon in July 1926, however, Rudy put a hand on his sleeve – 'I hear they're happy with your work' – and promised to do what was needed to 'regularise his situation'. If he continued to give satisfaction, Rudy would make him an American citizen, and that was a promise. It was nice of him, but Valentino died on 23 August, at midday, after nine days of dreadful suffering.

He felt responsible for that agony.

A rumour of unknown origin had spread, claiming that Rudy wasn't a whole man. Real women whispered it to each other. An anonymous reporter of the *Chicago Tribune* wrote an article: *Hollywood is the school of masculinity and Valentino is supposedly the model of the American male. Dear me, darling.* The article was entitled 'The Pink Powder Puff'. It was unsigned. It made Pola Negri choke with anger. She exhorted Rudy to 'do something, for God's sake!' Her outbursts of fury reverberated around the walls of Hollywood. That's because it was above all a question of her honour, her reputation as a woman! 'Can you understand that, Rudy? Can you understand that at least?'

Rumour attacks the belly. Something lodged in Rudy's stomach. Rudy was tender-hearted, and modest with it. He attributed his success to a series of lucky breaks. He didn't make the mistake of identifying with his film persona. At most he wanted to 'leave an image' behind him. And now there was a rumour eating away at Rudy's image.

Through the newspapers, Valentino challenged the

anonymous journalist of the *Chicago Tribune* to a duel in the boxing ring, whatever his height, weight or reach. He even went as far as training with the world champion, Jack Dempsey, in person. Rudy had a sense of honour, a great right hook and courage to burn; the scribbler didn't show up. But the rumour grew, and so did the thing in Rudy's stomach.

To make matters worse, in Italy a Pereira with shaven head and lantern jaw thundered against the son of the sheik. Benito Mussolini didn't like Rodolfo Valentino, a naturalised Yank, a traitor to the land of his birth. Shame on him! Friends of Benito took Rodolfo's picture down from the walls of Italian cinemas. They emptied the frames, left his name and draped a black ribbon across them. No more image. The thing in Rudy's stomach fed on this too. It made frightening progress. On Sunday 15 August 1926 in New York it exploded, devouring the poor man's entrails until Monday 23 August at midday when, despite the best efforts of the doctors, Rudolph Valentino died in appalling pain and stench.

It rained on the day of his funeral. Charlie Chaplin, Douglas Fairbanks, George Ullmann and Joseph Schenck were pall bearers. The cinematograph was in mourning. Though the rain fell heavily, Pola Negri's tears flowed even more heavily.

The coffin was put on a train to Hollywood.

32

'I'M THE ONE who should have died, not him.'
You could never convince him otherwise.

33

HE LEFT HOLLYWOOD and took to the road, without beard or wig, looking like Valentino (to the nth degree). Music hall, that was what he planned to do. Do Rudy on the boards; to restore his reputation, he argued. He would not play the sheik, the hussar or the wonderful *tanguista*. No. He would just tell the true story of Rodolfo Pietro Filiberto Raffaello Guglielmi di Valentina d'Antonguolla, alias Valentino, born in the same year as the cinematograph, 6 May exactly, at Castellaneta, in the Puglia region of Italy, near the Ionian Sea, an area of big landowners. He would describe his rise 'from the cotton fields of his childhood to the silk shirts of Hollywood'; he would praise his modesty, his doubts, his goodness, his generosity, his gentle grace, his sense of honour and his fidelity; he would say how their paths had crossed and how Valentino had saved him from everything, 'including myself', and what a worldwide success as a director Valentino would have become, had human malice not eaten him alive.

Rudy was the best of those good people who always die young: that's what he would say! And also that he himself, still on this earth, was but a pale imitation of him. His soul was as black as Valentino's was pure. He would say that and more. He would go right back to Valentino's dad, the cavalry officer who became a vet and died too young; he would describe his mama, Gabrielle Barbin, the heroic woman from Alsace; he would talk about the two brothers and the little sister Maria. They only had to hire him, and he would tell it all, the genuine, true story!

But there was nothing.

Nowhere.

The owner of one theatre explained to him that nobody in the world had the right to look like Valentino now. Had Christ ever had a double, someone just like him? Before the crucifixion, yes, there were prophets galore, but afterwards? One can't be Christ's double: his agents would object.

'All right, since they don't want me anywhere, I'll go everywhere.'

He was as good as his word.

Off he went, wandering his way all over the United States of America.

'Crossing continents is nothing new to me!'

Wherever people offered him a drink, he would put the record straight. When they gave him enough liquor, the stories would pour out of him. For example, when he described Pola Negri's grief at Valentino's grave, he was inimitable. 'She tore her heart out, she threw it into the trench, and had to be restrained from adding her liver.' According to him (screwing up his eyes as he looked at his glass), Ullmann had bought this despair from Pola's agents. 'It's true!' Ullmann absolutely had to have 'resounding female grief' to save Rudy's honour. Every tear of Pola's was negotiated for the price of diamonds. A shower of precious stones made a dead man potent for posterity. Thanks to Pola's tears, sixty-five women ('and real women at that!') declared themselves pregnant by Valentino in the week that followed his funeral.

'Lies! Bullshit! Talk!'

That's possible, but in the bars where he told stories like these, he was asked to repeat them. Prophets come from the outside and people want to believe the unbelievable. This one had a sense of detail, and a vague accent (but where exactly did he come from?) that gave his words the exotic aura of truth. They filled up his glass.

A few years passed. Hollywood dug up Valentino again. They wanted to make a film about him.

'I rushed there to get the title role.'

But time . . .

But alcohol . . .

'They didn't even want me for the father, Guglielmi.'

It was then that he remembered something Valentino had said (was it in the car, with Chaplin, had he read it in *Variety*, heard it on the set in Hollywood?). Anyway, something Valentino said, admitting that he dreaded the ravages of time, predicted that he 'would die young', refused to grow old, to 'tarnish his image', and that he wanted to stay just the way he looked here and now, '*ad vitam aeternam*'.

So somebody else would have to agree to grow old in his place.

'That's it. That's my lot. My penance. And when I see my face each morning in the mirror, I say to myself that Rudy was damn right: *metamorphosis*, changing into something else, in his case would have been a crime!'

He had a few months' remission in his rapid decline. A good-hearted lover briefly dragged him away from the bar, got him to rewind his monologues and go back to his real work: as a barber. She said she did it out of love. But he suspected that what she loved in him were traces of Rudy. Even though she kept asking who this Rudy was (she was a recent immigrant, from Hungary), she always received the same answer, 'You don't love me for myself!'

He also resented her for not being a 'real woman'.

Besides, the effects of alcohol left too many scars on the customers' faces; the barber was no more.

When you fall, you really fall. He went back to touring the country as a bachelor preacher. 'Let me tell you. Valentino was a saint!' He would beat his breast saying, 'I killed him.' He cried into his glass. 'It's my fault that he got the reputation as a cockless wonder.'

Ah! But, all the same, he did experience one small pleasure. In a motel in Arkansas, where someone had left a newspaper behind, he happened to notice a short item: a certain Manuel Pereira da Ponte Martins, the dictator of some banana republic, had been shot between the eyes on the national holiday. Bang! Nothing remained of his killer, who had been torn to pieces by the crowd. He feared for an instant that the assassinated president was his own double. But that wasn't the case. The paper reported that Colonel Eduardo Rist, the Commander-in-Chief of the army, had accepted the post. Therefore the dead man was the real Pereira. Someone must have got sick of the *bacalhau do menino* at last. That called for champagne.

One fine day he realised that he was wasting his breath. 'What! You don't know *The Four Horsemen of the Apocalypse*? Or *Alimony*? And *The Sheik*? Not even *The Sheik*? *The Sheik* doesn't mean anything to you? Or *The Son of the Sheik* either? No, not that either. Valentino had faded with time. His name got no response from young people. Even the old people lost interest once the movies learned to speak. Who was this guy boring them stiff with his tales about a ghost of the silent cinema?

Rudy and he were wrong: film did not confer immortality. Americky was forging ahead, and there was nothing but oblivion, on earth as in heaven.

'Amen.'

Henceforth his greatest claim to fame was his extraordinary

capacity for drink. The amount that guy could knock back! You had to see it to believe it. And he wasn't even Irish! They took bets as they filled his glass. He never collapsed. When asked why he drank so much, he replied that years ago the sun had turned him into a dry cuttlefish.

'You know, one of those white things you give to budgerigars to peck.'

34

HE DIED ONE winter evening in 1940, in a cinema. They were showing Charlie Chaplin's *The Great Dictator*. The film tells the story of a barber who turns out to be the double of a dictator. The dictator juggled with the world and the barber was nameless.

The usherette thought the last person left in the audience had fallen asleep. When she shook his shoulder, the body collapsed at her feet. To the policemen who asked her if she had noticed anything in particular, the girl replied that the dead man's face was 'bathed in tears'. (These are her own words.)

'He died laughing, then,' the younger of the two cops suggested.

'No, it was murder with two killers,' the other replied.

He pointed his foot at a bottle of J&B under the victim's seat. Empty.

'Dirty cops,' the young usherette muttered later that night. She couldn't sleep. She kept seeing the dead man's face, wet with tears.

IV
THE LURE OF THE INTERIOR

1

'**D**IRTY COPS...'

Yes, I know there's a terrible lack of women in this story, and I'd love to take advantage of this hour or two in my hammock to slip a woman into these pages, to tell your story for example, little usherette, a story that may not have ended yet, as it's not impossible that time has brought you to us still alive today...

Tell me, what do you look like on this 1 December 1940? (It will be another four years to the day before I'm born.) What do you do, when you're not showing these popcorn munchers to their seats? Are you a real usherette or a student? Are you learning to be an actress? So you like the cinema, eh? Do you feel that it's always been there? It's 'your whole life'. How old would you be? Sixteen, seventeen? And your favourite actor is Bogart, Humphrey Bogart. Come on, don't deny it. I knew it when you whispered 'Dirty cops' (an expression of Bogart's, with the 's' typically pronounced more like 'sh'), and you look so cute in that Bogart trench coat your parents don't want you to wear, with its knotted belt that makes you look like a spy... Where do you hide this gabardine raincoat, since they won't have it in the house? Here in the cinema? Do you have a locker? One of those metal wardrobes? With a photo of Bogey behind the door? Or is it the manager's idea, dressing the usherettes like Bogart?

How I'd love to meet you today, now that you've become an old lady, and a Parisian, still looking discreetly American despite all these years in France... Of course I'd have to write to you first and introduce myself in a polite letter before coming to ask you these questions for documentation, to get the right detail, to fish for first-hand information, as I did in Venice with the collector Montanaro, Carlo's friend, a walking encyclopedia of the silent cinema. It was he who gave me the name, the year, the instructions, the advertising of the Motiograph projector, and contemporary magazines: *Screenland*, *Moving Picture News*, *Motography*, *Photoplay*, the *New York Dramatic Mirror* . . .

For example, what was the name of the Chicago cinema where the double died? Did movie-goers stuff themselves with popcorn in the dark back then in 1940? Did men keep their hats on? Did they whistle when the vamps appeared on the screen? Or is it just our impression of it, which also comes from the cinema?

That sort of information . . .

Of course, like everyone else, I know a few things about what happened when Chaplin's *Dictator* first came out: the deluge of anonymous letters than rained down on Charlie for daring to debunk Hitler, the threatening phone calls from American Nazis, his fear of seeing the film banned following protests from the German, Italian and Argentine govern-ments, the accusation of being a Communist sparked off by the barber's final speech haranguing the armies in place of the dictator: 'I should like to help everyone, if possible – Jew, Gentile, Black Man, White . . . The misery that is now upon us is but the passing of greed . . .' I know all that, and how Chaplin had held out against everything and how, two years later, when the winds of history changed direction because of Stalingrad, the very people who accused him of warmongering when *The Great Dictator* came out, sought his aid in hastening the opening of the Western Front . . .

I know all that.

But tell me, what was the weather like in Chicago on that night? Was there one of those north winds that blow down from Canada, become more biting as they cross the immense flat surface of Lake Michigan, then slice into the legs of people on the sidewalk where you come from? Was it the blizzard that made the double take refuge in your cinema? Wind and snow?

At the beginning of that December, how many weeks was it since *The Great Dictator* was first released? Did people really talk about it a lot? Was as much revealed then about films before they were screened as there is today, when you have to make yourself deaf and blind if you want to have the faintest hope of coming fresh to one? Was there the slightest chance that the double could have gone into that cinema quite unprepared? Could he have sat down in his seat knowing nothing about *The Great Dictator*? Do you think that's possible? Or better still, that he took shelter there not knowing what was on the programme, and that without warning he found himself looking at the story of the barber and the dictator on the screen, the very one he had told at Morasecchi's table? Is it conceivable? Think before you answer. Think hard, it's very important. The meaning of his tears depends on it. Those tears that had dried before the police arrived: 'His face was bathed in tears,' you said. Do you remember?

Unless, wait a moment . . .

No . . .

Those tears didn't dry on their own . . .

They didn't disappear before the two cops arrived.

It was you, wasn't it?

It was you. You wiped his face.

Yet he was the first dead person you had ever seen.

But you took it upon yourself to hold that neck in the

159

hollow of your hand and wipe away the tears with your handkerchief . . .

And you must also have closed his eyes.

Yes, it was you.

Of course . . .

Of course it was you.

2

AT THIS STAGE I must open a separate little chapter as an aside, since intuitions of this kind, which are really certainties (you, young lady, wiping away the tears of the dead man and closing his eyes in this empty cinema), don't suddenly appear and take over a novelist's imagination by chance.

It's a memory, actually, a picture that suddenly surfaces in this narrative without warning, a moment of my youth brought to life again by my trying to imagine yours.

This is the memory:

We're at the very beginning of the seventies, in Paris. It concerns my friend Fanchon. (We're from the same village, La Colle-sur-Loup in the Alpes-Maritimes, we've done part of our studies in the same arts faculty in Nice, we'll teach together for a while in the same high school in Soissons, then we'll lose track of each other.) My friend Fanchon and I are going down into the Métro, I forget the name of the station. It's rush hour at the end of the day, there are lots of people streaming in, all hurrying to get home. A tramp has fallen asleep on a seat, overcome by alcohol. He's dirty. His face, chest and hands are mottled with dirt, as if social decomposition was already laying the colours of death on him. And the smell . . . People avoid him. They suddenly move aside, leaving an empty space in front of his seat. But I'm mistaken, it's not because of the smell. It's something else: his fly is open and his dick is lying limp and heavy across his thigh. That's what it is, and the travellers look away – all taking a sudden interest in what's happening on the opposite platform – and there's Fanchon walking ahead of me. She stops when she reaches him, leans over, puts his penis back into his trousers, also tucks in the ends of his shirt, zips up his fly and buckles his belt . . .

That woman's gesture done without fuss – a real woman's gesture! – it's you wiping away the dead man's tears.

3

RIGHT, SO NOW you have Fanchon's face. (She was more or less your age when I knew her.) It's easier to imagine you and your gabardine raincoat since Fanchon's right upper lip had the same scar as Bogart's – his came from a war wound, hers from a dog bite.

Dirty war!

Dirty mongrel!

As for me lying quietly in the hammock where I've been musing for hours (while Minne, who has left her own typewriter for the moment, is trying her best to make the southern

Vercors bloom – two pick handles have gone by the board since the beginning of summer; the ground here resists flowers . . .), I'm thinking of the question sometimes asked of novelists: 'How are your characters conceived?'

Like that. From the unpredictable and essential combination of thematic demands, narrative requirements, deposits left by life experiences, the vagaries of daydreams, the arcane mysteries of a fickle memory, events, books, images, people . . .

Besides, the conception of a character is not important; it's whether they spring to life that counts. As far as the reader is concerned, characters aren't 'conceived', they exist from the moment they appear in the text. No conception, no birth, no growth, no initiation, just one mission: to be there from the very beginning. Of course they can fill out as the book proceeds, but first they must 'be there'. Now a character is only really *there* if he or she escapes from the incident that demanded their appearance, from the function that ostensibly defines them, in a word, from the strings that the author thinks he is pulling.

This unexpected gesture, inherited from Fanchon (wiping away the dead man's tears), has saved you from the strictly utilitarian role I had planned for you: i.e. discovering the double's body, *basta*, that's it.

Well done! You've escaped.

4

A LL THE SAME, I can't really say that I can *see* you. And
even if I endowed you with all of Fanchon's particular
attributes (the brown shimmer in those blue-green eyes, her
quick gestures, her short brown hair, her high cheekbones, the
whiteness of her skin, the slightly nasal vehemence when she
spoke . . .), I would see you no better. You characters don't act
on our senses. And you don't make any greater impression on
those of the reader than you do on the novelist who imagines
you. You don't make yourself seen or heard. It's your way of
having an intimate relationship with all of us, as well as each
one individually. And when a film-maker claims to present
you for our collective consideration, we obviously never
'imagined' you like that.

'Is that the way *you* saw the usherette?'

5

H ERE'S ANOTHER FEATURE of characters: each one of
you is a snowball rolling down the incline of the author.
Your ball is formed as much from what happens to us by
chance as from our quiet meditation and reflection, and you
pick up everything on your path that can give you meaning.

An example? You've taken up residence in this book for
scarcely two days and your existence has already been

enriched by a comment from my friend Jean Guerrin, to whom I've dedicated this story of the double. When he finished reading it, he asked me, 'Do you think that Chaplin made a habit of plundering human wrecks?'

The expression 'to plunder wrecks' (although it doesn't concern you directly) opened my eyes: the thought immediately came into my mind that you knew the double.

You knew the double!

You couldn't *not* know him. He was the local wreck, the mythical drunk of that part of Chicago, the all-round champion of downing a drink in one go. Exactly the kind of boozer whose tackle Fanchon had put back in its place as he was lying on the seat in the Métro. Maybe he was a regular at the bar where you gulped down your hamburger before going on duty at the cinema. Night after night you heard his Hollywood chronicle, his pathetic attempt to clear Valentino's name, all the talk that no one but you ever listened to. You saw the punters fill his glass. Would he fall or wouldn't he? They lined up the dollars. The winner was the one who bought him the fatal pot. The boss took the bets and got his cut; legit. There was a real bundle to be won in the end, since they spent the night trying to knock him over and the pot increased with every contestant who collapsed into the sawdust before him. But for him, of course, not a cent. The glass he drank only gave him the right to down the next. It was the local lottery; a great way of sucking in the customers. People came from far afield to challenge him: brakemen from the railways, butchers from the abattoirs, dockers, Irish, Poles, Lithuanians . . . The bar was never empty. Every night there was the same competition for the last man standing; one glass after the other, straight down, until he collapsed. Despite the fact that I wrote he never fell, of course he finally let go of the bar and the winner pocketed the kitty. His fall, which never happened before dawn, was the signal for closing time. They carried him out and put him away in his cardboard packing case (in the lane just behind the bar, relatively sheltered from the wind, where your cinema came out). They tucked him up well and he even had several layers of blankets. There was no question of letting the hen that laid the golden eggs turn up its toes with pneumonia; no one want to see this small business die.

There was an unspoken agreement that the winner bought him the first glass on the following day.

6

So you knew him.
'Dirty cops!'

You're lying on your bed with your eyes open. You hate the cynicism of the cops who questioned you; they seem to you to be terrible stereotypes of their profession and nothing more, not worthy to be considered real individuals. But you're not stupid, you know very well that those policemen were not dealing with their first dead body, that in their line of work joking is a necessary protection for their mental health, just as it is for surgeons or firemen (the scream of an ambulance siren outside is proof that their lives are not a bed of roses), but you don't care, you're like Fanchon at your age, you don't pursue these thoughts, tormented as you are by a dead man's tears.

'Dirty cops!'
You on your bed.

Me in my hammock.

(And Minne outside, this time with Dane, breaking pick handles to win the battle of roses over flint.)

7

THE BIOGRAPH THEATER, was that your cinema? 2433 North Lincoln Avenue, right? Six years earlier, Mr John Dillinger, the Robin Hood of those days, got himself shot right in front of the entrance. You were a little girl at the time, but it was still talked about when you began as an usherette. The woman who betrayed Dillinger to the FBI agents wore a red dress so that she could be identified.

For the purposes of the novel, it would be a stroke of luck if it was the same cinema. Added to that, Dillinger looked vaguely like Bogart and was easily as popular. Legend has it that women soaked their handkerchiefs in the hero's blood after the ambulance had taken the body away.

Does the back of the Biograph Theater open on to a lane? This needs to be verified.

8

I<small>T'S YOU WHO</small> invited the double to see *The Great Dictator* (he hadn't even dared *think* about Chaplin since the episode in the car when he arrived in New York!), and you feel responsible for his death. You think of yourself as the woman in red. Maybe you even gave him the ticket – always supposing that you weren't in the habit of letting him in on the quiet through the door that opens on to the lane. By doing that you reconciled him with the cinema. He'd lost his taste for it and no longer had the means to indulge it. In short, you re-educated him. You reintroduced him to the cinema out of gratitude for all that he'd taught you about the cinematograph of the twenties. The guy really had spent part of his life in Hollywood; you checked his stories, all confirmed down to the last detail. You already know enough to separate what he had read in magazines or made up, as the drinks went down, from what he had actually experienced. Although he no longer looked anything like photographs of Valentino, he was his lighting double for *The Son of the Sheik* in 1926; you have no reason to doubt it. Your passion for the cinema has largely been inspired by his insistent monologue, and your discussions after seeing films finally shaped your taste.

In your memory today, he's still your film-buff angel, the Aladdin of the Motiograph, the legendary hobo whose story you've told to your children and grandchildren. One of them – Frédéric, your youngest grandson – will write a screenplay about him, which he'll think is original, poor fellow.

The story will be a flop for your grandson Frédéric, but that's not the point here.

The point is you lying on your bed in tears on that day, 1 December 1940, certain that you have hastened the poor man's death by inviting him to come and see *The Great Dictator*, a film whose theme Chaplin apparently stole from him.

He died of rage.

Because of you.

9

YOU CAN'T SLEEP.

You get up, sit down at your table and draw the dead double's face.

(Fanchon had this amazing gift for drawing . . . Two or three lines were enough for the things in her head to come to life before our eyes. Her drawing was light and clear-cut, but also tortured, the line often breaking at a disturbing angle.)

You stand up; you go to get your charcoal pencils . . .

. . .

While at the same moment, but sixty years later, here in my hammock, I feel a strange need coming over me:

The desire to create you as a living person.

That is to say, the need to write *as if you really existed.*

To carry on as if we knew each other *in real life.*

You now an old lady, me now respectfully calling you 'vous' instead of the familiar 'tu' I used for you as a girl, and the reader reaching the last pages of this book having completely forgotten *that you're just a fictional character*, my dear Sonia.

. . .

A mad impulse.

It had to happen. Since I've been shamelessly using certain characteristics of my friends to flesh out my fictional characters, one day I would inevitably feel the need to draw on the human qualities of a character to make a living creature.

. . .

And it's not really difficult.

. . .

You just have to imagine a dinner that took place, last month in Paris, say, where someone (our friend Catherine, for example, who is much more into art shows than Minne and me) exclaims: 'What! You don't know Sonia Ka's work?'

'Sonia Ka? No, we don't.'

'Not her retrospective exhibition at the Pompidou Centre last year?'

'No, sorry.'

A retrospective show of your fashion drawings, Sonia, your theatre sets and your story boards that attracted the whole Parisian fashion and theatre scene. Newspaper and magazine arts supplements did great spreads on your charcoal drawings, with punchy titles like 'Sonia Ka, Life at a Single Stroke', to quote just one.

'Herma and Anita' (two of our friends), 'did a great interview with her,' Catherine adds. 'Would you like to read it?'

Sonia Ka . . .

. . .

It's a detail in that interview that made me decide to write to you care of the Pompidou Centre, dear Sonia. In a reply to one of Anita's questions, you mention that job as an usherette at the Biograph Theater in the forties. Growing up American-style, with those little part-time jobs. Your father was very keen for you to try your wings, 'when they were still only stumps,' you explained.

And so I write to you. And lo and behold, you reply by return mail saying, no, no, not at all, it's no trouble, on the contrary, you'd be happy to see me, and besides, you know something of me as a novelist and you find it stimulating to help a writer 'carve out his slices of life'.

'And also,' you add, 'if I understand you correctly, I'm both a character and an informant in your book. Do come, dear author, and question me as much as you like. It's not a very frequent occurrence to have someone offering to present one's youth on a platter in fiction.'

. . .

Despite the hint of irony, I came. I even turned up in record time since, to my great surprise, not only did you live in Paris but in the rue des Envierges, just a stone's throw from me, in the building with the sharp angle rising up into the Belleville sky. And I recognised you as soon as you opened the door, having gone past you several times pulling your shopping trolley on the rue Piat rise, or at the butcher's in the rue de la Mare, and Minne and I even shared your table at the Mistral in the rue des Pyrénées one lunchtime when the restaurant was crowded. (You hardly noticed us as you were reading the TLS while nibbling at a salad.) Minne thought that you looked like 'an old Apache', then, after further detailed consideration, we agreed that you actually looked like the novelist Nathalie Sarraute: 'The same smooth hair and the same keen eye . . .'

If at that moment you'd started writing in a little exercise book, we would definitely have taken you for her.

'How old would she be?'

10

So, on that awful night in your adolescence, dear Sonia, you sketched the dead double's face,

a charcoal drawing you found sixty years later,

among the stuff in your studio

in the rue des Envierges where you can see all of Paris from your window,

and which you held out to me over our glasses of Vouvray

(when you come to think of it, that taste for our 'little Loire Valley wines' is the most American trait you still have)

and said,

'Here you are. That's him.'

What you held out to me wasn't a piece of art paper, but a bit of cardboard: 'The bottom of a shoebox, the first thing to draw on that came to hand that night when I got home.'

' . . . '

' . . . '

'Is that really him?'

'Yes, it's him.'

' . . . '

' . . . '

' . . . '

' . . . '

I expected to see a broad drunkard's face sagging down to a still shiny lower lip, and the liverish flesh that precedes tissue decay . . .

It's not like that at all. The face is emaciated, rather long, with a noble bone structure. The skin is stretched over the bones by the plumb line of wrinkles. The temples are hollow and the eyelids heavy under the greying mass of hair; the mouth is firm, closed, on a glass jaw; it looks like *a mouth used to staying shut.*

. . .

I didn't imagine him at all like that. And yet his face seems familiar.

. . .

It could be the face of a Corsican peasant, the impassive face of my distant cousins, the Lanfranchis from Campo, or the Prunettis from Guarguale, neither of whom were peasants, but they were oh so Corsican, and definitely silent; or the face of Minne's father Roger, a wind-blown Breton of few words, or perhaps – though I've never been there – one of Valentino's ancestors from Castellaneta in the province of Puglia. And perhaps in the end, that's what Valentino would have looked like – that severe, pensive, lined face – if he'd been given the chance to reach the age of wrinkles, and if he'd escaped the beauty masks the stupid image-makers would have forced on him. They're obsessive illusionists, cheating nature and making the skeleton vanish . . .

But, ladies and gentlemen, the skeleton always has the last word. You can smooth the rough edges, polish, remove, pad and stretch all you like, one day soon it will appear: the skeleton will bring out the astonishing, universal truth of what you are. Even Hollywood can't do anything to change the truth the skeleton reveals!

'That was one of his last tirades,' you told me as you put down your glass. With this comment: 'All drunks are inclined to preach. Besides, theirs is the only "Internationale" that lasts.'

Then she said, as she stood up: 'When are you leaving for the Vercors? Take the drawing with you. You can give it back to me when you've finished.'

11

I T WAS MY turn to wake up in the middle of the night.

Waking up: you dream, then suddenly you're thinking.

Last night I dreamed of two pictures of the liver that hung on the back wall of the classroom when I was a child at the local school in Savigny-sur-Orge: the alcoholic's liver and the healthy liver. Then with eyes wide open I remembered how, to my young mind, the excrescences on the liver with cirrhosis looked like a bouquet of flowers, especially as it was done in pretty colours, while the other, the healthy liver, was rather dull and unattractive. I didn't understand why you should be afraid of that burgeoning beauty. (The rest of my schooling was affected by that.)

Tonight I've been woken up by Malcolm Lowry. He drank twenty times the amount it's humanly possible to drink in forty-eight years of writing and travelling, then he fell through a window. The autopsy showed he had a perfectly healthy liver.

It's the dead of night. Minne is sleeping. The house, which is empty for once, groans in the Vercors wind. Outside, the hollyhocks are battling squalls and hail with a tenacity which seems miraculous when we go out with our bowls of coffee, prepared for the worst, only to find them standing there in the early-morning light, windswept but still standing!

. . .

Right. Lowry didn't have the liver that goes with the occupation, and the double didn't have the face.

. . .

I get up. Espadrilles. Office. Light. Portrait.

For the umpteenth time I scan the face of that dead man, trying to find what inspired the emotion I felt when Sonia put the drawing in front of me.

. . .

It's definitely not the face of an alcoholic non-stop talker.

It's not a Corsican peasant either.

Nor a Castellaneta cotton-picker.

Yes, it's a face formed by dry wind and silence, but also from somewhere deeper, more distant. He looks as if he's listening.

He suddenly makes me think of Erri de Luca, the Neapolitan writer whose face is like a parchment that history, rebellion, action, work, exile, reflection, reading, solitude, wind and silence have creased, and stretched.

. . .

That pensive reserve . . .

. . .

That inner strength . . .

. . .

A *sertanejo's* face . . .

That's what you've drawn, Sonia!

. . .

That night you drew a native of the Brazilian sertão on your shoebox! A native of Teresina or somewhere like it. (And isn't that what the double was, after all?) A *caatinguero*: one of those long-suffering people of the continent who are capable of anything.

It could be the face of Seu Marins, the father of Soledad and Néné, the husband of Mãe Martins, the silent and prolific patriarch of the Martins tribe. One of those faces . . .

His mop of hair is like a *cerradões* bush, bleached white by the sun.

If I dared, I would take my pencil and go on with your

drawing: I'd put a *vaqueiro*'s toughened-leather hat on that head. Then I'd place the head and hat on shoulders – shoulders, chest, arms and legs; shirt and trousers of denim or twill – I'd give him sandals that the cobbler in Maraponga made for Irene and myself from tyres, and I'd stand his two feet firmly on the hard-packed ground of a marketplace: in Teresina, Sobral, Canindé, Juàzeiro do Norte, Catarina, Crateús, Quixeramobim, Canudos, somewhere in the vast expanse of the sertão . . .

An old *vaqueiro* without a horse, leaning against a mud-brick wall with a bottle of *cachaça* in his hand, in a marketplace: that's what you've drawn, Sonia.

Look at him.

He's listening.

With his eyes closed.

What's he listening to? The poetry of the *cordel* duo.

He knows these poets who sing in the markets around there; he knows them well. Especially those two: Didi and Albão da Casa, father and son. Didi on the accordion and Albão on the guitar. He's known them for as long as he can remember. *They* haven't been tempted by Americky; they've never left the sertão, they've never gone down to São Paulo or Rio, they've been through the most terrible droughts without ever giving in to the lure of the coast. They've refused the fate of the *retirantes* swallowed up by the *favelas* in the big cities. They sing here, going from market to market as Didi used to do with his father, Jorge Rei da Casa, *o famanaz do desafio*, the master of the challenge! You see, they improvise. They hurl verses at each other. The verses are challenges and the voices are blades. It's like swords clashing in the hot sun. That's what the *cordel* duettists do. They're poets who have been defying and replying to each other in the white heat and dark shadows of the market for as long as anyone can remember. They embody the imagination and the memory of the sertão.

He's listening to them, Sonia, the man you drew.

Negociar com a ilusão
Pra muitos é profissão
Vender sonhos é bom negócio
Quem sabe disso é o palhaço
Também o politiqueiro
E eu, poeta boiadero

Using illusion to turn a penny
Is the profession of many
Selling dreams will make a profit
The clown knows all about it
And the wily politician
And me, poor poet and musician

Não vou dizer, meu irmão
Que palhaço é um mandão
Mas no Sertão uma história
Fica ainda na memória
Aquelo do presidente
Que virou-se comediante

Brother, I won't own
That the boss is just a clown
But in the sertão there's a story
That is graven in our memory
Of the President-Dictator
Who then became an actor

Lhe devorava a ambição
De reinar no coração
E se transformar num mito
Tal qual um novo Carlito
Virar santo ele podia
Do cinema fez a escolha

One ambition would remain
In every heart to reign
A living legend he'd become
Like a new Charlie, number one
He could turn saint, but there you are
He chose instead the cinema

. . .

It's the story of what happens before that, followed by a huge number of verses that give countless versions of the same story.

That's the man whose eyes you closed in that cinema when you were a girl, Sonia: a native leaning against a mud-brick wall, listening to the spirit of the sertão. He slowly raises the bottle of *cachaça* to his lips, thoughtfully takes a drink and, behind closed eyes, gives a title to the duettists' poem: '*Coronel Carlito*' ('Colonel Charlie').

12

I SAY A NATIVE, but I could say *cafuz*, *mamaluco*, *pardo*, or *mulato*; I could mix the various colours of the Indian, the black, the white, the half-caste and the mulatto, make up nuances of skin tone and give them new names, but I would still end up with this dry body and silent face that the caatinga gives the men who live there. It could also be the face of the Jesuit interviewed earlier by 'the Sleeper in the Sertão', or that of '*doutor* Michel', the French doctor from the Jura I met on the road to Aratuba, and who became a friend. The wind had spread whispers of this unusual presence even to me in my hammock at Maraponga. It was said that he was alone, had no name, no origin, belonged to no government, no humanitarian organisation, that he had appeared in the sertão a few weeks earlier between Aratuba and Capistrano, that he treated newborn babies without asking for any kind of payment, and that at night he took part in secret union meetings with the peasants.

No one had seen a foreigner in that part of the Ceará since a Dutch pastor had been there in 1948. The case was unusual enough for me to drag myself out of my hammock and go looking for him. The next day when I asked the first *sertanejo* I came across on the slopes of Aratuba if he had heard about a foreign doctor wandering around in the area, he looked at me placidly, put down the two huge bags of aubergines that were weighing him down, and replied: '"*Doutor* Michel"? I do believe that's me.'

The *sertanejos* were in their third year of drought, and he in his third week of dysentery.

'Hence the resemblance,' he said with a smile. 'We're all the same weight here.'

13

SONIA, YOU HAD nothing to do with the double's death. Nor with his sorrow. Just think for a moment. He'd been making a feature of public vilification for years. You can be sure that if he thought Chaplin had stolen his film, he'd have shouted it loud and clear in your cinema. I can just imagine it. He would have suddenly stood up between the screen and the beam of light from the projector, casting his gigantic shadow over the walls, and the whole cinema would have heard him yelling and making a tremendous scene, 'It's my idea! My film! A dictator and his double, the barber! It's my idea! My life! They've stolen my life! Morasecchi, you son of a bitch, how much did you get for selling my life to Chaplin? My film! You pack of bastards! What a country of thieves!' All that verbal gesticulation, so unlike his death mask . . .

You wouldn't have heard any more because the people in the audience would quite simply have thrown him out.

And you'd have lost your job.

I'll tell you something that you probably don't know, Sonia. When *The Great Dictator* was first released, Chaplin received so many threatening letters that he decided to get Bridges to protect his film. Doesn't that name mean anything to you now? Bridges? Harry Bridges, the all-powerful boss of the longshoremen's union in the forties. Bridges, king of the wharves! Chaplin asked him to plant a few dozen of his boys in the cinema on the day of the premiere to ward off any attack by pro-Nazi strongmen. Bridges said no. 'There's no need. Your public loves you, Charlie, and you're promoting a just cause. They won't dare show themselves.' And that's exactly what happened. The Nazis did not show themselves; Bridges was right. If a single one of those madmen had dared heckle *The Great Dictator*, Chaplin's fans would have thrown him unceremoniously out.

That's what would have happened to the double that night if he had acted as he usually did in the bar.

No, Sonia, your film-buff angel did not think he'd been robbed by Chaplin (who had probably forgotten him anyway). It was Hitler that Charlie had it in for. Not content with leading mankind to a common grave, Adolf wore the same moustache as Charlie. That was the plagiarism Chaplin couldn't tolerate.

14

LOOK AT *The Great Dictator* through the double's eyes. Draw on everything you know about him and look at the film as if we were in his seat, *sitting inside him*. Taste the salt of his tears and you'll find the reason for his death.

To begin with, remember this: the story of the barber and the dictator does not come at the beginning of the film. You have to wait a good ten minutes. First we see Charlie alone, the Charlie of the silent films. We see Charlie rushed into the 1914 war. We see him in the trenches, we see him as a gunner for Big Bertha, we see him manoeuvring an anti-aircraft gun, we see him on parade, we see him go over the top, we see him trying to dodge machine-gun fire and bomb blasts, we see him lost in enemy lines, we see him run, we see him replace a machine-gunner who deserts his post, we see him fight heroically, we see him save Schultz, the aristocratic aviator who becomes his friend, we see him in Schultz's plane, we see the plane crash. It's here that the first part of the film, and the First World War, end.

During all this time, we don't hear Charlie talk, yet everyone around him talks: the officers talk, the NCOs talk, the enemy soldiers talk, the machine-gunner talks, the narrator talks, Captain Schultz talks interminably. As for Charlie, just a few snatches of words here and there. He's like the last survivor of the silent cinema in a talkie. The lone innocent thrown into the talkers' war.

From the very first scenes, we hear explosions, bursts of fire, orders barked, bullets whistling, soldiers yelling, the plane engine throbbing, the awful impact of the crash, the crumpling of metal plates, all the frightful din of war . . .

The audience howls with laughter as Big Bertha coughs up a pathetic shell that lands at gunner Charlie's feet, as the live grenade slides down infantryman Charlie's sleeve, as Charlie, who has gone over the top with his mates, finds himself surrounded by the enemy when the fog lifts, when Schultz's plane flies upside down without Charlie noticing, when Charlie's fob watch stands straight up on the end of its chain like a rattlesnake, as the plan crashes, as Charlie's head emerges from a pit of liquid manure . . .

In the cinema, there's the audience roaring with laughter.

In the loudspeakers, there's the din of war.

In the double's head, there's Charlie's silence.

And all the reasons for him to weep are already there in this silent choreography.

Look at him. He's just found Charlie again! The Charlie of his revelation! The Charlie of *The Immigrant*; the same! The emotion with all its original force suddenly sends him back a quarter of a century in time. He sees himself in the stupid role of Pereira, in Pereira's absurd uniform, in Pereira's gloomy office, that night when he was in ecstasy – the night he discovered the cinematograph! . . . But that night the ecstasy was entirely his own! And he experiences it all over again as strongly as ever! Look at him, look at him. His heart stopped beating as suddenly as a mind stops doubting. His face is the face of a child on the day of his first communion. Sadly there's nothing else of the first-communion child about him! Sadly a whole life has gone by! But what has he done with that wonderment? *What has he done with that wonderment?* Whereas Charlie on the screen, Charlie rediscovered, Charlie in his mad dance over the world in ruins, he hasn't changed at all! He's the Charlie of *The Immigrant*, he's the same! Yet the years have left their mark on his face, you can see it under his make-up, he's no longer a young man; and trials too, and no doubt a few dirty deeds, he's no longer a simple soul; and the effects of fame, and the disappointments, he's no longer an unknown artist; and love problems, money worries and persecution by rivals, he's an idol who has become a target. Decades have passed for him too, but Charlie, oh! the Charlie on the screen, despite the crow's feet in the corner of his eyes, despite the slightly sagging skin on his neck and the new line at the corner of his mouth, the Charlie on that huge screen is the same, exactly the same, as the one who projected his cheeky life on to the rectangle of light above Pereira's desk!

That was real life then, and it's still real life, life that withstands life, the lively intelligence that gives freedom from everything that would weigh it down, art thumbing its nose at the world, poetry, poetry, poetry, and he, the double, sitting in his seat, feels that extraordinary revelation come over him again, but weighed down now with the unbearable knowledge of his unfulfilled life, and he lets the tears flow and fill his eyes, tears of gratitude and despair, which now stream down his face. With his eyes fixed on the screen, he feels about under his seat, trying to find the bottle . . .

And the film goes on to the next part. To show time passing, Chaplin uses the metaphor of the rotary newspaper press. The presses turn: 1918, 1919, 1927, 1929, 1934 . . . Newspapers are followed by other newspapers in quick succession, titles by other titles, years by successive years, alarming news by devastating news . . .

15

NEWS . . .
A memory comes to mind in this kind of intermission (without any noticeable connection with what precedes it): Michel, the solitary doctor in Aratuba, telling me about Sartre's death.

'Do you remember the boy who fell with his face against the mantle of an oil lamp?'

Yes, it happened late at night down Capistrano way, in an isolated hut in the caatinga, a kid of five or six disfigured by an oil lamp. After vainly calling on the best efforts of two or three healers, the parents finally took the child all the way up to the Aratuba hospital, under a leaden sky, hoping to find Michel there. The child's face was being eaten away. What the burning oil had not ravaged, the glass from the lamp had deeply gashed, and wasted time had done the rest. It was no longer merely an emergency; the child was dying. He was delirious. 'And of course I hadn't any antiseptic at all; that lousy hospital was nothing but a shed for the dying. No one wanted the child to die. I no more than the family.' In desperation Michel had to remove the dead skin from the little face with a laundry brush. 'Yes, a big brush for scrubbing clothes. It's all I had, and without any sedation . . .' The parents sat through this agony without a word, then took their still delirious child back home into the burning heat of the caatinga. Two days later Michel joined them, stumbling down the slopes of Aratuba under the weight of a bag of peppers and a large hand of bananas.

(The day we met, when I asked him what on earth he was doing in the area, he replied, 'I'm trying to understand why people die of hunger in a region where there is enough to eat for everyone. Drought or no drought, Aratuba Mountain could feed all this part of the sertão.' And in fact, every time Irene and I came across him, Michel's back was bent under phenomenal quantities of fruit and vegetables, which he distributed. Later, he swapped semi-precious stones for medicine.)

Well, there he was at the door of the hut, carrying his peppers and his bananas.

'I was sure that the child was dead.'

But the child was not dead; his face was healing up. And the penicillin that Michel had procured in the meantime would pull him through. The peasants welcomed the *doutor* with quiet gratitude.

'The wife gave me a plate of rice and *feijão*, sprinkled with *farofa*. She even added an egg – a great luxury! And her husband unrolled a hammock so that I could rest.'

The child was watched over by his brothers and sisters sitting around him on the earthen floor. They would not let a fly anywhere near his face. During the siesta the man, lying in his hammock, listened to a little transistor radio that hummed like a bee, a barely audible but very distinct sound in the silence of that single room. (These transistors were found even in the furthest corners of the sertão. They buzzed with news, advertisements, songs, football commentaries, as if from a distant hive, and the sound was so thin – to save the batteries – that it seemed to increase our distance from the rest of the world. It was like the faint noise of a forgotten planet.)

'And there, in the midst of all that silence, the radio announces Sartre's death.'

'. . .'

'. . .'

'Well?'

'Well, nothing.'

16

TWENTY YEARS LATER, he added: 'All the same, Sartre was one of the few authors I allowed myself to read when I was studying medicine, and I really liked him. If I'd heard of his death in Paris, maybe I would have cried like a baby.'

17

THE ONLY SOUND the *sertanejos* ever heard above their fields of manioc was at 3 p.m. precisely and 10,000 metres up: it was the mail plane passing overhead.

18

THE DICTATORSHIP HAD banned the word 'peasant' (*camponês*), which suggested the idea of landownership. They had to be called 'farmers', a word which retained only the function.

19

'WHY DID WE like the sertão so much?'
    '...'
  'I mean, in spite of everything ...'
  'Do you remember what you said about Brasilia?'
  'Yes, that it felt as if we were living on the world's back: "The earth is round. Brasilia proves it." That's what I wrote to friends.'

'Well, the sertão proves the opposite: the earth is flat and the interior is everywhere. Hence the empathy the *sertanejos* feel for each other. It's those people we liked, and the great silence of their landscape . . .'

'. . .'

'. . .'

'. . .'

'We cursed the drought, we condemned local feudalism, we wanted land and water to be distributed to the peasants, we disapproved of the way their superstitions affected food and health, but we admired their capacity for resistance, the wisdom they employed in not being understood by their oppressors.'

'. . .'

'. . .'

(Yes, and the way the people on the coast began to perspire when we talked to them about the interior. Oh yes, I liked that too! It was as if the demons of the interior still terrified the coast dwellers, driven back against the emptiness of the sea, a century after Canudos was wiped out.)

'. . .'

'. . .'

'I spent my nights with the peasant unions and my days playing the health worker, but at bottom, we loved the idea that here at least, even if it all changed, *that* would not.

'. . .'

'. . .'

'. . .'

'. . .'

'. . .'

'And there's something else.'

'. . . ?'

'The best violins are made of wood from the sertão.'

20

A ND SO CHAPLIN's rolling presses show the passing of the years as the double watches: 1918, 1919, 1927, 1929, 1934 . . . It's historical time but also his own; and his own story is that of a *sertanejo*, no longer of the interior, a wandering clown, a bloody *palhaço* forgetful of his land, indifferent to the fate of the world and who, going from stupid choices to foolish illusions, from bad luck to repeated blunders, has drifted so far in the unchecked course of his life that he has washed up here in Chicago on 1 December 1940, his face bathed in tears looking up at the huge screen of the Biograph Theater, where Charlie Chaplin's *The Great Dictator* is showing.

It's the hour of reckoning, and he knows it.

It will be paid in gallons of tears.

Watch it! He's about to start *thinking*.

For the first and last time in his life.

He should never have done it.

It'll be the end of him.

. . .

The presses stop rolling.

Charlie makes his ear-splitting entrance into talking pictures.

Listen! Look! Listen!

The dictator Adenoid Hynkel is haranguing a monolithic crowd from his dais high above. For the first few seconds, the audience doesn't know what to make of it: What's he saying? What's that language? Then come the first, small bursts of laughter: Chaplin is speaking German! No, he's pretending to speak German! No, he's not pretending to speak German, he's imitating *Hitlersprache*, Adolf Hitler's speech! No, not even that! The *sound* of Adolf Hitler's voice! There are no distinct words; Charlie is only making sounds! Charlie is taking the mickey out of Hitler by making noises with his mouth! He croaks, he barks, he belches, he chokes, succumbs to a fit of coughing, recovers, whispers, coos, spits like a feral cat, explodes . . . God, that Charlie! It's Hitler, it's him *exactly*! Amusement becomes hilarity, the audience falls about, the laughter swells into a gale, to such an extent that while he's declaiming, Charlie is effectively crushing the vile creature under an avalanche of gags: see how I stop the cheers short with that marvellous little flick of my wrist, and how I scream into a microphone that bends back in fright, and how I cool my Führer's red-hot balls by pouring a glass of water into my trousers, and how I pour another into my ear then spit it out again in a virile little spurt. Like a crazy machine, a broken jumping jack, which is both rigid and uncontrolled, frenzied and constrained, Chaplin goes wild and the audience in the Biograph Theater begin to chant the name of their idol: Char-lie! Char-lie! Char-lie! Char-lie! Two syllables that beat like a gong in the double's heart. Char-lie! Char-lie! Twice the emotion in the double's pounding heart. Char-lie! Char-lie! A highly explosive mixture of warring feelings in the double's twice-moved heart. 'Shame on me and long live Charlie!' the double is thinking, something of the kind, shame on my shitty head and long live Charlie Chaplin, who has just exhausted all the possibilities of talking pictures in one go without actually saying a single word! *Every one of them*, and perfectly! The talking cinema may last for a thousand years, but Charlie has just done it all in five minutes! No film will ever express the truth of what's being said there, no director, never, in any film, even if it were filled with all the words in the world, with the best chosen, the most apt, the most spontaneous expressions, it would not say as much as Charlie, there, now, with his goobledegook, the double is thinking, Charlie *went straight for the tone*, straight for it, eliminating the words! The only truth in speech is the tone, the right noise conveyed by man's intention, and the intention of that man there on the screen, Adolf Hitler, whose true intention Charlie extracts through the tone, the intention of that man, whom Charlie reveals rather than caricatures, is to lead the monolithic crowd to death, the crowd that idolises him, to death, the crowd with its automatic responses that will applaud or be silent at a single gesture, to death! And the rest of humanity, beyond every horizon, all the crowds in the world, in uniform or not, to death! There's the truth of that tone, the single-minded *intention* of that man! The whole human race, to death! But the crowd thinks that this man's voice is demanding only the death of Jews, for the word, the sound of the word 'Jew' is spat out, spat, spat, spat: Jews! Jews! Jews! The crowd hears nothing but that word, which gives it a taste for killing. Preparing itself to sacrifice all the Jews in the ghetto to the disgust of the voice that spits them out, the crowd does not know that it is also preparing its own annihilation, 'because', the double thinks, a voice that demands the destruction of a particular people is a voice that wants the destruction of all people, the sacrifice of all, down to the last baby wailing in the furthest hut in Africa, and the double – he gropes around again under his seat, raises the bottle to his mouth – and the double between gulps thinks that the other crowd, the laughing crowd, the Biograph Theater crowd, the one all around him slapping their thighs, will soon join the dance. Volunteer! Volunteer! Can't allow the enemy of the human race to do that! Volunteer! Give

Hitler a hiding! And he also thinks that the session will hardly be over before real life outside will be the dead spit of what Adenoid Hynkel's wordless voice predicts: a bloody world war! The Second and the best, the universal set-to, not one country will escape it. It's a question of tone, *churrasco** for all, the great planetary spit-roast, that's what Charlie twigged, that's what he's saying to those idiots killing themselves laughing: it's the final orgy and you'll be part of it too, a bloody, planet-sized cauldron, just the right size.

And I know all about tone too, for Christ's sake. As the ex-double of the late dictator Pereira, I've given speeches with it, I've controlled crowds with it, I have no equal at getting the right tone, I was well taught! *I'm not one of those European politicos who read their speeches to the public. I'm a president who is not alone when he speaks: the people have a voice through my mouth. It's my little bit of vulgarity! The tone is everything, do you understand?* Did I understand, you old bastard? I understood, and how! Who turned the peasants of the North into miners? Could it have been you? You, Pereira, you were lazing around in Europe with your Scottish whore while I was sending my brothers down the mine. I had the exact tone all right, and the gestures, more's the pity! Could you have imagined imitating a peasant waiting for an aubergine to grow? Could you have done it? No, you couldn't, you couldn't! I had the tone, I had the gestures. Shame on me! They died because of me; buried them alive, I did, took away their sky, from all of them, from those men of wind and sun who believed me because they liked laughing with me. They wanted to laugh, always, those *sertanejos*, basically so serious,

Churrasco is a Brazilian barbecue, originally the traditional food of the gauchos or cowboys of southern Brazil, but now spread all over the country and around the world.

to laugh like brothers, a trusting laugh, trusting me who they thought was one of them! My tone was right and the aubergine trick worked. All it took was a joke between brothers for me to change these birds of the open skies into moles, for me to send the sun down the mine and put out its light. Shame on my shitty head, shame on bloody me, and long live Chaplin!

'Char-lie! Char-lie!'

Waving his bottle, he also began chanting Char-lie! Char-lie!, but offbeat and, as often happens in the cinema, this lone voice fired the audience's enthusiasm again and they fell in with a new wave of Char-lie! At which point he was overcome by a long series of sobs which passed unnoticed in the loud peal of laughter. He was caught by one of his sudden bursts of self-pity, the kind of tears he had shed over his impotence in the arms of 'real women' . . . Because, he thought in his own defence, he wasn't so bad after all; at least he wasn't Adenoid Hynkel! *He* was only a double, and he had made his escape; he had chosen redemption through the cinematograph; he had handed everything over to another double who could always do the same if he got sick of it! Individual freedom, hell, it's basically a question of choice, of conscience!

Of conscience?

Of conscience? Did you say conscience?

Conscience!

You?

The image of the projectionist came suddenly into his mind.

The projectionist being dragged away by Guerrilho Martins' men.

'Take the man and leave the machine.'

That's what he said.

Had you forgotten that?

The projectionist, had you forgotten him?

What? What!

It was true. He had handed the projectionist over to Guerrilho's men before the Motiograph had even cooled down. 'Take the man and leave the machine.' Oh, the last sight of the projectionist's poor battered face when the padded door was opened and swallowed him up! Oh, that last expression! Oh, the final exit, when he disappeared for the last time! Because that was exactly what Pereira's telegram ordered a few days later: 'Get rid of him!' Not 'Deport him', not 'Into the nick', not 'Shoot him', no, 'Get rid of him', implying: leave no trace of him, nothing. I don't want any evidence; he never existed; or I'll have your balls, double! 'Get rid of him', make him disappear, as if the projectionist had really been nothing but a picture, and all you had to do was . . . And he, the double, had let him disappear, the poor wretch, the angel of his Annunciation! He had made him disappear as simply as pressing the little electric banana he described in his speech to the peasants: light and dark, that's all it was, the picture; and then click!, no more picture; the projectionist, and click! no more projectionist. How the hell had he been able to forget that murder, blot it out so effectively? He'd never thought of the projectionist again. Oh yes, once, to serve up the stupid story of the widow and orphans to Chaplin, who hadn't believed a word of it anyway. And suddenly it was worse than if he himself had buried the projectionist alive – which Guerrilho Martins' goons loved doing . . . It was, it was . . . he couldn't even take refuge in reasons of State, as he did for Pereira's other 'disappearances' ('For reasons of State: my personal cellar, where you go down and don't come up again'). No, the projectionist's death was his own personal crime, a murder for theft: he had killed the man to pinch his projector and his films. It was quite simply . . . oh! it was . . . another measure . . . drown all that . . . and as he drank, his eyes and nose flowed. While on the screen Charlie, who had now become a barber, once again produced gales of laughter as he shaved a customer to the Brahms 5th Hungarian Dance – his gestures were perfect! God, that Charlie! His skill with the brush! His mastery of the shaving cream! His artistry with the cut-throat razor! The sweep of his blade! You'd think he'd been a barber all his life! While Chaplin's razor flew back and forth to Brahms's violins, the thought struck the double that all the tears he'd shed for Valentino were really meant for the dead projectionist; all that sincerity put into mourning Valentino's death was to lay flowers on the projectionist's grave, the grave so deeply buried in his memory, so indistinguishable in the darkness of his conscience, that by some trick he couldn't explain, something in him felt the need to pour out his heart for a death in the outside world, a tragedy in the full light of day. And so he had chosen to pay for the humiliating death of Rudolph Valentino; he said he was responsible for that! *The actor's reputation as a cockless wonder? That's not him, it's me!* He had taken that alleged infamy upon himself on his own initiative, without anyone asking him to. Expiation! Permanent, public expiation! Ah! Heady stuff! He had spent fourteen years of his life (fourteen years!) assuming the ridiculous posture of a Christ trying to crucify himself, determined to hammer the nails in with his own hands, without help. But that's impossible, my lad, just think for a moment. How are you going to manage the last nail, eh, little Jesus? During all that time, people naturally laughed at the ridiculous position he had adopted (a fellow saying he caused Rudolph Valentino's death . . . there are people out there who think they're Jefferson . . .), and after all that interminable palaver, the only thing that remained now was a sense of the ridiculous.

Oh! the ridiculous . . . It eats away at you far more quickly than remorse!

It wasn't enough for you to be a murderer; you had to be a *ridiculous murderer* to boot?

For the first time he felt how absolutely alone he was, for nothing makes us more isolated, more turned inwards, than being convinced we are ridiculous.

He was surprised how loudly his laughter burst out.

But he wasn't laughing at himself.

It was Adolf Hitler.

He remembered having seen – it was already a memory – Adenoid Hynkel climbing up the curtains in his study in a fit of escalating megalomania, and playing with the inflatable globe, which finally burst in his face . . . That was ridiculous! As ridiculous as it gets! Chaplin had made Hitler look terminally ridiculous! He began shouting again, 'Char-lie! Char-lie!'

This time no one joined in, as the scene with the globe had come and gone; the film had moved on to an extraordinarily peaceful moment when the ghetto was enjoying a miraculous state of grace: Hannah was making herself look pretty to go out with the barber, the barber was sprucing himself up to go out with Hannah and, grouped around Mr Jaeckel in the courtyard, the neighbours were amicably commenting on the idyll unfolding before them . . .

'Shut your mouth!' a voice shouts at him in the dark cinema.

'Pipe down!' says another.

'For Christ's sake, shut up, will ya?'

He did, once and for all, drowning his merriment in another swallow of whiskey.

21

SIXTY-TWO YEARS LATER, at the end of October 2002, when *The Great Dictator* was being rereleased in French cinemas and I was writing these pages, Minne and I invited Sonia to see it again.

Paris, 19th arrondissement, Métro station Jaurès . . . The banks of the Seine . . . The Bassin de la Villette where rowing boats glide peacefully over the water . . . After the screening, night had fallen, we were in a restaurant beside the cinema. Over dinner, Sonia told us that Chaplin very much regretted having made those scenes of happiness in the ghetto.

'Yet from the scenographic point of view, they're quite justified,' she argued. The Dictator Hynkel wants a loan from the Jewish banker Epstein, and to help him get it he decides to get on the right side of the people in the ghetto. A sure-fire comic effect: the people who were previously persecuting them become as considerate as guide dogs, happiness enters the scene as naturally as could be, and life goes on again as if nothing had happened.

Sonia was gazing at the water, where the glowing façades of the houses were now reflected on its surface.

'But when the scale of the genocide became known to all,' she explained, 'Chaplin's usual critics accused him of having watered down the horror, and he who had so brilliantly foreseen the course of history with this film believed them; he believed the fools! He felt ashamed of having filmed those few carefree minutes . . . and even of having made people laugh with the horror of Nazism.'

She was seething with anger. I never had a better glimpse of how she must have been as a young girl. She slapped the table with her open hand; our glasses tottered towards the edge.

'For God's sake! These are the most poignant moments in the film! Because, by blotting out tragedy for a while, they herald the systematic horror to come. In the midst of the general madness, normal people can live normally for a few seconds, with their little virtues and their little faults . . . Tomorrow they'll be dead, nearly all of them, and the few survivors will never be carefree again . . . That's what Chaplin filmed! He didn't know it at the time, but he was filming the last moments free of care.'

When Minne asked her why Chaplin had been so harassed throughout his life, Sonia replied, 'It's always the same. The only choice my America has ever offered is between murderers and Bible thumpers. Chaplin didn't like either. He had to pay the price for that independence of mind, and a high price at that!'

Then coming back to the subject of my book:

'But if I've read you correctly, the double wasn't particularly affected by this peaceful interlude in the ghetto.'

22

No, IT WAS something else that affected him. He was astounded by an obvious fact that rose up from the bottom of his bottle: *No one in the ghetto noticed the resemblance between the barber and the Dictator!* He was so staggered by it that he wanted to point it out to the people around him, but his instinct told him to desist. All the same, all the same, the fact that no one reacted was . . . Now let's see (with his eyes opened wide as if to take in the whole screen), let's see for a moment: after fifteen years of amnesia, the barber finally comes back to the ghetto. Everyone watches him, and only him, talks of no one but him, and nobody notices that he's a true copy of Adenoid Hynkel whose face is stuck up on posters everywhere! Not Mr Jaeckel, nor his wife, nor Mr Mann, not even Hannah! Nobody! Not the slightest mention of the slightest family resemblance between the Dictator and the barber. God, what's wrong with their eyes? Hannah's going out with the tyrant's double and Mrs Jaeckel's getting her all dolled up as if she were sending her off to meet Prince Charming! The whole ghetto is delighted to see the little orphan girl offer herself to the double of the Ogre! Even the audience inside the Biograph Theater seems to find it quite natural and desirable that Paulette Goddard is about to make a life with Adolf Hitler's twin. He's the spitting image of Hitler, for Christ's sake, the double screamed inside himself. You must warn the girl! Maybe not, he said to himself, revising what he had just thought, *it's a convention*, pal, *acinematicconventionmeoldpal*! Yes, and one that everybody swallowed without question. It was another example of Chaplin's genius! Charlie, you're the king, there's no doubt about it! But if you look at it seriously, he argued, *ifyoulookatitseriously*, he slurred to himself, what does it mean when nobody notices the resemblance between the barber and the Dictator? Or rather *when they notice it but accept it without batting an eyelid*. What does that mean?

The question took his breath away.

That means . . .

He prepared himself for another attack of despair . . .

That means . . .

. . .

It meant that though they looked the same, the barber and the Dictator had absolutely nothing in common: word for word what Chaplin announced after the credits: *Any resemblance between the Dictator Hynkel and the Jewish barber is purely coincidental.*

That's it! Nothing to do with each other . . . not a thing . . . two people so different that nobody would think of comparing them; the audience sees them *on the ins—* . . . *on the inside,* so different from the outside, as men I mean, that even if they were walking along hand in hand with one cap on both their heads, nobody would see the resemblance between Hynkel and the barber! *Nooobody!*

So . . .

So if that's it,

if that is it . . .

If that was it, the moral presented by Chaplin was the most lethal blow one could deliver him, to him personally.

To me *personally,* the most utter condemnation.

'I'm in total agreement with you on that point,' the voice of Pereira says in his head.

Pereira in my head!

This time it was his bladder that gave way.

'To be a double, you have to really want it,' Pereira explained. 'I've told you a hundred times. Resemblance is an act of faith, as your Jesuit would have put it. I wanted you to look like me, you wanted to look like me, and so we looked like each other. That sums up our story . . . There's no way you can be innocent in any of that. As far as the barber is concerned, he never wanted to look like Hynkel that I know of.'

Am I pissing on myself?

Could I be going to . . . ?

Well and truly, but another detail stopped him from following this line of thought to its conclusion: Mrs Jaeckel suggested putting mittens on Hannah's hands so that the barber wouldn't see that they were red and wrinkled from doing laundry. Now Hannah is all dressed up. She leans over the banister and asks little Annie to go and see 'if he is ready'.

'Annie, go and see if he's ready.'

The child, who was playing with her doll, runs off happily towards the barber's little shop in the row of houses.

This time it was the pronoun that caught the double's attention.

'Go and see if *he* is ready.' . . .

Who is this he?

The barber, of course!

He had just realised that since his return to the ghetto, no one had called the barber by his name. He took it as a personal matter: hasn't the barber got a surname? Or a first name? Is he just 'the barber'? Even for his girlfriend? 'The barber'? Is Hannah going to spend the rest of her life with this man calling him 'the barber'? All the others have names: Mr Jaeckel, Mrs Jaeckel, Mr Mann, Mr Agar, Colonel Schultz, Mrs Schumacher, little Annie herself . . . but not him . . . ?

Oh, my God!

The thought of it filled him with the sadness of an abandoned child. And now there he was, finding enough tears in that almost completely dried-out body to weep over a nameless man. He no longer had the capacity to reason, to think for example that the barber was Charlie's last incarnation, and that Charlie had never had a name in any of Chaplin's films.

Me neither, I haven't a . . . With his fists in his mouth, his knees pulled up to his chin and his elbows pressed to his sides he was vainly struggling against . . .

I've spent my life . . . Even the girl doesn't know my name . . . He was thinking of Sonia, the young usherette who had taken a liking to him. Or more exactly, Paulette Goddard made him think of Sonia. Hannah delivering the laundry . . . with the basket on her head . . . I haven't even told my name to her . . . as I go out, I must . . .

He suddenly felt cold.

I'm cold, I . . .

He was terrified, as at the moment of birth.

Then he pulled himself together and thought 'that wasn't the point': Charlie the barber was a 'symbol', the symbol of all those people, doomed to sacrifice, who would no longer be there tomorrow, who would no longer even have a name: all the Hannahs in all the ghettos, all the Jaeckels, all the . . .

He was swept up in a wave of empathy, a nameless victim among all those anonymous victims. He willingly let his last tears flow. That fraternal sorrow calmed him a little, a warm current in an icy sea that was taking him far from shore, in the company of the martyrs to come . . .

I'm warm now . . .

I'm . . .

On the screen, the film went on. After the banker Epstein refused Dictator Hynkel a loan, the death squads burst into the ghetto again, destroying everything in their path . . . 'God, their uniforms are awful!' It was true. Chaplin had raided the Nazi wardrobe. He'd made those actors wear the frightful uniforms of the Storm Troopers, which seemed tailored for children who would grow to be fat and self-satisfied . . . 'Their trousers made them look as if they had babies' bottoms –

pants filled with shit that would overflow if it weren't for the belt and boots . . . !'

He was about to laugh again, but another idea came to him, or rather leaped at him like a wildcat; the *coup de grâce*.

Those men who were shouting, breaking shop windows, that vile mob unleashed into the ghetto, those pig snouts that would eat the barber alive . . .

They had no names either!

'And tomorrow they'll say they weren't part of it,' he thought, seeing them rush at Charlie . . .

They were the anonymous ones *he* belonged to, not the victims. He was Guerrilho Martins' man, a connoisseur of human death, a specialist in making people disappear.

'I agree with you there, too,' said Pereira's voice.

His hand felt around one last time for the bottle.

Empty.

23

D EAR SONIA,
    I have almost finished with the double. I would like to return your drawing. If you're not roaming about somewhere, we could meet when I get back. My wife and I are coming up to Paris during the week, taking back roads for the pleasure of reading Philip Roth's latest novel aloud en route.

24

*D*EAR AUTHOR,

Why do you imagine I would be 'roaming about'? Do you think that once they get past a certain age, all women with artistic leanings are affected by the Riefenstahl syndrome? Hitler was not my kind of youth, and I have no liking for deep-sea diving nor the slightest desire to go and do portraits of handsome lads from the Nuba Mountains (whom the local authorities slaughter left, right and centre to the indifference of the population, I might add). To be honest with you, as the result of a recent sprain, I haven't even the strength to go down to the Belleville market. My grandson Frédéric is seeing to my meals while I wait for the swelling to go down. That's my whole day. So on the 11th you'll find me sitting near my window at the rue des Envierges, as you did on your last visit. Come and join me for a glass of Vouvray.

One favour I do ask. Send me what you have written before you come. I'm curious to know what kind of a garment you've made of my bits and pieces. In return I'll tell you a few little things about myself as a young girl which may make you think of your friend Fanchon.

Oh! I nearly forgot. Did you know that The Great Dictator *is being re-released towards the middle of October? Does news of this kind reach as far as your place in the Vercors?*

25

A T THE OPENING of the hunting season, all the guns in the Vercors fire their first volley at 7 a.m. precisely. That's the signal for our departure. Minne and I leave the forest animals to the mountain men. Once the car doors have slammed shut and the engine is running, we're quite on our own. We've had this delight in travelling together for so many years now . . . How come we feel more together in a train, in the bus, in the Métro or in a lift than anywhere else? It's not that we love getting out on the road; actually, we're more the sedentary type. It's not the excitement of travel, not the journey itself or the destination; it's not the pleasure of departure, the expectation of arrival or the interest of the route; it's not even the book one reads to the other who is driving. No, it's something else . . . As soon as we have left together for wherever it may be, time stands still for both of us.

If the magic lasts until the end, don't dig a hole for two; just send us off into orbit in the same rust-bucket bubble. That's all we ask.

26

T HE LAST THING seen as we left the house: the foliage of the old sorb apple tree where the thrushes will soon be targets for the hunters. Does that old man of a tree with the red topknot know that he reminds me of the flame trees of the sertão? And do the offshoots that Minne plants under our windows know it when they burst into colour in mid-August? It's true that the whole southern part of the Vercors – a sea-less islet where tractors battle the flint and the peasants don't talk about their history – makes me think of that silent land of the sertão, although it's no more like the Vercors than a flame tree is like a sorb apple or the silence here like the silence there.

27

THE BRAZILIAN SERTÃO is three Frances of loose stones and greyish thorn bushes under a white sun, and here and there that gold-fringed red blaze – a flame tree! The most beautiful tree in the world, which does not even enjoy the luxury of being rare.

28

WE'RE DRIVING ALONG a road in Burgundy . . .
We're in the middle of reading Roth's latest novel . . .
She's been reading for three full hours without a break. She never uses too much expression but anticipates, scarcely emphasising the author's intention. Once she begins,

travelling means letting my mind drift along with the lucid flow of her voice. Most of our itineraries are inextricably linked with these hours of reading, and the novels are read between two towns: Jonathan Coe's *What a Carve-up!* between Paris and Nice, despite the Route Napoléon (the bends in the road don't make my reader dizzy). *The Story of Gösta Berling* by Selma Lagerlöf, read for the umpteenth time, between Biarritz and Paris (what were we doing in Biarritz? No idea). T. C. Boyle's *Water Music* is an exception: three days lying in a hammock between two ash trees that didn't miss a word of it. *A Tomb for Boris Davidovich*, by Danilo Kis, Cahors–Paris, a true novel about disappearance, read twice rather than once, as it happens. *Disgrace* by Coetzee from Nice to Quimper, crossing France on the diagonal (so many repressed tears in Coetzee!). *The Feast of the Goat* by Mario Vargas Llosa between the Vercors and Lagrasse in Les Corbières, for a good part of the return journey on the motorway, while the last lot of cep mushrooms we collected went bad in the overheated boot of the car. The deeply moving *The Girl from the Chartreuse* by Pierre Péju between Valence and Nice in icy-cold weather. A day in the Métro with *La Dernière Nuit* by Marie-Ange Guillaume, published by the attractive Éditions du Passage, or twenty-four hours in a plane with *The Manuscript Found in Saragossa* by Jan Potocki, the traveller with so many pairs of glasses, when we were flying to Nouméa, on the other side of the planet.

So, she has been reading the story of Coleman for a few hours . . . (the slow disintegration of those socio-human entities that are Roth's characters . . .), when she suddenly looks up.

'By the way, what's the situation of your double at the moment?'

'He's had it.'

'Is he dying?'

'Yes. Total dehydration. His body has lost all its fluids; now he can release his soul.'

'Is he sort of mummified?'

'Like the scrawny little donkeys he left to die when he was crossing the continent. He's burning up with fever, the same kind of fever he got from the snake poison, do you remember? He's delirious. He sees only snatches of the film now. The images of Chaplin become part of his own hallucinations. While the skies grow dark above the barber giving the famous last speech in *The Great Dictator*, he sees whole lakes drying up beneath his feet. Irene and I had lakes like that next to where we lived in Maraponga, a fairly big pool where zebus and dogs went to drink, and the kids from the *favela* played while their mothers did the washing. Almost a lake really. It dried up in the drought; sucked up into the sky and swallowed by the ground, almost before our eyes. In the course of a few weeks it became a pond, then a puddle, an eye of water, a bit of spit, then nothing; just scars on the silt, like swollen eyelids.'

'. . .'

'In short, the double is dying, going back home. He's given in to the lure of the interior.'

'The opposite journey from ours, you might say.'

'That's right. He's not "returning home to Paris", he's not "making his return", he's found the exit at last. He's walking on ground that loses its colour with its water. All around him the earth is hardening and the eyes close. Thirst makes him dream of the dried cuttlefish his mother used to hang in the budgerigar's cage. Budgerigars are very important in the sertão – budgerigars in particular and birds in general. There are bird markets in the remotest villages. The Indians almost worship them.'

'. . .'

'The birds . . .'

'. . .'

'It's not only because of their song in all that silence . . . It's something else . . . For the people of the sertão, I imagine that the bird must be living proof that the outside world really exists, and the budgerigars spread news around. If they're in cages, they invent it, which is just as good. The boundless imagination of the *sertanejos* does the rest.'

'. . .'

'Like all the kids who grew up in the caatinga, the double spent his childhood among budgerigars. And maybe there was an armadillo too. Until the day came when they had to eat the armadillo and sell its shell to a wandering musician who would have used it to make a *charango*, the kind of mandolin they play in the foothills of Amazonia.'

'Can you really eat armadillos?'

'Yes. They're like turtles.'

'. . .'

'Did I ever tell you the Brazilian story about the Dictator who ate nothing but turtle soup?'

'I don't think so.'

'He was an obese Dictator with jowls that came down to his fat chest. You get the picture? Every evening he had to have his turtle soup. Well, one evening the soup fails to appear. The Dictator throws a fit. His major-domo goes down to the kitchens. They show him the turtle, which won't put his head out of his shell. Now everyone knows that you have to cut off the turtle's head to make it fit for eating. Leave it to me, says the butler. He lifts up the turtle, sticks a finger in its backside, out comes the indignant turtle's head, which is immediately cut off by the major-domo. The kitchen staff are full of admiration: How about that! Where did you learn a thing like that? The butler replies: How do you think I get the President's ties around his neck?'

'. . .'

'Indeed.'

29

HUNGER DROVE THEM to eat the armadillo.
Then the Jesuit arrived on the scene,
taking him to town,
and his salvation,
or his downfall,
it all depends.
In either case, life has passed; now he is dying. As he sits there below the huge cinema screen, at the point of death, he goes back into the interior, guided by the chatter of a budgerigar: his own evening star. Apparently it's an Italian budgerigar. In any case, it's reciting Italian poetry to him. It seems to be mocking him:

> *Eri pur bella, o di Colombo terra*
> *avventurosa, e l'ospital tuo seno*
> *al proscritto porgesti!*

This ironic cackling reminds him of someone who certainly

did not have a voice like a bird and who never used irony:

> But you were beautiful,
> Oh adventurous land of Columbus,
> And you generously offered your breast to the exile!

Behind the screeching of the budgerigar, he recognises the stentorian voice of the Garibaldian barber from his youth. Every time the old man recited Garibaldi, the budgie would protest, trying to drown out the song of the revolution.

'Just our luck to get the only papist budgerigar in the interior!'

The old man cursed, but he held his ground. Of course he had to teach his apprentice the art of curling beards in the style of Garibaldi, but above all he had to make him learn Garibaldi's poetry, especially 'Montevideo', so that the promise of the sister continent could be realised.

'You shouldn't just become Garibaldian; you must become Garibaldi in person! Repeat after me:

> *'Una daga per combattere gli infesti,*
> *ed una patria non di rovine seminata.'*

And he repeated:

> 'A dagger to fight the corrupt,
> and a land that is not strewn with ruins.'

The old man would shout with joy: 'My red shirt will be your flag!'

All that comes back to him as he crosses the sun, in step with Garibaldi's verse:

Un cielo come d'Italia, abitator fratelli,
e donne impareggiate

Ah, yes! . . .

An Italian sky, friendly inhabitants and incomparable women . . .

God . . . those 'incomparable women' . . .

While on the screen of the Biograph Theater, Hannah, weeping on the ground, also hears a voice from on high: 'Look up, Hannah' . . .

Did he just imagine them, those *donne impareggiate*! How often had he fallen asleep dreaming of those *incomparable women* after his days of scissors and combs?

'Look up, Hannah. We are coming out of the darkness into the light . . .' says Chaplin's ethereal voice.

Now he dies. He is going back to the interior. He is going home. He sweeps over his continent, his alone. He is enormously light and yet he raises the dust of a thousand horsemen as he advances.

He is flying to his forgotten brothers and the incomparable women . . .

A budgerigar guides his way.

The old barber's red shirt flaps in the wind.

'Look up at the sky, Hannah. The soul of man has been given wings and at last he is beginning to fly . . .' says Chaplin's voice.

And, while Hannah raises her eyes to the sky,

dark grey clouds roll towards him from all sides, roll and gather, gather and merge,

just above his head,

and burst like a water gourd,

all the clouds in the world,

just above his head,
like a water gourd that is cut
and releases its contents
all at once,
he sees the water falling on him,
all the drops together,
and each drop separately,
all together
and each drop, a world in itself . . .

'Will they reach the ground?' he wonders, offering them his burnt skin, open hands, closed eyelids and cracked lips. 'Will they reach the ground?' . . .

. . .

It is the end. While the rain falls in the sertão, while the waterholes fill up, while the sky seeds the ground, and nature held in check for so long now covers itself with a carpet of amaryllis, flowers open without waiting for leaves, insects buzz and birds fly, while the vocabulary in books by botanists, entomologists and ornithologists has such richness of colour and variety that novelists will borrow from them, while the end of the drought, that instantaneous and age-old miracle is played out, turning hell into heaven, a young usherette finds a body in an empty Chicago cinema, a dead man as dried out as a goatskin, but wet from head to foot.

'. . .'

'. . .'

'Have you written all that?'
'It's written and sent to Sonia.'

V
SONIA'S OPINION

1

WRITERS WRITE TO be rid of themselves, but also to be read. There's no way of escaping this contradiction. It's as if one were drowning and shouting, 'Look, Mummy, I'm swimming!' Those who scream the most about being authentic jump from the fifteenth floor in a swallow dive, 'Look, I'm me and me alone!' As for claiming to write without being read (keeping a personal diary, for example), that's taking the dream of being both author and reader to ludicrous lengths.

These were my thoughts as I went up the rue Piat towards Sonia's flat in sunny weather that promised a mild autumn. *Come, dear author, I've read what you've written and we'll have a chat about it.* She annoyed me with her frequent use of 'dear author', but it was done to annoy me. Her note had filled me with that ambivalent excitement I know so well: feeling curious about being read, and guilty at being curious; wanting to be flattered, and ashamed at wanting it; seeking objective criticism, and protesting one's independence; the whole thing based on false modesty. What does it matter? Who do you think you are? And, tired of all this questioning, the consequence of a depressive upbringing, the conclusion: Yes indeed, who do I think I am, and what does it matter?

In short, I was indulging in a little bout of my back-to-Paris blues, made worse by the fact that my book was nearly finished. A few more weeks of that imprisonment and I'd have to come out . . .

2

SONIA GREETED ME holding the bottle of Vouvray and a corkscrew. Then she trotted off towards her living room with two glasses in her hand. Her ankle seemed all right again.

'Well now, did you have a good trip? Did you enjoy reading Roth?'

That face like an old Apache . . . It's true, she does look like Nathalie Sarraute. How old could she really be? (When I was little, I thought my grandmother was immortal. Her great age guaranteed that she would live for ever: since she had lasted so long, there was no reason why she should stop! The others, who were younger and so full of energy, seemed to me to be in much more danger.) Looked at from this perspective, Sonia's wrinkles, ravines, husky voice, mica hands and bright deep-set eyes offered her a serious option on immortality.

As I was opening the bottle, she began to talk about Roth.

'I have to say that your Roth annoys me. I love it when he examines his subject in depth, but he gets on my nerves when he finishes everything off too meticulously. That young man hasn't the slightest confidence in his reader. When I'm reading a book of his, I always have the feeling that he's going to suddenly appear over my shoulder and ask me if I've understood everything. The more he writes, the more he gives the impression that with each novel he's casting pearls before swine. He reminds me of one of my lovers who would cry out "My semen! My semen!" every time he came in me, as if I were robbing him.'

That made me look up, somewhat taken aback. Sonia gave a little smile as she took the bottle from me.

'It's a joke! And the last sentence isn't original . . . a quotation from someone or other. I can't remember who.'

(Ah! Right . . .)

'I wanted to get a smile out of you. You seem rather gloomy. Sit down over there.'

As I've already mentioned, the sharp angle of her building rises up into the Paris sky. She indicated the armchair facing the window – her chair.

'Please, do sit there . . .'

She turned another chair around and there we were seated side by side, glass in hand, looking down on our city.

Silence.

More silence.

Paris.

(I'm not wild about panoramic views. The bird's-eye view, in this case the pigeon's-eye view, doesn't do much for me. It's too abstract or too realistic. These flying rats never find the right distance: either they glide over the whole layout of a town, or they peck about among the dog shit on the ground. A metaphor for literary debates.)

More silence.

Then she quietly came out with this comment: 'I was right to tell you as little as possible about my adolescence . . .'

' . . .'

'It allowed you to create a charming picture of me.'

' . . .'

'You're rather partial to idealisation, you know. Someone shows you a little old woman who has given up everything and you turn her into an angel of the night . . . Is that what you do with love, friendship and family? Those close to you must have very little to complain about!'

She gave another gentle prod.

'That and your need for redemption . . .'

'. . .'

'The double's gradual repentance during the screening of *The Great Dictator*, for example . . . Do you really think that a man can die experiencing such a change of heart? I'm nearer the end than you, and I have some reason to doubt it.'

Nearer 'the end' . . .

I watched the blue patch of the Pompidou Centre fade as the sun sank in the western sky.

'Coming back to actual facts,' Sonia continued, 'the double was dead when the ambulance took him away, that's true. The forensic pathologist diagnosed a relapse of malaria, something of that kind, which was a medical curiosity. Just think of it: raging tropical fever in midwinter Illinois! This combination didn't agree with all the alcohol he'd consumed. I think he also drank to keep warm, you know.' (A short silence.) 'You're right on that subject: he died of both heat and cold . . . and from a severe attack of delirium.'

With the next comment, she succeeded in making me smile.

'It would take nothing less to make someone recite Garibaldi when they're dying!'

At this point she started to explain to me that in her opinion the novel itself was of the alcoholic genre.

'How can one explain the intoxication that is life, other than by diving into the bottle that lets you do or say anything, which is the novel?'

Granted, granted, but I was asking myself a much more prosaic question. I was wondering how a young girl of her age could have got hold of a forensic pathologist's report on the death of a nameless tramp in a Chicago movie theatre in 1940.

To which she replied, indicating that I should fill up our glasses again, 'So, we want our little reality check?'

3

WHEREUPON SHE INFORMED me that her father was an undertaker. Not a gravedigger, an embalmer, a monumental mason or a hearse hirer; no, in charge of the whole thing, the chief undertaker, a big man in the industry, at the leading funeral directors in Chicago, a financial metropolis where, as everyone knows, death was not a rare commodity.

'Which didn't prevent him regretting his early years in the business,' Sonia explained. ' "In those days," he used to say, "people really died; they didn't hang about waiting to go." '

'Those days' went back to 1918, when the Spanish flu ravaged Chicago, dispatching far more old men and babies than any others. Sonia's father had been a carpenter at the time. He struck while the iron was hot and turned his roof beams into coffins. Then came the Prohibition years . . . another form of slaughter: the bodies were fewer, but the coffins were top of the range. Any third-rate gangster got a national funeral.

'When asked what he did, my father would just laugh and say that he was in "import-export". He had a playful character, found everything entertaining, and was completely uneducated, unfailingly optimistic and fiercely didactic. If he'd been able to read, he'd have made a wonderful character for your friend Roth.'

'. . .'

'Where did you get the idea that he had forbidden me to wear my Bogart trench coat? On the contrary, he loved to see me done up in that detectives' raincoat. He even bought me the felt hat that went with it. Which was something, as he never gave presents and hated Bogart. Bogart, Chaplin, Fairbanks, "all that bunch of bloody Communists". Do you know what he called his funeral business?'

No, I didn't know.

'The BDTR, which officially stood for Better Deal Truer Repose. But it took on a quite different meaning at the family dinner table or with his whiskey pals: Better Dead Than Red.'

'. . .'

'That's the sort of man he was. A fairly common type in my home town. He died in his bed at a canonical age, without the slightest doubt ever impinging on his convictions. He booted the backsides of my brothers who slaved away in the business with him, but he adored me. All the same, I had to earn the money to pay for my studies. Hence the usherette's job . . . and my charcoal sketch . . .'

Then followed some details about how she began drawing. Her father had set her to work as soon as she had shown the first signs of liking to draw: he got her to sketch the profiles of the people lying in the funeral parlour where their relatives came to mourn.

'Yes, do it! It'll be a nice memento for them,' he insisted.

At $5 per 'nice memento', she earned more than her pocket money. As a result, she spent her teens sketching corpses smelling of carbolic acid to the accompaniment of sniffing and nose-blowing.

'You could say that, in my own way, I was an undertaker too.'

It was a very small step from that to doing the portraits of all the members of the deceased's family, which she did with no difficulty. Hence her rapid technique. Going from one chapel of rest to another – they were side by side and numbered like beach huts – she would often sketch thirty relatives in a day.

'It wasn't very hard. Mourners hardly move more than their dear departed.'

She corrected herself.

'Except for Italian women . . . Yes, Southern European grief taught me a sense of movement.'

Here she gave a little half-smile, and said confidentially, 'I'm telling you all this so that you'll know how touched I am by the picture you give of me: the brave girl in an empty cinema who wipes away the tears of the first dead person she has ever seen . . .'

(OK, OK.)

Then she began to talk for her own benefit. A short retrospective trip into her past.

'That experience in my father's business was tremendously helpful when I went into fashion drawing. The only living thing about the mannequin is the dress. They've killed the girl. Have you looked at their faces? There's nothing going on there. The couturiers eliminated them in favour of the material. In the seventies they went as far as making them skeletons. They all look like brides of Frankenstein as they walk with that loose, mechanical stride towards a destination they disdain. When I was drawing dresses, I always began with the portrait of these dead girls. It's incredible how alive a scrap of chiffon can look on them.'

She embroidered on this subject for a while. In her opinion, our society tended to produce an imitation of life to the detriment of the real thing, and in every possible context. Her grandsons were 'the dying proof' of it: young corpses spending their time rotting away in front of screens where 'all that stuff' was doing the living instead of them.

'No one is brave enough to haul them out of their rooms and sit them at the dining table, or even to get them into a girlfriend's bed.'

I let her ramble on on that theme, and then, as she drew breath, slipped in a question: 'And what about the forensic pathologist's report, Sonia?'

It was as though I'd suddenly woken her up.

'Oh, yes.'

'. . .'

'Yes, yes, how I got the pathologist's report.'

She gave a slow smile.

'The novelist's question . . .'

She gazed into the distance.

'Are you in a hurry?'

No more of a hurry than the sun taking its time setting in the distance behind the École Militaire.

'Well then, tell me why you went off to Brazil. You don't explain that anywhere.'

4

I'D NEVER ASKED myself that question. It was Irene's first job: a position became vacant at the University of Fortaleza, we jumped at the chance and there we were. But this explanation doesn't explain the 'why' of our decision. Irene was a real Parisian girl born and bred; I was a stay-at-home (of the Charentais type) and decidedly sedentary. A childhood buffeted around to the four corners of the globe had made me immune to travel. In theory I should have objected, stuck to my Belleville rock; instead of which I contributed to the decision by giving up my own job. Rereading today what I wrote to my friend, I think that what decided us, both Irene and me, was the fact that we knew nothing at all about Brazil, didn't speak a single word of Portuguese and hadn't the slightest idea of what awaited us at 'Fortaleza', capital of the 'Ceará', a town and a state that only seemed to come into existence when we heard their names for the first time. We were being presented with the chance to see with new eyes and hear with new ears; better not miss that. And another thing: it was imperative to get away from the idiots who tried to hold us back by saying that leaving Paris was virtual suicide. Cutting the cord once and for all, putting an ocean between us and this so-called hub of the world, was what we needed at the time. Get away! Get away! Break free, get away and see what Giscard's France looks like from afar.

'...'

'And?' Sonia asked, not satisfied by these generalities.

'And I had just handed over a novel to the publisher. There's no better reason to slip one's moorings.'

'. . .'

'. . .'

'And then?'

Then our arrival in Fortaleza, that concrete block, the Hotel Savannah, and the street behind it where gap-toothed prostitutes plied their trade in the steamy tropical heat. Our amazement at the phonetic gulf that separated Portuguese from Spanish and Brazilian from Portuguese . . . Our brief stay in the restricted Aldeota quarter where armed patrols and a host of servants recruited in the interior gave us our first opportunity to gauge what seemed to be an auto-colonial society. *Empregadas sem escola*, the employment notices stated, which could be translated as: 'We want ignorant servants who won't try to better themselves.' Then came our flight from Aldeota to Maraponga, a suburb of Fortaleza, and the white house that seemed designed for Corto Maltese, which no one had rented for several years because a *favela* had grown up on the other side of the road and the middle classes feared being near people with empty stomachs. It was a *sítio*, an abandoned tropical farm. The roots of the mango trees had split it down the middle, coconuts shattered its tiles, cockroaches filed through it while the trapdoor spiders that inhabited it resisted all efforts at expulsion, our shoes, which mildewed during the night, harboured translucent scorpions by early morning, the snakes our cat Gabriela proudly brought to Irene were of the most venomous kind, the proprietorial monkeys in the mango trees looked on us as intruders, the water in the well was full of iron, enormous anthills marked the four corners of the orchard, and in the evening, after the sudden dying of the light, three fat toads kept us company at the foot of the veranda while the bats circled around above our heads and the moths buzzed like high-tension wires.

211 Avenida Godofredo Maciel, Maraponga, was the address of that house, which has now disappeared and which we loved like a real person.

'...'

'And?' Sonia asked, not satisfied with tourist reports.

And then we got to know the people, then the language, then the land. There were the teachers and the Rector at the university whom social propriety prevented from visiting us in Maraponga, and the French voluntary service workers – nostalgic, gregarious, superior and interested in folklore – for the most part to be avoided. But there were also Sergio, Expedito, Bete and Ricardo, Arlette and Jean, or Soledad, Néné, Nazaré, Juan, the too numerous to mention members of the Martins clan whose lives we shared, the children who called me *vovó* (grandmother) when I smoked my pipe (which old women of the sertão do when they're looking after the sick); Irene's first classes when she communicated in gestures to students who adored this semaphore, Soledad learning to read, write and count, and to accept with some puzzlement that for eighteen years she had been living on a round planet that revolved with a few pals around the sun, but who obstinately refused to believe that the Americans had landed two men on the moon: *Tá brincando, rapaz! Acredita mesmo?* ('You're joking, man! Do you really believe that?'); the delight in learning that language whose vocabulary has mostly slipped from my memory, but whose music is still in my ears, as one remembers the smile on a face, a look in the eyes, the exuberance of a personality: *sertão, sertanejo, caatinga, saudade* ('saoudadji'), oh! writing is so inadequate in transcribing the melody of foreign words, the sound paths of the languages that criss-cross everywhere beyond our borders!

Geraldo Markan arrived on the scene, the keeper of all

things magic, with his charisma, his moustache and comb, his lucky charm, his *macumba* and his *candomblé*. Then came our first incursions into the sertão, meeting Michel almost hidden under his bags of vegetables, exhausted with dysentery, plagued with boils, dedicated to caring and understanding; Mãe Martins' words as she stood by her dead daughter: 'I slept well, thank you. Disturbed sleep is for rich people. I know that anything can happen to me. Look . . .' Her girl lying there (the lighted candles in her hands to show the way to heaven). She had caught something as a prostitute in Fortaleza and the wrong dose of antibiotic had killed her. As there was no carpenter, we were going to bury her in a hammock, which added the shame of being poor to the family's grief.

What more can I tell you, Sonia? The tropical green strictly limited to a strip along the coastline and the cracked earth as soon as you approach the interior, the hoarse voices of the *cordel* guitar duos, the joyful energy of their fierce exchanges, the contrast between the *sertanejos*' superstitions and their political awareness, the correspondence with my friend to whom I told everything as it came, a good thousand pages that were rare moments of happiness during my professional writing, for writing to someone you like liberates you from the worry of having to write . . .

' . . .'

I managed to go on for a good half-hour, gathering together the little I knew about Bahia, São Luís do Maranhão, Belém, Portuguese architecture of the sixteenth century, Brazilian literature, the poetry of Drummond de Andrade, the novels of Machado de Assis, music of all kinds, that fabulous jester Ney Matogrosso, the extraordinary linguistic phenomenon of the language in Brazil (how did so few men spread Portuguese to the four corners of a continent that is so huge and varied in so short a time?), the *telenovelas* that were as long as Amazonian rivers, *tabaco natural*, recipes for duck in *tucupi* sauce,* *vatapá* (spicy shrimp puree) and the national dish, *feijoada* (rich meat stew with black beans), the ubiquitous drink *caipirinha* (*cachaça*, lime, ice cubes, cane sugar) of course, and the *codornos*, those tiny roast quail from the Texaco station next door ('It's strange,' Irene said when Gabriela and I were eating our *codornos* together, 'I feel that we're separated by millions of years, but it's nothing really'), the shrill chattering of the monkeys in the mango trees, the zebu I had tamed and brought into the house to Gabriela's horror (it had to turn its head so that its huge horns could get through the door), panic the first time it saw itself in a mirror (even though its eyes looked as if they were beautifully made up!), the stray dog that took refuge under my hammock (a good fellow but with impressive fangs, so that no one dared come near me). There was the paradox of the waning military dictatorship when television comedians openly made fun of General Figuereido, the red Church of Dom Hélder Camara, 'Long live the Pope and the working class!' the demonstrators shouted in São Paulo, the first appearances of Lula on TV, the hope the *sertanejos* (and we with them) placed in that guy from the North-East who had become a distant metalworker from São Paulo – and whom they elected president last week, twenty-three years later, Sonia. How about that! I mentally cracked a huge bottle of champagne to make up for the lack of response from our government, which did not deign to go and honour the old fighter who was now Head of State . . .

'. . .'

'And?'

Tucupi: a golden yellow liquid extracted from grated manioc root.

'. . .'

'. . .'

'And the hammock, Sonia. The hammock under the veranda at Maraponga. One writes for lack of anything better; lying in the hammock is definitely better. The hammock must have been invented by a wise man to resist the temptation to become something. The species won't even reproduce in it. It inspires you to make all the plans in the world and excuses you from accomplishing any of them. In my hammock I was both the most inspired and the most unproductive novelist alive. It was a rectangle of time hanging in the sky.'

'. . .'

'. . .'

'What else?'

'Nothing at all. It's your turn now. How did you get that pathologist's report? Where did a girl of your age get an idea like that?'

5

FIRST SHE HAD wanted to know the double's name, nothing more.

'It's not what you might think,' she said, 'I wasn't looking for a father figure. I'd had enough to do with fathers, believe me: the best and the worst by turns. Was he Aladdin come out of the Motiograph projector? The mythical tramp? Yes, if you like, there was something of that about him, but nothing more. At sixteen I was already grown up, if you please, and I didn't need that kind of crutch. And besides, he wasn't the discriminating critic you show him to be. Apart from Chaplin's work, there wasn't much he admired in the cinema. But he was an intriguing person. He was very handsome, you know; he held his back very straight . . . and his neck. He was taut and sinewy. You had to be an Irish ox or a Polack pit pony to see no more in him than the alcohol. He was hiding something. He was hiding someone. You say he was the double of a South American dictator? Manuel Pereira da Ponte Martins? It's possible. You have that freedom as a novelist. He never mentioned that name to me. He talked about everything: his wanderings as a projectionist in the interior, the *Cleveland*, Valentino, Chaplin, all that, but not a word on what went before, nothing about his childhood, his youth, complete silence about anything to do with Teresina. And this "before" was the very thing that interested me. You're right: his endless drunken ramblings were a smokescreen. He had to watch out for the immigration people as well. But – and this isn't made clear in your book – most of the time he didn't talk at all. To my mind he was a unique, silent man who was systematically destroying himself in the company of people very like my father. Yes, that's quite a paradox, now that I come to think of it: as I was reading your book, I thought that the others were the doubles, that lot who challenged him at the bar, all exact replicas of each other. To my mind he was the only real person. That at least is one definite memory. I really knew very little about that unique individual: his worship of Valentino as a person (by the way, where did you get the idea that Valentino wanted to be a director? That's news to me!) and his boundless admiration for the genius of Charlie Chaplin. There again you're mistaken when you say that from his arrival in New York he didn't dare to see a single Chaplin film. He knew the three that came out between 1926 and 1940 very well: *The Circus*, *City Lights* and *Modern Times*. He said some interesting things about them. In his opinion, Chaplin was the only free film-maker in cinema; the length of time he took shooting is a case in point. He was really amazed that Charlie could find the means to finance this artistic freedom. It was above all when he was talking about Chaplin as an artist that he opened up a little. That was why I thought he would tell me more about himself after the excitement of seeing *The Great Dictator*. But he died during the screening. No, I didn't seriously think that I'd killed him.

'To answer one of your questions, *The Great Dictator* came out in October; it was December then, and of course everyone knew what the film was about, including him. The resemblance to the subject he'd related at the Purser's table didn't seem to affect him. Perhaps he'd become American after all? In our country, an idea belongs to the person who carries it out, and that's all there is to it. No, really, I didn't feel guilt. Sorrow, yes; his face sketched on my shoebox, that's true . . . But I think that what I felt most was anger. I was shocked. Looking down at his body, I thought that I would never know anything more about him, and I couldn't accept that. When the policemen took him away, I insisted on knowing his name. To put some pressure on them, I mentioned my father's name, which opened doors and chequebooks. The reply from the relevant authorities: no name. He had no name. He was not registered anywhere. Not with Immigration, Hollywood, or anywhere else. No legal existence before his death. Now he was someone. So I simply had to find out. It was obviously my father who got the forensic report for me. My father never thought my stubbornness was just a whim. As far as he was concerned, it was enough to want what you wanted, but woe betide anyone who didn't carry out an expressed desire, however absurd it might have been! I insisted on having that report, and I got it. What the forensic pathologist wrote didn't teach me anything new. A bout of tropical fever . . . probably a Latino . . . I knew that already. By this stage, there was nowhere else for me to look. Not me, not the Chicago police, not the FBI, nor all their wherewithal. The man was just one of those nameless bodies of illegal immigrants in America. There must have been several thousands like him every year, including several hundred in the state of Illinois alone. I could not accept that. Him in a common grave? It was out of the question. If he had no identity, I'd give him one. A permanent one! A reason for *having lived*.

'How?'

'This is where I'll remind you of your friend Fanchon.'

'. . .'

'I decided to bury him myself.'

'. . .'

'In Hollywood.'

6

SINCE HE WAS nothing but what he had told her, Sonia was going to bury him at the very heart of his story. He would become what he said he was: Valentino's shadow. He would spend his eternity in the Hollywood cemetery. The idea of this funeral amused Sonia's father, who thought that actors were nothing but 'bloody ghosts' anyway. It was therefore quite fitting that ghosts should be buried in the actors' cemetery: The Hollywood Forever Cemetery, 6000 Santa Monica Boulevard, in Hollywood, California.

'Your father gave you his blessing?'

'His blessing, as you put it, yes, but not a cent. What fascinated him was how I could find the money to cart a body all the way from Illinois to California, which wasn't exactly next door. He was prepared to arrange the legal side of it on condition that I paid every cent for the coffin, the trip and the burial.'

'So?'

This time she held out her glass with a encouraging smile.

'So, what then?'

'. . .'

'. . .'

'So, my dear, I became your friend Fanchon, or Joan of Arc herself, if you will. The next day, at 6 p.m. (note the time; it's important), I went back to the bar where men who were doubles of my father used to get my unique individual dead drunk, and I decided to strike a small spark in their brains, which had ossified through exile, work, struggle, family and booze. Not possible on the face of it, but I had an ace up my sleeve: do you know, they missed the dead man! They weren't aware of it yet, but they missed him terribly. After all, he was their champion. He had drunk them all under the table more often than anyone else. No one came near him for endurance; you wrote that and it's true. Now that he was dead, they hadn't the heart to challenge just anyone. You don't box with people who have wandered in from the street when you've shaped up to the world champion. I made a speech to them that went something like this: Who are you now that he's not here? At first they looked down their noses at me. Who was this slip of a girl who had come here to lecture them? But I hadn't come to preach to them, I'd come to make them understand that, without him, they'd lost their whole *raison d'être*, or at least their *raison d'être* there. After all, they were there every evening, it was their refuge, almost their home. I knew the lot of them by their first names, and I spoke to each one individually. At that time I was about the same size as I am today – but less stooped. Just imagine a matchstick taking on Stonehenge. But the match was aflame, I can tell you! So, Felix, who are you going to challenge tonight? And you, Brian, how are you going to get the bids to rise? Horst, can anyone make the pot climb as high as you, now that he's not there? How high? Are you taking the bets, Jerzy? (Jerzy was the boss, a real beanpole from Poland with paws always ready to swipe the stakes.) Well, boys, he's dead. Not here any more. He was your champion, and now he's gone. How many nights have you spent with him? Are you going to let that man be thrown into a common grave? A guy like that! Like a dead dog? And so on. When I told you that the drunks' 'Internationale' is the only one that lasts, I wasn't joking. It's even the only one worth anything. Drunks share a brotherhood in being broke and it's worth all the others put together. With them at least, the theorists wake up from time to time, while an ideologue or a monk never sobers up. In short, they quickly understood that this man was one of them. There's something in what the kid says. A guy like him didn't deserve to finish up in a hole with all the others. A funeral, that's what they should do; they should pay for his funeral! Yeah! OK, but where? Was he from Chicago? No. That's right, where did the guy come from? Was he a Mex? An Eyetie? I told them that he was from Hollywood. Everything he told you about Valentino was true. He was an American from Hollywood. They obviously saw straight away that money would be a big problem. Shit, Hollywood! That's where we're going to bury him all the same, I said. Where's the cash coming from? With the cash from bets, of course! Jerzy, how high did the pot go on pay days like today, on Saturdays? It was high, but as you know, it all went. You haven't lost tonight's bets yet, have you . . . tonight's? Who are we going to bet against tonight, since as you say, he's no longer with us?

'Against me.

'And I laid down the symbolic rules for our contest: they would have bourbon and I would have water. A duel with shot glasses until they collapsed or my bladder burst. Who would begin? Jerzy was the first to line up the glasses and put his money on the bar, without a word. The only reason he was doing it, challenging a girl who only drank water, believe me, was in honour of the departed! The others not only followed but called their mates to arms, and that night the final of finals was played. My bladder swelled like a balloon, they fell like flies, bodies lay all over the bar, whole pay packets were bet. Their wives must have cursed me, and at the end of the week the debt collectors must have knocked harder than usual to call in their bills. But when I totted everything up, there was easily enough to bury a large family in Hollywood.'

'. . .'

'. . .'

'And then?'

'And then I spent the rest of the night on the toilet, and the next day, with six of them who were going to be pall bearers, we boarded the Union Pacific Challenger headed for Riverside, California. I'd booked a sleeper where my companions and I spent three days and three nights with the coffin – my longest vigil ever! I had plenty of time to draw the portraits of my pals. I'll show them to you if you like. You'll see that they're a delightful bunch who never sobered up during the whole trip. At each stop, Omaha in Nebraska, Ogden in Utah, and even in Oakland, a telegram from my father would be waiting for me with congratulations and advice on how much ice was needed to preserve the body. Dried out as he was, the body would have lasted to the end, but the ice was a pretext to stash away my mourners' supplies. Those flasks of whiskey were the only material contribution my dad made. He also spent those three days getting smashed; he was proud of his daughter. As I said, they were simple men.'

'And what about the actual burial?'

'Less colourful than you might imagine. It was at night, of course, and on the quiet. A few people had to be bribed. I had names, I had money, it wasn't difficult. And so, since the night of 4 December 1940, your *sertanejo* has been sleeping in the Hollywood Forever Cemetery, in the shadow of Rodolfo Guglielmi Valentino, his patron saint.'

'. . .'

By now it was dark. The only light in the room came from the city outside.

'As for me,' Sonia said in conclusion, 'I never went back to Chicago.'

'No?'

'. . .'

'. . .'

'No. But I'll tell you about that if you take me to see *The Great Dictator* in a nice cinema. What about the MK2, quai de Seine, for example, tomorrow evening, with a good dinner thrown in?'

7

A s we were leaving the cinema, Sonia pointed out to me that 'here too' I was mistaken.

'When you say that Chaplin doesn't speak in the 1914–18 part of the film, you're mistaken. He does speak! He even says a few complete sentences.'

'Well, we did take the trouble to see the DVD several times over,' Minne explained.

'Even if you'd seen it a thousand times, you wouldn't have heard Charlie speak,' Sonia replied. 'It's not your fault: Chaplin's mime makes the audience deaf, it's as simple as that. Even when he speaks, his body is expressing itself. No actor has ever been more *looked at* than he has. Hence the impact of that famous final speech, which absolutely reverses his usual acting technique. Suddenly there's no more body, only the head, the look, the hair against a background of clouds, and his voice bursting forth, in his own words. We are really seeing Charlie Chaplin for the first time. Then, oh yes, then we hear him . . .'

We took Sonia's arm and walked slowly in the direction of the restaurant. Her ankle wasn't actually very strong.

'I heard you laugh quite spontaneously, and several times, as if the film still held some surprises for you,' she said to Minne. 'It got me in too. "As in 1940"!' she chuckled. 'That Chaplin, there's always something more to see in him . . .'

She was hardly any weight on our arms. Bones like a bird.

'Always something more,' she repeated, watching two people paddling a canoe over the water on their way home.

'. . .'

Once the meal had been ordered, Minne asked Sonia what had kept her in Hollywood.

'There was a smell of sage in the cemetery,' Sonia replied. Once the meal had arrived she put her head down and began eating.

Then, after her first swallow of wine, 'You were expecting a love story, weren't you?'

She was a good sport and admitted that there was a love story. You mustn't forget that Hollywood had been her girlhood dream too. It didn't take her long to 'get into the cinema scene' through an apprentice cameraman she had met at Palm Springs and who was 'keen on' her. In fact, he was her first lover. He gave her the opportunity to do pencil drawings of locations, sketches of sets, of set designs, costumes, story boards, etc.

'But the only interesting thing about love stories,' she said in conclusion, 'is knowing what happens afterwards. The couple think their lovemaking takes place behind closed doors, but when those doors open, what lies beyond?'

Those particular doors did not open on to a cradle and baby babble for the seventeen-year-old girl, but to four years of war in the ranks of the British Secret Service.

'My little cameraman was part of Korda's entourage. You've heard of Alexander Korda, I suppose? He's the one who gave Chaplin the idea of playing the dual roles of the Dictator and the barber. Well, Korda was part of the Intelligence Service. From 1934 onwards, his crews filmed thousands of kilometres of the Mediterranean coast, under the guise of making sword-and-sandal epics. What they were really doing was locating and documenting all the possible landing beaches in preparation for a war that Churchill thought unavoidable.'

Sonia paused for a moment, then said to me, with nonchalant sarcasm, 'By the way, did I thank you enough for the little history lesson you gave me when we came out of *The Great Dictator*? The reaction of the American Nazis, protests from the embassies, Bridges and his dockers, etc. . . .'

And turning to Minne, 'It must be such a comfort to share the life of an educator!'

Minne replied that I sometimes very wisely and cleverly convinced my students that they stood several heads taller than I did. 'And that's his gift to you, Sonia,' she said. 'It's very good for morale.'

They exchanged one of those looks that alternate between cold war and light-hearted regard. Apparently it was the second that won the day. Sonia kissed my wife's hand before coming back to the main subject.

The fact is she knew a little more than I did about the amniotic fluid surrounding *The Great Dictator* during its gestation. According to her, it was a carefully planned war film and anti-Nazi weapon refined by the people in the Intelligence Service. Korda had been their Hollywood agent since 1937 when he joined Chaplin at United Artists.

'All the more credit to Chaplin for making such a personal masterpiece out of *The Great Dictator*. That's the true mark of genius!'

Then she came out with a series of names, dates, initials and acronyms, all readily produced from a memory for history which can easily recall the most distant past.

'Korda was also a friend of Claude Dansey, himself a close friend of Churchill since the Boer War. Dansey had set up an autonomous network within the Intelligence Service, the Z network. Korda was their man in Hollywood. One of these days someone should write a history on the role of the cinema in Second World War Intelligence. Identifying landing beaches wasn't the only contribution. There were also the fictitious armies set up in the Libyan desert to trick Rommel, for example: huge encampments that were only sets, fake artillery, cardboard tanks, plywood planes, regiments of scarecrows, deployments of an extraordinary force, all to trick the Germans, immobilising whole divisions . . .'

She stopped and asked us: 'Do you remember the part where Hynkel crosses the hall in his palace and stumbles over the emblem of the double cross, which Chaplin used as the symbol of Nazi Tomania?'

Yes, we remembered the scene.

'And did you wonder how anyone could trip over a smooth mosaic in the floor?'

'It was symbolic,' I replied, hazarding an opinion. 'A sign that Hitler would soon get his feet caught in the swastika . . .'

I was right, but the irony of the scene was far more murderous that I suppose.

The double-cross, Sonia explained to us (double-cross: trickery, deceit, misinformation) was the name given to the most secret, devious, deadly counter-espionage service that the English had ever set up. The top chap was called Masterman. A tough customer, Masterman. Considered from this point of view, the scene is a direct message (like a straight right to the chin, really), sent from Churchill to Hitler: 'You've had it, you bastard. It's as though you're already dead. My friends and I are seeing to it personally.'

8

Sonia explained, 'You ... you've gone and bored them ...
... to tears with all of that ...
... there was nothing ...
... admitted my suspicion ...

T HE RESTAURANT EVENTUALLY got us to leave by
turning out the lights. That was because Sonia had spent
part of the night telling us what happened to her after that.

Being in love, she soon told the story of the secret burial to
her young lover. 'It was a good subject for a film, after all!' So
good in fact that the subject came to the attention of Korda,
perhaps even to his boss Dansey or Churchill himself, who
loved amusing stories and especially determined characters.
To cut a long story short, the Intelligence Service recruited the
heroine, and a year later, Sonia landed in Paris as a milliner
with Coco Chanel, where they were very cosy with the
occupying forces.

'The fact is that it was the best springboard to jump feet first
into the Nazi upper crust!'

So there she was, a spy at seventeen who 'had done what was
necessary' until a certain Adolf Hitler got his feet well and
truly caught on the double cross.

We were careful not to interrupt her. People left the
restaurant, but we listened to her describe four years of a
youth that would have filled four whole lives.

It was well past the time for the last train. After a long
silence in the taxi taking us back to her flat, Sonia leaned over
to me.

'I know just what you're thinking.'

I didn't exactly know what I was thinking myself. I was
trying to take in the story of that extraordinary life, sitting
there in a daze like a young boa constrictor with eyes bigger
than its stomach.

Sonia explained. 'You think you've got a wonderful subject for a novel in all of that.'

The rest was not long in coming.

'I forbid you to write a single word about it.'

There was anger in her voice.

'With your penchant for hagiography, I can just imagine how it would turn out . . .

'Daniel . . .' (it was the first and last time she called me by my first name), 'try to see it as it really was. Of course we were twenty, brimming with enthusiasm. It was an exciting cause which we defended with fierce commitment and courage sustained by a kind of blind determination and watchful daring. We were heroic, there's no doubt about that, and yet the memory I have of those four years is one of dreadful fear, fear every minute of the day. It was degrading, unspeakable. Leave that alone . . . please.'

But when the taxi came to a halt outside her building, she suggested in quite a jaunty tone, 'Would you like to come up for a cup of hot water?'

During the herb-tea ceremony, she asked me: 'And what about you? How does your story end?'

'My story?'

'Your story of the doubles! How does one end a novel like that? I'd really like to know! You don't really mean to leave us high and dry after the death of the first double, do you? And the second? What about the second? And the others? How many were there again?'

Minne was having a quiet giggle, with her nose in her teacup. I'd been boring her for more than three years now with this book written in the conditional tense, so she allowed herself the pleasure of a tiny act of treachery.

'Yes, *it would be the story* of what exactly?'

'We want to know,' Sonia exclaimed.

Both of them looked at me as if they had been doing this double act for ever.

'Well –' I began.

'No, no,' Sonia said, cutting me short, 'we don't want you to *tell* us, we want to read it!'

Then she launched into a series of demands.

'But please, have some consideration for my age. Your wife may belong to a generation that can read anything, but you must treat me like a centenarian, almost like a survivor from the nineteenth century! I want it classical: well constructed and well written, with verbs in the traditional tenses. And fiction, if you please. Give me a rest from your mixture of the real and the imaginary. You'll almost have me doubting my own existence soon! Clear, concise writing to tell a focused, linear story – that's what I need. Do you understand me? I want the story to be *focused*. Spare me the digressions. I don't have my whole life ahead of me, you know.'

She was slightly out of breath as she finished.

'And when you've finished, write "The End", as novelists used to do. This was a useful device which closed the book and locked it up before it found a place in the library.'

And as we were going down the staircase, she leaned over the rail with a final piece of advice.

'Oh, yes. And do begin by giving us a nice portrait of a woman. It's quite true, there are not enough women in this thing of yours.'

VI

FROM DOUBLE TO DOUBLE

And so for Sonia, the 'focused'
conclusion with portrait of a woman.

1

SHE WAS RACINE'S Bérénice. She was Racine's Bérénice with every ounce of her skill. She had been Bérénice since the first time she read the play at the Institution de la Légion d'honneur when she was still a child. Her family thought she had the vocation to be an actress, which they resolved to suppress. But she didn't want 'to be an actress', she wanted to play Racine's Bérénice, and nothing could change that; neither the wishes of her father the Colonel (when you come to think of it, this banishment scene, with the father in full uniform, booted and spurred, pointing a threatening finger towards the front door, declaring 'I disown you!' – no, really . . .), nor the opinion of her teachers at the Conservatoire (they saw her as the Soubrette, the Ingénue, the Girl in Love, the Grande Coquette, the Prima Donna, the Young Romantic Lead – 'She has a wide range, yes, and personality, most certainly, but a tragedienne, come now!'), nor even the well-disposed older actresses at the Comédie Française – 'Bérénice, oh, my dear . . .'. She suffered the paternal wrath, stood up to her teachers' assessment, slammed the august portal of the Comédie Française and vowed never to play any role but that of Bérénice. (Racine's Bérénice.)

At this juncture the First World War broke out; the father died with his boots on, leaving her one of the tidiest fortunes in the almanac of aristocrats. She hired a Titus and an Antiochus from among her contemporaries at drama school, and she could at last be seen by the public in the role of Bérénice. Some critics found she had a cast in her eye, others disliked the supple movement of her body or the liveliness of her gestures, still another thought he saw an irrepressible gaiety in her voice, which he also found too young. Generally speaking, they condemned a *joie de vivre* that did not suit the proper image of a Queen of Palestine chosen before all others by the future Emperor of the world, but obliged to sacrifice her love to the laws of Rome. No, this Bérénice was decidedly too lively. 'Lacks gravitas' was the conclusion of the most influential critic.

The lukewarm reception by the public had no more effect on her than the cutting comments of the newspapers. She played Bérénice every evening to almost empty houses for years. As her personal wealth compensated by far for the lack of takings, theatre directors hired her sight unseen. As for the other members of her cast, who were very generously paid, they steadfastly said their lines night after night. And so for years, alone in the world, she played Racine's Bérénice. The applause may have been scanty, but her incarnation of Bérénice was apparently sustained by something else. Nobody had thought of asking her what inspired such enthusiasm. Every evening, greeted by general indifference, she imperturbably defended Bérénice's love against the law of Rome.

In desperation, her relatives let her do as she wished (to tell the truth, they had kept their distance). And so, when she proposed a tour in Latin America, there was an influential uncle in Foreign Affairs at the Quai d'Orsay to arrange things for her: 'A good idea. She can go and play to the natives.' And play to the natives she did, among others. Caracas, Bogotá, Quito, Lima, Santiago, Buenos Aires, Montevideo, Asunción, Rio de Janeiro, Salvador, São Luís do Maranhão, Belém . . . One could even hear her happy voice floating in the pink opera house at Manaus on the banks of the Amazon, where the bats fly.

Manaus was the second-last leg of her tour of South America.

And the performance given in Teresina would be the last of her career.

I shall live, I shall obey your law
Adieu, my Lord, reign; I shall never see you more.

After a little polite applause, the curtain fell in the Manuel Pereira da Ponte Martins Theatre in Teresina.

As she was preparing to take off her make-up, the President in person suddenly entered her dressing room (she didn't know, of course, that he was a double). She saw him standing there in full dress uniform when she looked in the mirror. One glance was enough to know that it was Titus standing behind her in the room. She turned round and gazed at the man who dared not raise his eyes to look at her, or say a word or move a finger. One look from her and she knew what she thought of him, body and soul. She even imagined what he looked like naked under his ceremonial uniform, and she felt her own heart beating beneath her tunic. She decided that this President was not in his proper place, that the President's place was in her, and that no power in the world could prevent them from loving each other. In short, she became Bérénice 'for real', the Bérénice she was determined to be as a schoolgirl on that far-off afternoon when her first reading of the play had filled her with a passion for revenge. This time Bérénice would carry off Titus! A woman in love would conquer Rome and avenge the Queen of Palestine. Love had just won over politics! A tragedienne was wiping away the tears shed by all those who had preceded her in the role: La Champmeslé, Adrienne Lecouvreur, Mlle Gaussin, Julia Bartet, and the great

Sarah Bernhardt who had made her cry so much. There would be revenge too for all those women in the audience whose hearts were broken; and all those gently dabbed eyes, discreetly blown noses, silently wrung hands, stifled sobs! And on a more prosaic level, revenge for humble passions sacrificed on the altar of everyday duties: love wrecked by the factory, the workshop, the office, the business, the high school, the barracks, the harvest, the tide, even the theatre, the career, the career, the career!

. . .

In the name of all women in love, she carried off this Titus of the Tropics, and they were never heard of again.

2

BEFORE RUNNING OFF with his Bérénice the smitten double, who had to find someone to replace him in Teresina, came upon a pair of twins. What a piece of luck: two doubles for the price of one! Two interchangeable Pereiras. Two monozygotic presidents. A permanent presence assured in the event of death, lightning strike, laryngitis or desertion. One single course of training for both of them, but it was unbelievably strict, directed by a pseudo-president transformed into a mad pedagogue by the urgent fires of love.

'Two doubles can be replaced,' he shouted, brandishing his pistol. 'People just have to believe in the resemblance!'

These twins didn't come from the mountains of Ponte like Pereira, nor from the eastern plain or the countryside around

Teresina like the barber double or the lover double; no, they were natives of the North, of that northern frontier that had been devastated by the President who was a General, on the pretext that the peasants wouldn't go down the mine. The twins had seen their father and mother strung up by their feet and their heads buried in anthills. While the insects ate their parents' faces, the mother's upturned skirt exposed what the boys should never have seen.

A shock like that, the recruiting double thought, guaranteed the brothers' absolute loyalty to the President. Wasn't he the one who had executed the Butcher of the North? And the strength of that fidelity, he judged, would amply compensate for the slight deficit in resemblance that one might suspect if the twins were placed either side of Pereira's official portrait. It's true that the said portrait was taken some time ago, and one could hardly expect every feature of two forty-year-olds to look exactly like those of a putschist of twenty-five.

Nevertheless, the recruiting double shouted as he took out his gun for the umpteenth time, 'You have to make people want to see the resemblance!'

In short, as soon as they were adequately trained and utterly terrified, they drew straws to decide which of the twins would be landed with the job first.

3

So, the first one is landed with it. Like the doubles before him, he begins by playing his part as the bogus President to the letter, filled with doubt, fear, but eventually with enthusiasm. Then he calms down, grows weary of it all and, like his predecessors, decides to leave. The reason is that he, too, thinks he has discovered 'his true nature' (the constant preoccupation with 'finding oneself'). But this double doesn't want to be an actor or a bashful lover. He has no desire for a Bérénice and no taste for the cinematograph. He's a pragmatic character with a mind that can see the whole picture. Once installed in Teresina, it hardly takes him a moment to judge the limits of the President's power. He quickly comes to the conclusion that the power wielded by the President – the real one – is no more genuine that his. He realises that everything is in the hands of the big corporations. The President or his double may well speechify to tame crowds, but this hardly scratches the surface. The real power thrives 'underground', to use an expression of Sir Anthony Calvin-Cook, the British Ambassador (the son of the one who held the post when Pereira first took over). The new double very quickly understands that the most minor official on any board of directors concerned with nickel, silver, gold, oil or akmadon is sure to have far greater and more profitable power than his own job travelling the country giving the sales talk that Heads of State seem to love.

Lying awake at night, his eyes map his career plan on the ceiling of his bedroom. He pictures Teresina with its mineral-laden underground like a territory without borders, where a lode worked here under his feet could lead him to the other end of the continent, his fortune made, and a huge one at that, without anyone being the wiser. In a word, if he aspires to power, it is through wealth. He is more and more convinced of it. Leaving Teresina and entering the world of Big Business is jumping out of the goldfish bowl to rule the planet.

Nevertheless, he keeps up all his duties as double. The ceremonies organised to honour Pereira have more pomp with him at the helm. This is the time when Guerrilho Martins' men infiltrate various marketplaces and get the people to sing:

> *Maior do que um farão*
> *Mais forte do que um sultao*
> *Mais potente do que um czar*
> *Mais imenso do que o mar*
> *Juro que não é bobeira*
> *Eis o nosso pai, eis Pereira!*

> Greater than a pharaoh
> Stronger than a sultan
> More powerful than a tsar
> Vaster than an ocean
> I tell no lie, but rather
> It's Pereira, who's our father!

The day finally comes when this third double announces to his brother that he's leaving.

'OK, little brother, the party's over. I'm off to make my fortune. It's your turn to play the goldfish.'

4

THE FOURTH DOUBLE is as different in character as he is similar to his twin in physique and intelligence. Like him, he very quickly realises the extent of the power enjoyed by the big corporations and the correspondingly enfeebled state of the President's office. He also understands that laws promulgated on the surface only serve as a guarantee that foreign interests can plunder the depths. He sees a factor for revolution in that, but he remembers too well the savagery with which the oligarchy put down the revolt in the North. He and his brother had reacted very differently to the torture of their parents. His brother had decided to join the winning side, whoever they were, as soon as he had identified them.

'Because it's not enough to be in the winners' camp, little brother; you have to choose those who are *always* winners.'

He, by contrast, had assumed an absolute detachment from the things of this world. The sight of so much suffering, together with an instinctive understanding of the way humans behave, had brought out in him what you might call a fatalistic goodness.

It was this goodness that the fourth double put to work for the benefit of his fellow citizens as soon as his twin had left Teresina.

From this point of view, he was the best possible Pereira by far. He was no longer content simply to listen to the wretched, cutting off their confessions with a benevolent 'I have heard you'; he let them get everything off their chests down to the tiniest worry, pain, regret, resentment or despair. He listened very well. He looked at you, drinking in everything you said. You'd have sworn that he was filling himself with your woes. He gave each person the time that was needed: a whole hour, sometimes all night. No one in the queue grew impatient because they knew that when their turn came, they would have that ear to themselves. And besides, there was something soothing in the sight of the sun going down on that man devoting himself to his fellow creatures with unfailing wisdom.

Only the dawn brought an end to the session. The President had to go and listen to other people under other flame trees, and give other speeches on other steps. Although his speeches, written by Pereira down to the last comma, still inspired the crowds (the greatness of the nation, pride in being a part of it, the glorious past, the shining future, sacred tradition, indispensable hard work, gratitude of the President . . .), the President's voice, the *tone* of that voice, implied that time flows on and that man being what he is, one is quite powerless to do anything about it. In a vague kind of a way, people were grateful to him for expressing the truth while taking the trouble to be very encouraging. After listening to the President, the love they bore him was the same they felt for themselves in those very rare moments when, free of illusion and desire, they were content just to be themselves, just to be alive. At about this time, they began to sing these lines in the marketplaces:

> *Povo tem que ter cabeça*
> *Não vive só de cachaça*
> *Alguns querem ditadores*
> *Outros, reis, imperadores*

253

Pra gente essa maravilha
Nosso chefe é uma orelha!

The people should always have a head
Cachaça's not the whole of life
Some want dictators, I've heard said
Or kings or emperors to ward off strife
Ours is a marvel without peer
Our leader is a listening ear!

It's difficult to count the number of years Teresina lived
with the goodness of this man: the President was loved as if
time stood still.

But alas, time did not stand still; time ground him down.
Exhausted by sleepless nights and continual travel, crushed by
the burden of things he heard – and felt – weary of forcing his
voice to contradict his words, he seemed to shrink before their
very eyes. His joints began to swell and his limbs began to twist
to the point that, in the rare moments when he took off his
clothes to rest in a hammock, his uniform hanging on the back
of a chair still had bumps in the places where empathy was
causing him so much pain. When he woke, it was not unusual
to see a circle of peasants kneeling in adoration before this
piece of clothing that bore the signs of his stigmata.

The Bishop was struck (perhaps even touched) by this
worship of his godson.

He declared to old da Ponte Senior, 'Your Manuel has
reached eternity in his own lifetime. He's loved beyond reason
and for ever. There's no doubt about it; he's a saint. Who'd
have thought it, when he began?'

'I would,' the father replied.

The mother confirmed this in her motherly way.

'He never liked the *bacalhau do menino*, but now he's cleaning his plate to the last bean.'

5

THIS WAS THE man Pereira killed with a bullet between the eyes, before being torn to pieces by the crowd and replaced as Head of State by Colonel Eduardo Rist, his childhood friend.

(Is that concise enough for you, dear Sonia?)

6

AS LUCK WOULD have it, on the very day that the saintly President's head was blown apart in Teresina, another drama was being played out in New York. His twin brother was being dismissed from the big company he thought he was about to control. The Board of Directors, who had met to enthrone him in their Wall Street office, told him that he now had to go. A majority of the shareholders had voted in favour of the decision, which was final.

'For what reason?' the excommunicated member asked.

'The akmadon scandal,' was the Board's reply.

The twin raised an eyebrow.

'You all agreed to renew that loan!'

'No doubt, but it was not a good idea. It was up to you to reject it.'

'The idea' in question consisted of borrowing phenomenal sums from the shareholders to finance 'studies' on mining akmadon. If these studies – 'and there is no doubt about it', the advertising proclaimed – allowed for 'optimal exploitation' of the precious mineral, the company guaranteed 'comfortable dividends' to its backers. In the event that it came to nothing, it went without saying (and it wasn't said) that the time had come for the company to launch a new round of borrowing from the same shareholders to extend 'the studies', naturally 'about to come to a successful conclusion'.

And so it went on.

It had become a routine.

A lucrative one.

For decades.

'In what way was it a bad idea?' the twin asked.

'Look at this.'

They threw down on the table the draft of an article that would be all over the world press on the following day if the company did not immediately buy out the newspaper that intended publishing it. The article bore the restrained title 'Akmadon, a new Panama scandal'. It revealed that for a certain number of years, a certain company led its shareholders to believe in the mining of a certain mineral, akmadon, which quite simply did not exist. Unbelievable sums of money had been misappropriated to finance so-called 'studies' on the composition, extraction and innumerable properties of an imaginary mineral. What seemed to shock the author of the article (a certain Postel-Verdi) most of all was the word itself: *akmadon* could not be found in any dictionary. 'A common or garden swindle has been compounded by a semantic tall story!' concluded the journalist, obviously a poet who had strayed into the Business column by mistake.

The twin pointed out to the Board of Directors that this tale to relieve the shareholders of their money had been in existence for some time (akmadon was actually the brainchild of Pereira himself, and Sir Anthony Calvin-Cook had been the first to finance the said studies). It was then confirmed that this was the case, but that he was in charge of the programme, he had failed to keep the shareholders in a state of well-disposed torpor, and that their awakening demanded his departure.

In a word, which was delivered by the youngest member of the Board, the Frenchman Madricourt, he had 'screwed up'.

'You screwed up, my friend, and now you have to pay the price.'

7

FORTY-SIX DAYS WENT by in Teresina after the murder of the saintly President, forty-six days of national mourning ordered by Colonel Eduardo Rist. In every church there was a daily Mass to the martyr's memory. The Mass was said at the time when the saint was gunned down, and the host was raised in the priest's hands at the very second when the bullet of the unknown assailant set his soul free. Forty-six days during which the subject of the saintly President occupied every conversation and every silence. People prayed beneath the flame trees where he had listened; they listened around the steps where he had spoken. Statues were raised to him even in the remotest villages. These monuments did not represent the dashing young man who had earlier killed the General who was then President, but the pilgrim in the misshapen uniform that he had become through dedication and compassion.

On the morning of the forty-seventh day, in a mining village of the North, a man stood beside one of the many statues of the martyr President. The man was wearing the saint's uniform and looked strangely like him (and for good reason – it was his twin brother, the one whose company had recently dropped him from their Board.).

At first no one noticed him standing there, he was so much a part of the stone statue of his brother. The village lads were harnessing up, getting ready to go to the mine. You could hear their picks, billycans and sieves clinking in the early-morning silence. They adjusted the lamps on their helmets.

Without batting an eyelid, the sacked twin watched them buckle the last of the hooks on to their makeshift shoulder belts. Standing motionless against the cold stone shoulder, he gave no hint of the turmoil he was feeling inside. 'Here are my avenging troops,' he said to himself. 'Here is the sword of my revolution: peasants taken from the fields and sent down the mine, *vaqueiros* taken from the open plains to crawl like excrement in the bowels of the earth, proud hunters changed into moles . . . How they'll cry for vengeance when they find out who is robbing them, who is ruining their lives and working them to death! Oh, how their strength will be mobilised when they see the sunlight again! Oh, what a massacre when I let them loose on Teresina! A crusade led by their risen President! My God, they'll be invincible!'

For this was his plan: to present himself before the vast door of popular superstition as the reincarnation of his brother, and raise the troops needed for his revenge. It would be easy. Just think. Their saintly President come back from the dead! They would follow him to a man. Everything was ready: caves full of weapons in the border foothills, trucks and machine guns waiting under camouflage, agents infiltrated into the government of Teresina, collusion assured even in the presidential palace, including the immediate entourage of Colonel Eduardo Rist. The only thing left to do was to recruit the troops.

The moment had come. In a few seconds the twin would separate himself from the stone and make the risen President's speech to the men: 'Yes, it really is me. I am your murdered President. My only crime was wanting to give the riches of your soil back to you . . . And so they killed me! But I have come back to life! I'm coming out of the stone. I'm coming back! I have returned! I'm no longer that man whose goodness blinded him; that man they sacrificed like a lamb. I am the glorious Body of your Revolution. I see clearly, I am your rage, the implacable guide of your avenging arm, the living statue of your cause, the sacred sword of your age-old rights! Yesterday I spoke to you and you listened to me; you confided in me and I listened to you; today we will kill together!' Yes, that's what he intended to do: enter fully armed into the band of their innumerable saints. He would be the incarnation of the bogeymen of the interior, the Orixa gods of *candomblé* in the Caribbean, and the fury of the Old Testament all rolled into one; he would ride all four horses of the Apocalypse, overthrow Colonel Eduardo Rist, take Teresina, send agents to

New York to exterminate the Board of Directors that had ousted him, set up a new one in its place; in short, he would seize both power and wealth, and from there swallow up the rest of Latin America. (Ah! He'd have the Frenchman Madricourt kidnapped also, and the journalist Postel-Verdi. He'd concoct a particularly nasty death for them in his spare time.) The thought of it made the twin shiver with one of those pleasures that only truly speculative minds can feel.

'There, one of them has seen me!'

And indeed, Néné Martins, a peasant, miner and secret unionist, was the first to notice the man standing beside the statue. At first Néné Martins thought that he was seeing double. He thought he'd drunk a bit too much *cachaça* to celebrate the end of the national period of mourning. He rubbed his eyes, lit his acetylene lamp and came closer.

There was no doubt about it. The late saintly President was standing beside his own statue. But to put his mind at rest, Néné Martins asked Didi da Casa, poet, peasant and miner, if he was seeing the same thing.

'Do you see what I see?'

Didi was seeing what Néné was seeing.

The men made a circle around the statue. They couldn't believe their eyes. They lit their acetylene lamps. The twin was now standing in an assembly of Cyclopses. They touched him. They pinched the material of his uniform; it wasn't made of stone. Someone put a hand on the apparition's heart and immediately took it away again: the heart was beating like the call to fall in! The twin let them rouse the rest of the village. He only detached himself from his statufied brother when assembly was complete.

Then, as the light of the sun unfurled like a standard, he began to speak in a strong, clear voice.

'Yes, it's me,' he said. 'I've come back from the dead to show you real life.'

He left them enough time to take in the full extent of the miracle, then he took a deep breath to launch his call to arms. But another voice arose before his, a shrill voice, a rusty, vibrating guitar string, like an ancient fury. It was the poet Didi da Casa suddenly seized by inspiration and quite unstoppable.

> *No Saara de além do mar*
> *Há miragens de enganar*
> *Gente vê o que não é não*
> *Mas pra gente no Sertão*
> *Não funciona a ilusão*
> *Tampouco a ressurreição!*

> In the Sahara across the sea
> The mirages are illusory
> You see things there that are not real
> But we who in the sertão dwell
> Have no truck with vain illusion
> Any more than resurrection!

A few hours later, the twin found himself bound hand and foot, standing before Colonel Eduardo Rist.

8

'HELLO, PEREIRA,' THE Colonel said to the twin as he welcomed him into his office. 'So, what was death like?'

While he was speaking, the Colonel signalled the guards to untie the prisoner.

'Eduardo,' the twin replied, rubbing his wrists. 'Are you crazy, arresting someone who has risen from the dead? Do you know how much that can cost you up there?'

He raised his eyes to the sky.

Colonel Eduardo Rist unfolded a chessboard on his desk, scrabbled about in a bag of pieces, took a black pawn and a white pawn, then held out both fists in front of him to allow his opponent to choose the colour.

'What do you say to a little game?' he asked.

'As if my mind was on something like that!'

'Come on, Manuel,' Eduardo insisted, 'it'll remind us of our nights at boarding school.'

'We're not children any more!'

The Colonel made him a proposition.

'If you win, I'll stand aside for you; if you lose, I'll let you go back where you came from.'

'That's not the way to do politics!' the twin protested.

'That's the way to spare ourselves a revolution. The miners and peasants have more to do than massacre the city dwellers.'

'Eduardo,' the twin exclaimed, looking genuinely scandalised, 'I didn't go to all the bother of rising from the dead to play chess! Who do you think you're talking to, for God's sake? Have you no religion!'

Colonel Eduardo Rist heaved a sigh.

'I think I'm speaking to a halfwit who takes me for a bloody fool.'

'What are you saying?'

The twin, who had leaped to his feet, found himself seated as if he had never got up. The two guards behind him were attending to his comfort.

'I'm saying' (Colonel Eduardo Rist suddenly seemed tired), 'that you are not Manuel Pereira da Ponte Martins, my childhood friend; that you don't know how to play chess; that you take us all for bloody fools with your story of resurrection: the miners, the administrators, the politicians, God Himself and me as well, just as you did with the shareholders who threw you out of your company in what was your only previous life.'

'Eduardo . . .' murmured the twin, in a tone of hurt disbelief.

Colonel Eduardo Rist replied with a sweet smile: 'Call me Eduardo one more time, my dear fellow, and your brains will decorate my office walls.'

He had brought his service pistol out of a drawer. It was an impressive weapon. The butt alone was enough to frighten anyone.

They looked at each other for some time.

It was Colonel Eduardo Rist who finally broke the silence.

'Who, in your opinion, hired you and your brother as Pereira's doubles?'

'The President in person!' the twin declared in all sincerity.

'. . .'

'. . .'

'It's just as I feared,' the Colonel said quietly.

He then gave an explanation.

'It wasn't Pereira who recruited you, you poor clown. Pereira went off to Europe ages ago. You and your brother were a copy of a copy of a copy.'

He gave the twin time to get over his surprise, and made this comment: 'Your predecessors weren't too bright either, but you're a nasty piece of work as well as being stupid. A venal shark with a one-track mind and not an atom of good sense. Nothing but an appetite. As bloody stupid as our late President, the General.'

Then the interrogation began in earnest.

'Tell me,' Colonel Eduardo Rist asked, 'which of my men did you bribe first?'

'Callado!' the twin announced. 'Manuel Callado Crespo, the Chief Interpreter! He was actually the one who gave me the idea of the revolution! He's the one who made the arrangements to buy weapons, and he was the one who told me about the caves to hide them in and the village where I could recruit my troops.'

The Colonel looked sorrowfully at his prisoner. 'A grass into the bargain . . .'

But the twin was launched on his subject. 'He gave me the name of every state employee to be bribed, his rank and his price. He even recommended a poet to spread my revolution song: Didi da Casa, a genius according to him, a real pest according to the opinion-makers in Teresina!'

. . .

While the twin was denouncing Didi da Casa, the poet was still singing for the peasant miners of the North. This was his latest verse:

> *Ramo em ramo o passarinho*
> *Passarinho faz o ninho*

Canto em canto o passarinho
Passarinho faz um hino
De verso em verso o poeta
Do povo tece a revolta!

Twig by twig the bird
The bird makes up its nest
Song by song the bird
Makes its anthem heard
Line by line without a halt
The poet weaves the people's revolt!

'It was Callado who organised everything,' the twin shouted. 'I swear it on my brother's grave! He even recommended a unionist to lead my troops: Néné Martins. Sedition is in his blood! He's a public menace!'

Colonel Eduardo Rist stopped him with a wave of his hand, then leaned over to the intercom.

'Callado, could you come here for a moment?'

'I'm coming,' the intercom replied.

Manuel Callado Crespo appeared as if by magic. He had put on weight during those years. The hair on his huge face looked more like the Amazonian bush than ever. Only the crown of his head showed premature signs of deforestation.

'My eyebrows make it hard for me to see clearly,' he complained, catching sight of the twin. 'Who's that sitting there? It wouldn't be the fellow who tried to bribe me, by any chance?'

The Colonel confirmed that it was indeed the same man. Then with a hopeless gesture, he added, 'Callado, be a good friend and explain to this cretin how things work in Teresina. I've had enough.'

'That's what interpreters are for,' Callado replied.

Then, in clear, considered terms, as if he were speaking to a schoolboy, Manuel Callado Crespo told the twin about everything that had gone before: Pereira, Mãe Branca's prediction, the President's agoraphobia, his exile in Europe, the choice of the first double, then the second . . .

'And so on, until the death of your unfortunate brother.'

At this juncture Manuel Callado Crespo deviated from the subject for a moment to ask Colonel Rist, 'Eduardo, how could a woman's body harbour twins as different as the saint and this pimp here?'

'That bitch Mother Nature,' the Colonel muttered.

' . . .'

' . . .'

Admitting defeat, the twin asked this question: 'So, you knew all about the doubles?'

Callado explained to him very patiently that after Mãe Branca was killed, Pereira's agoraphobia was so plain to see and his desire for Europe so strong ('It's more than a desire, boys,' the young Dictator argued, 'it's a cultural imperative!') that the Colonel and himself had decided he was unfit to govern and should be encouraged to take up a life of luxurious exile. All Callado had to do to bring this about was to mention the subject of a double (so discreetly that Pereira imagined he had thought of it himself) and to stick the barber with the uncanny resemblance under his nose (so cleverly that Pereira imagined he had discovered the man himself), for the agoraphobic Dictator to have himself replaced by his double and drop out of circulation.

'And that was that . . .' Manuel Callado Crespo said in conclusion.

'That was that,' agreed Colonel Eduardo Rist.

'Then we changed doubles as soon as they began to wear out. Same plan: let each one think that he had the idea of replacing himself and put a double in his path whom he imagines he's chosen himself. It's easy, given human vanity. Eh, Eduardo?'

Colonel Eduardo Rist indicated that it was so easy that it became boring.

'What about the father?' the twin asked. 'Did the father believe it? I've always wondered whether he really saw me as a son . . .'

'Vanity again. Old da Ponte found that his boy was improving with each double, and thought it was due to him. When Pereira killed your sainted brother whom da Ponte Senior took to be his son, the old man died of grief. Did you know that?'

'Paternal instinct . . .' Colonel Eduardo Rist murmured.

'Was it Pereira who killed my brother?' the twin asked.

. . .

Meanwhile in the mountains of the North, Didi da Casa was singing to the peasant miners.

> *Naquela história de gêmeos*
> *De que fala o livro santo*
> *Quem foi que matou o outro?*
> *Foi Caim? Esaú? Quem?*
> *Deus sabe, eo povo também*
> *Foi Pereira! Disse alguém.*

> In the story of the twin who died
> As told to us in the Holy Book
> Which of the two the other's life took?
> Was it Cain? Or Esau? Who?

God knows who, the people too
It's Pereira! Someone cried.

. . .

'And the Bishop?' the twin asked. 'Did the Bishop know that it wasn't Pereira? He was his godson, after all! Well, he always treated me like a godson.'

'Bishops don't play politics,' Callado replied. 'Every time Christ comes back to life they're satisfied with crucifying him again so that the Church goes on, that's all.'

'Which tells you what awaited you with your story of resurrection . . .' Colonel Rist pointed out.

'And the people?' the twin finally asked in a voice that was no more than a whisper. 'Did the people believe in these fake Pereiras?'

'The people are more complex than a father or a bishop. The people pretend to believe what we want them to believe, to the point where they sometimes talk themselves into believing that they believe it.'

'Until the day when they decide to begin to think for themselves again,' Colonel Rist added.

'Then you can expect something new,' Callado commented.

. . .

In fact at that very moment, Didi da Casa was singing:

> *Se o papagaio recita*
> *Será que a voz exercita?*
> *Quando o macaco imita*
> *Será que ele vomita?*
> *Poeta papagueando*
> *Algo tá se preparando.*

When the parrot recites his words
Isn't it for his voice to be heard?
When the monkey does his copying trick
Isn't it like he's being sick?
When the poet does what the parrot's doing
It's because there's something brewing.

. . .

'There again, your stupid revolution was doomed,' Callado observed. 'Since you couldn't have stopped yourself bleeding them all dry, as numerous as they are – peasants, miners, tradesmen, villagers and city dwellers – and you'd have ended up stealing from the rich as well. In a few years they'd have pretended to believe someone else and would have crushed you as they did Pereira . . .'

Seeing the expression on the twin's face, Callado exclaimed, 'God! Didn't you even know that they tore Pereira to pieces after your brother was assassinated? Poor lad, you're a hopeless case! You don't know anything and you don't understand anything. Not a great recommendation for someone who wants to be a dictator.'

'. . .'

'Anyway,' Colonel Eduardo Rist said, 'by lynching Pereira they killed dictatorship.'

'The end of an era,' Callado added.

'. . .'

It was then that the two men revealed to the prisoner the plan they had been working on since Pereira departed for Europe: to give back power to the people, hand over the keys to their own houses to all the Néné Martinses, to all the Didi da Casas, and with the house keys, ownership of the land, and with ownership of their land, the job of watching over the mining of the substratum, and the obligation to resist foreign greed . . .'

'And consequently,' Callado explained, warming to this lesson in civics, 'the duty to elect good deputies and to install as President the one among them whose arse will be least glued to the power of the presidential throne. A Néné Martins, for example, or a Didi da Casa.'

. . .

Who, as it happens, was singing at the top of his voice:

> *Povo sua quer a terra*
> *Faremos democracia.*

> The people must own their property
> We will make democracy.

'Who knows how long it will last,' Colonel Eduardo Rist concluded, in a voice with no trace of illusion, 'but it will always be better than prostrating oneself before a moron like you.'

'It won't get rid of corruption,' Callado Crespo added, 'but it will make things difficult for the big corporations. It only needs more palms to be greased, a few incorruptibles to put an occasional spanner in the works, journalists to use their curiosity, the vox populi to voice their voices . . .'

'Absolutely no time to get bored,' the Colonel said, almost nodding off.

In the silence that followed, the twin whispered the last four words he was still capable of uttering.

'And what about me?'

Colonel Eduardo Rist's face suddenly lit up.

'Don't worry. Democracy won't happen overnight.

Meanwhile we'll indulge ourselves one last time.'

'A little game of chess?' Manuel Callado Crespo exclaimed, with almost childlike anticipation.

'Exactly,' the Colonel replied.

Turning to the twin, he added with a conciliatory smile, 'If I win, I kill you, if Callado wins, he kills you, if it's a draw, we'll hand you over to the future democrats who'll slaughter you before they come up with the idea of justice. How's that?'

Without waiting for a reply, he held out his two closed fists for Callado to choose black or white.

The End
(the twin concluded)

VII

THE QUESTION OF ACKNOWLEDGEMENTS

I don't like the word 'end'; it brings obligations. To come down to earth again, for example. And once there, to remember that you, dear Sonia, are not a person made of flesh and blood: you're a character, nothing but words. Which brings me to thank Sonia Paul-Boncourt, for having lent you her first name and her flat; Silvia Pollock who spent her youth in Chicago and like you made the trip to Riverside in a sleeper compartment on the Union Pacific Challenger; my friend Fanchon, who was the inspiration for your teenage years, my friend Jacques, who meticulously checked your historical memory; Yasmina and Monica, who urged me to 'develop' you, so that we could know you better; not to mention our friend Claude, with whom we used to talk about doubles, or Tonino, with whom we were still talking about twins just the other day . . .

So now the thorny question of acknowledgements has been stated. Between the woman who brought him into the world and the one who keeps him there, there's a whole world a novelist should thank. Those who live around him, those who write, those he has read, those he listens to, those who edit him and those who support him while he labours: first of all my daughter Alice, who knows the drawbacks of having a writer for a father . . . Jean Guerrin, an old friend, who was the first person here to listen to me, Jean-Philippe Postel, Roger Grenier, J.-B. Pontalis, Jean-Marie Laclavetine, the first ones to read me, Manuel Serrat Crespo in the role of Callado, Didier Lamaison as Didi da Casa, Franklin Rist as the eponymous Colonel, the whole Martins clan . . .

When you come to think of it, the number of these acknowledgements and the reasons for them could provide the subject matter for a huge novel in themselves. I can see the opening sentences now: It would be the story of an author who has to acknowledge the people who have helped him. The hammock where this idea came to him is not important. Just imagine . . .